It Happened One Christmas

A Special Edition Christmas Collection

Daphne Lynn Stewart

Volume Two of a special holiday compendium of novelettes also published independently as Amazon Kindle editions in Daphne Lynn Stewart's charming Merry and Bright series of romantic Christmas stories for pet lovers. Volume One, *Some Enchanted Christmas*, contains books 1-4. This volume contains books 5-7.

Dashing Through the Snow   1
When Chelsea Doll meets Jason Frost she realizes she is engaged to the wrong brother. She and Bryce are planning their Christmas Eve wedding at Langdon Hall, a luxury country estate hotel. It seems she and Bryce's brother have everything in common, including a love of dogs. If only she had met him first!

A Very Catty Christmas   92
Budding artist Lorelei is in love with art curator Harry Snowden, but he doesn't know she exists. By day she is Lori Channing, a docent at the Art Gallery of Hamilton; by night she is textile artist Lorelei. When Harry finally notices her he doesn't recognize her as the bumbling docent Lori. Between her two disguises and her cat's mischief, her boss begins to suspect her duplicity, and Lori begins to question her choices. Is she dating the right man?

Rocky Mountain Christmas   188
Joy Zamboni is a writer for a magazine called *Cats and Dogs*. Her Christmas assignment? To write an article about how dogs are replacing men in the loves of modern women. To aid in her research she adopts a dog, and through him meets Jack Tinsle, the man of her dreams. At her father's winter lodge in the Rocky Mountains, her dear cousin Ellie arrives for the holidays with her boyfriend—who turns out to be none other than Jack!

In loving memory of Ming

Dashing Through the Snow

A Love Story For Pet Lovers

CHAPTER ONE

I never thought it would happen, but I am getting married! To the most wonderful man in the world. And everything would have been perfect if I hadn't gone out to Langdon Hall on my own without my fiancé. It all began when my wedding planner called to ask if we could come to see the new venue she had chosen for our wedding. It has to be in Cambridge because that is where Bryce's Great Aunt Tessina lives. She actually lives in Langdon Hall, an historic manor that was restored and converted into a luxury estate hotel. Oh yeah, that's how much money she has. That family is loaded. She can afford to *live* in a hotel.

But it wasn't money that made me fall for Bryce Frost. It was his love of family, his irrepressible charm and his commanding manner. I adore a man who can make people respond. And everyone loves him—except his younger brother. I have never met Jason in the three years Bryce and I have been dating. Jason doesn't live in Rosedale or any of Toronto's other ritzy neighborhoods like his family; he lives on the outskirts of a small city called Cambridge—on a horse ranch. He owns the horse ranch by the way. Jason is a bit of a disappointment to his parents because he decided to start a small business of his own rather than join his father and brother in Toronto's financial district of Bay Street.

To each his own I had thought back then. But it was clear from Bryce's description of his brother that they clashed on just about everything. Jason was like his Great Aunt Tessina. Eccentric. I met Great Aunt Tessina once at a Christmas party. Like I said. *Eccentric.* She *lives* in a fancy hotel. Seriously? Who does that?

Oddly enough it was she who suggested a winter wedding. Despite her peculiarities, she loves Christmas, and when she planted that thought in my head, I couldn't get it out. I love the festive season and what better day to get married than Christmas Eve.

Bryce was cynical about the idea. "Who gets married at Christmas?" he scoffed. "Let's have a beautiful outdoor wedding in June—like everybody else."

But that meant waiting months, maybe years to get the venue that I wanted. June was the most popular time of year for marriages. "No, please, Bryce. I want a winter wedding. With ice castles and one-horse open sleighs. And thousands of twinkle lights. And my precious Honey dressed in a white shearling jacket with a green bow. Can't you see it now?"

He laughed. "All right, but seriously. No dog. I don't think Honey would enjoy being part of the wedding party. And I am not wearing a tuxedo in the snow."

That's what you think. Or so I had thought at the time.

So here I was.

"Chelsea!" Melinda called from across the airy, pillared space, as I entered the Firshade Room. I had my white leather coat with the white fur hood draped over my arm. I walked cautiously across the floor, wary of my stylish boots leaving traces of snow on the floor. "There you are. I've been waiting for you. You look gorgeous—as usual. Love the outfit, where'd you get it?" I wore a lightweight designer wool skirt in black and white checks with a sleek black turtleneck on top.

"Ports," I said.

"Simple, but so sophisticated." She turned to face the room where fresh, spotless tablecloths were draped over numerous tables with satin upholstered chairs. The tables were not set with silver, china and crystal yet, but I could imagine it. I wanted the flower arrangements to be in various shades of blue and lavender. "I'm going to make this dining hall into a winter wonderland. So, what do you think? They received a last minute cancellation and it's yours if you want it. It's even better than the Orchard Room. Now we can really spread out!"

My eyes took in its spacious grandeur, the floor to ceiling windows with French doors that opened onto the snow blanketed garden. Sugar maples, hickory, chestnut and apple trees stood root deep in a pristine sea of white.

"Seats eighty to a hundred and twenty guests. What do we have…?" She glanced down at her digital planner. "Last count was one hundred and five. It would have been a tight squeeze in the Orchard Room."

"It's perfect."

The Orchard Room was in the same hotel, so it was only a matter of redirecting the guests when they arrived. I shivered with excitement. Only ten days before the wedding and I was planning to move into the hotel in five. My dream wedding was coming true.

Melinda flipped through her digital planner. "So that's confirmed." She looked up. "Where's Bryce?"

"He couldn't make it this morning. Work you know."

"Too bad. Well, let's finalize some details, shall we?"

Before we could do anything more, I saw the blur of ruby fur spinning outside the crisply draped white latticed windows. My heart did a flip. Two dogs were frolicking in the snow. I had left Honey outside in the sunshine, her six-foot long leash tied to a tree. Somehow she had managed to unknot herself and was being chased by a tricolor cavalier.

She suddenly made a sharp twist and pursued the rambunctious young spaniel in turn.

"Does this door open?" I asked Melinda, frantically shaking the knob.

"Oh no, is that *your* dog?" She frowned, unlatched the French door. Then smiled. "I know who that is. It's Holly. She's a fixture around here. Don't worry, she won't hurt Honey."

"The owners have a cavalier?"

"That's not their dog. Here, come outside. It's Jay. I hired him for your transportation on the day. You can meet him. He must be early. I asked him to bring the vehicle that's going to convey you to the ceremony. You'll love it. It's going to be soooo romantic!"

At this moment I got the sense that Melinda's romantic feelings came from something more than just planning my wedding.

"Jay and I have known each other for ages. Since high-school. We both went into small business ventures. There he is—" We stood on the threshold looking out. She ushered me forward into the cold, damp air, my winter coat still slumped in my arms.

Something about the broad-shouldered, tall, good-looking man in the fleece-lined leather jacket and blue jeans—who had now joined the dogs and was throwing snowballs for them to chase—seemed oddly familiar.

"Jay!"

"Mel!" He tossed one more snowball into the air, at which my Honey snapped, and came up to us, smiling.

"I want you to meet the bride."

"So… this is the lucky lady."

"And, you're entertaining *her* dog."

In fact, he had released Honey from her leash, but for some reason she had remained to play instead of taking off to explore the grounds.

"No dog should be tied up on the grounds of Langdon Hall," he said.

"I don't trust her not to run off," I answered, quelling my anger. "She chases squirrels and leaves. Anything could have set her off and sent her into the woods."

"She's fine." He shook the last remnants of snow from his hands and wiped them on the thighs of his jeans. "She's playing with Holly."

I clenched my right fist—and tried not to. "Still, I'd feel safer if she was secured to that tree when I'm not with her."

"Sure. Let me just fix my mistake." He whistled and Honey looked up from her romping. He called her by name, then: "Come, girl!"

To my utter amazement she came. He reattached her leash to her collar and brought her to me. I took the leash from him. His own dog came trotting up, wagging her long luxurious tail, and shoved her nose into Honey's. "They seem to like each other," he remarked.

Which was more than I could say for us. It wasn't that I disliked him, but his recklessness and presumptuousness was annoying. One should not just unleash someone else's dog.

"Jay, this is Chelsea Doll."

He nodded. "Nice to meet you."

"Chelsea, this is Jay Frost."

I started. "Sorry, did you say *Frost*?"

"Jason Frost, actually," he cut in. "Mel's the only one who calls me Jay." Was he bowing slightly? And was he mocking me because of my concern for Honey? "Looks like we're going to be related. By marriage that is."

I have to admit, I was speechless. Nothing was coming out of my mouth.

"Jason Frost," he repeated. "Bryce's younger brother." He offered a sturdy masculine hand.

I felt like I was in some sort of time lapse. I watched my fingers reach out and take his. Everything was moving in slow motion.

I glanced at Melinda. Why had she kept this from me? Surely she must have known that the two were brothers.

"My apologies, Chelsea," he said. "I asked Mel not to

mention that Bryce and I were related."

Why? But the word made no sound.

Melinda appeared to be enjoying the joke. "I'm sorry, too, Chelsea. I really wanted to tell you, but Jason thought it would be a nice surprise. I'm stunned you two haven't previously met."

Jason squeezed my hand. "It was really inconsiderate of me. I shouldn't have asked her to do that. It's just that my brother and I are not on the best terms, and I wanted *him* to introduce us. Turns out it isn't going to be that way after all. He's not here, is he? The Universe is screwing with us." He grinned. "Melinda let leak that he was bringing you out here today. You see... he doesn't know that she hired me to convey you to your wedding. It was going to be a surprise. A nice one—or otherwise—depending on his reaction. We don't speak. Much. Hasn't he mentioned me at all?"

Beneath that rugged, handsome exterior I detected a note of vulnerability. It made it just a bit easier to forgive the deception. "He told me he had a younger brother who lives on a ranch outside of Cambridge. That's all." I paused. "Why haven't I ever seen you at any of the family gatherings?"

A slight sadness touched his clear grey eyes. Was I going too far?

Obviously, he didn't want to answer, but then he broke into that contagious grin.

"You will have to ask him."

At that moment Holly jumped up to hug his leg. She bounced up and down. *I'm hungry* her eyes said. He dug out a couple of artisan dog biscuits and gave them to her. He glanced up at me. Honey was shoving her nose into his hand. *I'm hungry too!*

My hands flew up in surrender. "Fine, but just one, she's on a raw food diet and I don't want to—"

"Really? So is Holly. Don't worry. These are all natural. Mostly oatmeal." His grin certainly was disarming. He slipped a biscuit to Honey who gobbled it down in two seconds flat before he returned his attention to us. "So, did you want to see the carriage?"

"Yes," Melinda said. "Let's go see the carriage."

"It's out front."

By this time I had tugged on my white leather coat and could feel the fur of the hood tickling my ears. It wasn't terribly frigid outside, not like it had been, but certainly cold enough for a coat. I knew my cheeks were flushed, and not from the weather. His eyes were taking in my whole appearance, making me feel something I'd never felt. Self-conscious.

"You two go ahead," Melinda said. "I have to go back and get my jacket."

For no reason at all I wanted to return indoors with her. But that would be rude and I had no plausible explanation for accompanying the wedding planner back inside. Jason's rugged casualness made me self-conscious. I was overdressed. But why shouldn't I be? I had a meeting in town when my business here was done.

The dogs raced ahead, me still clutching Honey's leash. Although Holly took the lead, she always checked to see if Jason was following. We trudged through the ankle deep snow around the three-story manor house to the U-shaped drive—in awkward silence. I was in shock from learning that he was my fiancé's brother. I was working triple time to keep from exploding with questions. He on the other hand was casual and aloof. It seemed nothing fazed Jason Frost—except maybe his brother.

We turned the corner and I raised my head from watching the dogs. My eyes widened with pleasure, as I stopped to appreciate the beauty before me.

CHAPTER TWO

The scene was spectacular with the majestic white pillars of the manor against the deep yellow walls of the main entrance, the elegant horse and carriage drawn up in front of it, and the bare trunks of the Carolinian forest coated in frost in the background. There was a single horse, a white one as I had requested, its pale satiny coat gleaming in the sunlight, wearing a red bridle with silver jingle bells that glinted along its entire length. The carriage was in shadow due to the angle of the morning, red in color and open because it was a sunny day, but it had a retractable cover in case of foul weather, and the seats were piled high with soft scarlet and silver plush throws. The sight sent a tremor up my spine. My fairytale winter wedding. Secretly, I *did* hope it would snow on the day, just *ever* so lightly.

"You can have two horses if you like," Jason said. "But I have only the one white animal."

"No. It's perfect."

"Glad you like it." He hesitated a second, then added, "So I understand that everyone will be staying here for a few days before the wedding. I am to pick up the bride here,"— he gestured at me—"that's you, and take you to the church. After the ceremony I'm to take the newly married couple for a ride while everyone gathers at the entryway and then bring you back to make your entrance as husband and wife after the photographers set up?"

I nodded. Was he laughing at me? I know it was a little over the top but this was a once in a lifetime thing. I could feel Jason's eyes on me, and a sparkle in his smile. Why did I feel like a spoiled debutante?

"*What?*" I asked, annoyed.

"Nothing. It's just that my brother always knew how to pick 'em."

"What do you mean?"

He had no time to answer that. His dog had run onto the grassy boulevard and was now barking like crazy. She snapped first at the snow, then at the air demanding he throw a snowball to her. My own dog was tugging at me to cross the drive so that she too could play. By now Jason was tossing snowballs at Holly who leaped after them. To Honey's delight he tossed a snowball at her, too. She gleefully leapt for it and shattered it with her jaws. The second ball that came for her smashed right into my stomach. I glared at Jason in outrage, before I burst out laughing. The horrified look on his face was all it took to send me into peels of hilarity. I cupped a palmful of snow and shot one right back at him. He retaliated and before I knew it we were both flushed with exhilaration, we were having so much fun.

A car drove up the long, winding tree-lined road. It was a vehicle I recognized, a dark blue Lexus, and it stopped short of us. I straightened from where I was crouched to cup more snow, and brushed myself off.

Just as the driver's door opened, the front door of the manor swung wide and Melinda came skipping down the stairs in her high-heeled boots and a smart wool coat in grey with a red scarf. "Bryce!" she called out to my fiancé.

From the day we met, Melinda had always called Bryce by his first name. Her high heels tapped across the plowed drive as she hurried to greet him. Jason, oddly, had his eyes affixed to both of us. I wondered if he thought her behavior as strange as I did. Although Bryce and I had both worked with Melinda on the wedding, it was I who did most of the consulting as he was too busy or just not all that interested in the details of flower arrangements, cakes and hors d'oeuvres. He had warned me from the beginning that as long as the wedding venue was nearby—so that his great aunt could attend—he didn't care all that much what we did. He knew he was in good hands because I had excellent taste. Now, as I thought about it, watching Bryce and Melinda greet, it dawned on me that they were awfully chummy for two individuals who were simply acquaintances. Then I realized that of course he must have known Melinda back in the day—if Jason did. And wasn't it she who had pointed out that they had known each other in high school? That got me to thinking. Maybe there was more going on here than I was privy to.

Melinda seized Bryce by the wrist as his right hand formed a fist. If I didn't know better, I could swear Bryce wanted to slug it out with his brother. What was he so angry about? Earlier Jason had revealed that his brother was unaware of Melinda hiring Jason's horse-and-carriage company. But that wasn't all. He was staring at the state of my snow-frosted clothes.

Nothing a little brushing off wouldn't cure.

"Why are *you* here?" my fiancé demanded of Jason. "And just exactly what were you two doing?"

"Showing the bride-to-be her conveyance to the nuptials," Jason answered amenably.

"With a snowball fight?"

Jason shrugged. "*She* started it."

I frowned at Bryce. He caught my look. "Hi sweetheart," he said. "Sorry about this." He came over and gave me a peck on the cheek. He would have kissed me on the lips, I know, had I not been wearing lipstick. "I see you've met my rogue of a brother."

"What's going on between you two?"

The pause that followed was awkward. Then he said, "You know what? Nothing. Nothing is going on. You are going to have the wedding that you desire. You want this horse and carriage? You've got it."

At that moment Holly broke free from Jason's grasp and leaped onto Bryce like a squirrel on fire. It surprised me to see her act like that, and it surprised me even more when Bryce dropped to his knees and allowed her to lick his hands and face.

"I wouldn't let her do that if I were you. I know where that tongue has been." Jason's comment was intended to be funny, but Bryce wasn't smiling. He gave each of the dogs one more pat on the head, before he withdrew a tissue from his jacket pocket, and dabbed at his nose and lips. Then he grabbed my hand and led me inside. Melinda followed. Jason remained.

"Thought you couldn't get away," I said.

"Meeting was cancelled." He glanced at Melinda and I did also. Their eyes touched lightly—like inverted magnets forced to reject one another.

"Glad you could come, Bryce. I *so* wanted you to see the Firshade Room."

After that unexpected meeting with his brother outside it was clear to me that he was in no mood to assess wedding venues. Besides, it was done. We had made the switch from the Orchard Room to the Firshade Room, and I had confirmed the last minute booking.

"Just a minute," I cried. In my distraction I had forgotten about my dog. I had left her outside. I raced through the lobby to the front door. In the broad, elongated, snow-coated boulevard in the center of the enormous U-shaped drive, Jason was playing with Honey and Holly.

"Lose something?" he asked, jerking his head up after tossing a snowball.

I just could not be mad at Jason Frost. And why should I be? What had *he* done? This discord between siblings was something I refused to let affect my wedding. I took the leash Jason handed to me. "You *are* coming to the wedding, aren't you?"

He sighed. "Well, I *was*. But I'm not so sure big brother wants me to."

He was squatting in the snow scratching the ears of his sweet spaniel. Now, Honey moseyed over to him to get the same treatment. If my dog liked him, he couldn't be *all* bad.

"What happened between you?" I asked.

"Shouldn't you be asking your fiancé?"

He was right, of course. I had only just met Jason.

"Thanks for keeping an eye on her." I raised the hand with the leash. "Come on Honeypot. Time to come inside. You're cold."

My Honey Bear was not as rugged an outdoor dog as Holly. Jason's dog clearly spent a lot more time in the wild.

I made a stop at my car to retrieve a holiday flower assortment that I had meticulously arranged myself. My hobby was floral arrangements and I dug my hands into the copious blooms and greenery whenever I had free time, which lately between work and wedding stuff, wasn't often. When I went back inside Melinda was packing up. Bryce was nowhere to be seen. I had set the flowers down on a table and wiped off Honey's feet with some tissues I had in my purse, but now I had no idea what to do with them, and I didn't want my dog to soil the hotel's floors.

"He went to say 'hi' to his great aunt," Melinda informed me. She took a tissue and blew her nose. "Here give those to me." She dropped her own tissue into a white wicker, plastic-lined container that she extended towards me, and I did likewise.

"Is it okay if I take Honey upstairs with me?" I asked.

"She's only allowed in the Cloisters."

The Cloisters was the French-inspired extension behind the main house, with rooms meant to accommodate visitors with pets. It was located across the courtyard, past the gardens in view of the dining room's windows. The rooms were just as lavish as the others in the main house and the Stables, with marble bathrooms and individual fireplaces, and terraces that opened out under arched pathways to a croquet lawn and swimming pool (both now empty for the winter) and a sleeping vegetable garden. The Cloisters was where I would be staying (until my wedding night) because I owned a dog.

Great Aunt Tessina however was housed in one of the most luxurious of the hotels offerings, on the top floor.

I recovered my flower arrangement, and left Honey with Melinda, who had pulled out another tissue while offering to dog-sit, and clicked across the marble floors. I remember vaguely hoping that she wasn't coming down with a cold. That would be *all* I needed. To be sick on my wedding day!

I waved to Honey. She attempted a lunge at me but Melinda held her back, and when she tried to leap up on Melinda, the wedding planner recoiled. "Be good," I shouted to my dog.

The Pine & Orchard Suite showcased a lovely living room with hardwood floors, a wood burning fireplace and hospitality bar. Overlooking the garden was a private balcony with an outdoor sitting area that at this time of the year was unused. Set off from the sitting area was a private bedroom, and as I walked past after being let in by my dashing fiancé, I caught to my left a glimpse of a king-size bedroom and spacious dressing room which flowed into a luxury marble bath with therapeutic soaking tub and enormous glass walk-in shower. The suite also had a generous day bed, which could accommodate overnight guests, plus an additional powder room.

In the living room Bryce's great aunt sat on a gloriously upholstered gold and cream divan. She looked every inch the regal matriarch of the family Frost. I lifted my gift of a flower-filled porcelain bowl towards her, and she smiled.

"Why Chelsea, what a beautiful and festive arrangement. White amaryllis and holly, and what are those beautiful white berries? Did you make this yourself? Bryce has told me what a whiz you are at home décor."

"Yes, I did. So glad you like it. Shall I set it on the sideboard?"

"I simply adore it. The last time anyone made anything for me was when the boys were little tykes. They use to love to draw me pictures. Here, take your things off. Bryce, help her. Lovely to see you again, dear." She gestured for me to sit when I was free of my cold weather trappings. She did not rise as her osteoporosis made standing difficult. "Darling boy, go and fetch us some tea. I wish to visit with your bride-to-be."

"Auntie," Bryce said. "We can't stay. We both have to get back to work."

"Oh, excuses, excuses. Are you going to deny an old woman the chance to visit with your lovely fiancée?"

Bryce smiled good-naturedly. "Anything Auntie. I'll order the tea." He turned to me. "Chelsea did you want to stay? I have to get back to the office."

I told him I had an hour before I had to leave. He left to make the call in the bedroom before letting himself out. "I'll see you later." He came to me, and under the amused eye of his great aunt planted a kiss on my forehead.

The moment he was gone, Aunt Tessina hoisted herself out of her chair. "Help me to the window, dear," she said.

I understood why she might like some fresh air, since living partially disabled and spending so much time indoors could not only get boring but was not conducive to good health. However, the urgency with which she rose not only startled me but also had me panicking because I thought she might injure herself.

Her arm weighed heavy in mine, but it allowed her to rest her weight on me as we made our way to the window, which I swear must have taken ten minutes. The sheers were swept to the sides and below in the U-shaped drive I could see Jason packing Holly into the carriage and preparing to leave. Just then, Bryce appeared on the veranda. When he saw Jason he marched over to him. His face was in profile and obscured from this distance, although it wouldn't have mattered even had he been facing me because I could tell from his body language that he was flaming mad. Why?

A sigh came from beside me. Aunt Tessina detected his rage also. I turned to her and wondered whether it would be presumptuous of me to ask.

"I wish those two would make up," she moaned.

I helped her back to the divan just as a knock came at the door. A glance at her indicated that I should answer it. It was

Room Service with the tea. The young man wheeling the cart stopped in front of the coffee table and began to lay out the tea service. He poured us each a cup. I inhaled the warm fragrance of Earl Grey. He and Aunt Tessina seemed to know each other quite well. They joked and he called her 'sweetheart' and then he left with a wink at me.

I sat down again, and tested my tea with two fingers and a thumb to the side of the cup. Aunt Tessina did likewise. It was too hot.

"What happened between them, Mrs. Frost?" I asked.

"Please, dear, call me Aunt Tessina. After all we *are* going to be family."

"Aunt Tessina, then," I said, feeling just that little bit awkward, but she quickly put me at ease. She was a delightful old lady with none of the pretentions I had expected.

"Oh, it was such a long time ago. And such a silly thing. Those two boys have done so well with their lives and I am very proud of them. Yes, they are as different as potatoes and peas, but both so smart and talented. I wish they could put their differences behind them. They were just schoolboys back then."

"It was a fight then? A disagreement?"

"It was more than a disagreement. It was an entire soap opera if you must know, and I suppose you *must* if you are to marry into this family. So where to begin...." She took the porcelain creamer and spilled a generous amount into her steaming cup before stirring it with a silver teaspoon. "Sugar and cream, dear?"

I accepted the sugar but opted for milk instead. I took a sip. The tea was divine. And waited.

"It happened when they were still in high school. It was Bryce's graduating year and Jason only a year younger. Every two years the big American corporations give away a business scholarship worth a hundred thousand dollars; both Bryce and Jason were candidates for it. But in the end the scholarship went to Jason." I nodded beginning to understand, but Aunt Tessina stopped me. "No, it's not what you think. Bryce was not angry because Jason won the scholarship instead of him. In fact, the good brother that he was, he was happy for him. No, what placed the initial rift in their relationship was not that. It was because Jason, after a year at business school at Yale, dropped out. He didn't consult with anyone, didn't discuss his options with his family. He just quit. It was—*is*—such a prestigious school. For a foreign student to get accepted into Yale on a scholarship was rare and impressive. But he had decided school just wasn't for him."

"But surely that wasn't all there was to it? I mean sometimes that happens. Just because someone is smart doesn't mean they want to go to school."

"Oh, I agree with you completely. But Bryce thought it such a waste. He went to the Rotman School of Management at the University of Toronto, and then he followed in his father's footsteps to Bay Street."

"And he is a very successful stockbroker."

"Yes, he is. But I think when he was in school he had higher aspirations."

True, I knew about those. He had thought at one time that he would be a top bank executive, even a CEO of a large corporation. "And Jason just wanted to build a small business?"

She nodded. "His brother thought it was such a waste of a scholarship and his education. And then of course there was Melly."

"Melly?"

"Jason's young lady. They were so close in those days. Knew each other since they were children."

Suddenly everything clicked into place. Melinda was Melly was Jason's Mel. I clasped a hand to my mouth. *Why didn't she tell me?* I shook my head, squashing the thought. Why *would* she tell me? We were practically strangers.

"My wedding planner is named Melinda," I said cautiously.

"How did you know about her?"

"Bryce gave me her card, said his secretary recommended her."

"And you went along with that?"

"I had no reason not to. When I looked up her credentials she was rated as one of the best in the city."

Aunt Tessina smiled. "I'm sure she is. Nice girl too. I thought for sure she and Bryce would get married."

Now, I was stupefied. She and—*Bryce*?

"But then she met that scoundrel whom she married and later divorced. All I can say is: thank goodness they had no children."

CHAPTER THREE

My jaw must have dropped three inches. Which is physically impossible, but you know what I mean. This was all news to me, but then like I said, we were practically strangers. I drew my mouth closed and tried to look unruffled. But there was no fooling Aunt Tessina. "You didn't know?"

I shook my head.

"Well, not to worry. It's all in the past. When Jason went away to Yale, Bryce and Melinda started dating."

"Was Melinda Jason's girlfriend?"

"I'm not sure I would exactly call her that. They were close. Maybe they were more like best friends. Although he did take her to prom."

Definitely girlfriend, I concluded. I wondered why Bryce had never mentioned any of this to me. And why had he given me her business card? It was as though he wanted me to hire her. And that is exactly what I did. "How long did they date?" I asked.

"Oh, all of this was long before you came into the picture. Let me see. Bryce graduated from business school when he was twenty-two. Jason was away at Yale for a year. He was nineteen at the time. He moved to California and worked on a ranch for a couple of years before returning home. In that time Bryce and Melinda were an item. When Jason learned of their relationship he was quite gracious about it, but of course I knew he was upset. He just wasn't sure why he was."

I remained silent the entire time she was talking. That happened seven years ago. It should all be water under the bridge by now. Jason had made a good go with his horse and carriage business. He was making a living. And Bryce had already made his first million.

"It seems to me that maybe Melinda and Jason had more in common than she did with Bryce."

"Oh, certainly that's true. I don't really see why the dear girl didn't resume her relationship with Jason. They are more like business associates now."

"But they're on good terms."

She smiled. "Well… as I said, it was a long time ago. Too long to hold a grudge for either of them."

I couldn't agree more. And it was at that moment that I made up my mind to fix their relationship. Both were wonderful men. Jason and I were practically strangers but from what I had seen of him this morning, my impression was positive. I couldn't wait to see Bryce tonight. It was inappropriate of me to ask his great aunt to explain why he and Melinda had split up. But I was desperate to know. *Why* did I want to know? Maybe it was just morbid curiosity, but I sensed she had something to do with the bad feelings between the two brothers. For a second, I wondered if Melinda and I were on friendly enough terms for me to broach the subject, but then I felt a twinge of guilt. None of this was really my business. Or was it? If knowing more about Melinda's connection with the brothers would help to repair their relationship, then I had to do something—didn't I? Bryce was going to be my husband. Jason would be my brother-in-law and Melinda, through no fault of her own, was my chosen wedding planner. Wow, was it tasteless for me to ask about something that had occurred so long ago?

No. I had a right to know the truth. And Bryce was the one to tell me.

Dinner reservations were at Scaramouche, Bryce's favorite restaurant and pricy. It was one of the last fancy eateries in the city offering an intimate dining experience. The others squeezed in so many tables it was like dining at the same table with strangers. So close did customers sit at most of these places that every word of their conversations was audible.

Not so at Scaramouche. The restaurant hummed quietly with voices in the distance. Almost every table was privileged with a stunning panorama (through semi-wraparound windows) of Toronto's glittering skyline. I loved this place, but Bryce didn't reserve it for special occasions. He frequently wanted to eat here because of the great food and ambiance, and the outstanding wine list. But I told him many times over that if we kept spending money in this fashion, we'd be through his millions in no time. In fact it was after our tenth dinner at Scaramouche that I wondered if our attitudes towards finances were a little conflicting. Oh, well. He was paying, and I told myself it was the risk analyst in me that felt nervous. Yes, that's what I do for a living; I am a risk analyst. My job is to identify and scrutinize possible risks that will impact on the financial success of a business. So it's no wonder that the same kind of thinking enters my real life.

I was waiting at the bar when Jason Frost walked in. Startled was the least of how I felt. Unlike Bryce who would have been wearing a stylish three-piece suit, Jason was outfitted in dress pants, a nice shirt and tie and a mismatched jacket. Still, he looked good which was why he had caught my eye. He recognized me instantly and approached to say hello.

"The Princess Bride," he said. "What are you doing here by yourself? You look sensational by the way."

I had gone home to change after my meeting and wore a champagne-hued cocktail dress and gold spike heels. "Thanks." I glanced down at the plunging neckline before adding, "I'm waiting for your brother. What are *you* doing here?"

"I'm meeting a client for drinks."

"Another gig?"

"You might say that."

A movement out of my corner vision made me turn.

"Melinda? You're here too?"

"Hey Chelsea! What a coincidence. Are you meeting Bry for dinner?"

Bry? "Ye...s," I replied, frowning. I was beginning to get the sense that this was not entirely a coincidence.

"Your... *client?*" I said to Jason.

He grinned. "Shall we keep you company until big brother gets here?"

Melinda did not object, although a very slight contortion in the muscles of her carefully made-up face indicated she was none too pleased with the suggestion. Her lips were 'hooker red' and her eyes seemed over-mascaraed. And the normally loose honey blonde hair was swept up in an attractive up-do. Her intended plans for the evening had not included me.

Jason appeared quite relaxed and oblivious of Melinda's true feelings, and her 'night out' look only added to the sense that my earlier instincts were correct. Something was going on between those two, but it seemed a little one-sided. How I wished I could bring up the subject of their past relationship and get the truth out of everyone. I glanced briefly at my smartphone. But that was Bryce's job. He should be the one to tell me of his previous entanglement with his brother's girlfriend.

However obvious the disappointment in Melinda's face, I couldn't bring myself to decline Jason's invitation to keep me company. I hated to drink alone. And that was why I got irritable when Bryce made me wait.

Jason ordered a scotch with water, and Melinda had a cosmo, while I nursed my martini. "Aunt Tessina said she had a nice chat with you this morning."

Was this an opening for me to plunge in with some direct questions? I answered, "We did. She told me some family secrets." I grinned slyly, trying to make light of things.

His eyes had a gleam in them that caused me inexplicable discomfort. I realized then that no matter what secrets I dug up about him, he'd brush them off. A glance at Melinda informed me that for her it was otherwise. And I knew for a fact that Bryce *would* care. After all, wasn't that the reason he had kept this feud with his brother safe from me all these years?

Melinda's phone chimed. She glanced down to read a text. A frown creased her forehead. "Dammit," she said. Then she covered her crimson lipsticked mouth and giggled. "Pardon my French. It's one of my other client's. Wedding emergency." She smiled brightly at me, and I knew from that moment that something had changed in our relationship. I also knew that if she minded the change, it was *her* fault because she had hired Jason's horse-and-carriage business without first revealing his true identity.

"I gotta go." This to Jason. "I was so hoping that we could catch up... Another time?"

"Absolutely," Jason said.

Melinda turned to me and waved. "See you later? Text me if you're concerned with anything about the wedding. Bye!"

Her excessive friendliness seemed forced. I glanced at Jason. He shrugged and returned my look. "Do you want me to leave?"

"No, why should I want you to do that?"

"You look perplexed."

"I am perplexed."

He raised his hands in an innocent gesture. "Care to explain?"

Was any of this my business? I hesitated, but my curiosity got the best of me. "Your great aunt told me that you and Melinda were once engaged to be married."

All right, so I was exaggerating a little. She hadn't exactly said that.

"Huh." His head hung thoughtfully for a second before he raised it to capture me with his startled eyes. "How on earth did she know? We never told anyone. We were planning to elope."

What? I clamped my lips shut before any sound could escape. This was not what I was expecting. I had assumed he would call me on my lie. Then tell me that it was Bryce who Melinda was engaged to. Or, at the very least I had expected him to say, *'isn't that something you should be discussing with your fiancé?'*

I was mortified, and totally confused. I cautiously met his gaze. In the restaurant's romantic lighting his irises were a lovely clear grey color, lighter in tone than his brother's, which were a deep slate blue. "You were engaged to Melinda?"

His eyes brightened a shade. "Past history. Don't look so upset. It was a mistake and I told her so before I left for college. I didn't want her to give up her dreams for *my* sake. She was willing to move to Yale with me and be my wife. We were nineteen. It was stupid." He looked past me at all of the colorful jewel-like liquor bottles backlit against the bar's wall of mirrors. "Besides. She was allergic to dogs. She would never admit it, but she was constantly sniffly and teary-eyed around my dog. I couldn't do that to her."

Wow, maybe *that* was love I thought. "Funny she never mentioned it to me."

"What, our teenaged engagement?"

"Well, that. Plus the fact that she was allergic to dogs."

I looked steadfastly into his face, which in some ways reminded me of Bryce. But something was definitely different. The pervasive seriousness wasn't there. In fact, this conversation seemed to amuse him. I ventured a thought. "Looks like she wants to pick up where you two left off."

"Honestly, we haven't seen each other in years. We were just catching up. After all"—he squinted humorously at me—"I'm sure you know that Bryce asked her to marry him shortly after he graduated college. You see, I didn't return straight away when I decided to quit school. I knew everyone was disappointed in me. But I had no idea *how* disappointed I had made my big brother. He was breathing fire. It was so bad, Aunt Tessina told me to stay away for a while. So I moved clear across the country to California."

I nodded.

"You know the story. She told you."

"Some of it."

"Well, you should probably get the rest of it from Bryce."

I sipped my martini, stirring the toothpick-pierced olive with my left hand. He tasted his scotch, but by the expression on his face I couldn't tell if he was enjoying it. I sincerely wondered why Bryce had neglected to mention his liaison with Melinda. It was unfair for her to be tangled up in their feud. "Do you know why they called it quits?"

Jason shrugged. "He broke it off with her when he heard I was coming home. Accused her that her heart was elsewhere."

"You mean with you."

"That was ridiculous. We hadn't communicated since our split up—at that time—four years back." He sighed. "Poor Melly, heart broken by both of the Frost brothers. And still keeps coming back for more."

"From what I can tell, she doesn't seem to mind. It's you two who have the problem."

"*I* don't have a problem," Jason said, looking up. He studied me under that impervious gaze, causing me to squirm under my dress. "You are gorgeous, obviously intelligent, and if that flower arrangement you sent my aunt is anything to judge by, talented too. I couldn't be happier that big brother is marrying the Princess Bride."

I flushed. "You are a charmer, Jason Frost."

"Be careful, I might just cast you under my spell."

I smiled. Then my eyes widened, and a wave of heat touched my cheeks, as I caught a reflection in the bar's mirror behind the colorful liquor bottles. It was my handsome fiancé entering the door.

Jason also noticed. "Looks like this is my exit cue."

"Wait, Jason. You don't have to leave."

But by the look on Bryce's face I changed my mind and

decided that perhaps it would be best.

Jason gave me a thumbs-up, saluted his older brother as he waltzed out the door, and Bryce came over to sit down on a barstool beside me. He scowled. "What did *he* want?"

"Nothing. He just happened to be here to meet Melinda for dinner, but she got called away by a client. Your baby brother is very nice. He offered to keep me company until you arrived."

"Left in an awful hurry."

I stared at Bryce, trying hard to understand him. I thought I knew this man that I was about to marry. In nine days I would be Mrs. Chelsea Frost. Only I planned to keep my maiden name for business purposes. "Can you blame him? After this morning? You weren't exactly the picture of brotherly love. I almost thought you were going to punch him in the face. What I want to know is why?"

"You don't know him, Chels."

"Well, I'm beginning to think that maybe you don't either. He's not the same as he was seven years ago."

"Seven years ago?"

I felt the color swim up to my cheeks. Oh no. Now I'd done it. He knew I knew something. He just didn't know what it was.

"I knew I shouldn't have left you alone with Aunt Tessina. She's a talker, that one."

"She's worried about you and Jason."

"She of all people knows why Jason and I aren't best buds. What did she tell you?"

"Only what happened with the scholarship. And...."

"Oh, the scholarship. That was nothing. I had high hopes for Jason. They just didn't pay off. What else."

I clamped my mouth shout. Should I mention the subject or not?

The maître d' saved me by appearing just at that second to take us to our table. When we were comfortably seated at a prime spot overlooking the cityscape, Bryce put his hand out to touch mine. His forefinger gently ran over the huge diamond he had given me last spring. "What other sordid secrets did my great aunt let slip."

My eyes were following the circular motion his finger was drawing on my ring. He had a habit of making nervous gestures with his hands when he was uncomfortable. This conversation was *definitely* making him uncomfortable.

"She told you about Melinda?"

My head rose.

"She was a mistake."

Poor Melinda. Both of the Frost brothers thought she was a mistake. And yet there must be something about her that had attracted them. Sure she was nice-looking but not exceptionally. For the life of me I could not understand it. How could an average woman like her make two men so crazy. At one time each was engaged to her.

"She came on really strong to me when Jason left. At first I ignored her because she was Jason's friend, but then she persisted and finally I gave in. We seemed to hit it off, but there was always something..."

I understood what he meant. When I met Bryce the chemistry between us was gentle and comforting. But ever since I met his brother I had been wondering...

"Chelsea. Are you listening to me?"

"Of course, darling. I was just thinking."

"Stop thinking. Thinking too much never solves anything. Go with your gut instinct. That's what I always do."

My instinct right now was telling me that he was being a might bit too bossy. I still wanted to know why he had hidden his *so* intimate connection with Melinda. What *other* secrets was he keeping?

He picked up his menu. "Shall we order? I'm starving."

I glanced down at the sumptuous menu and made my selection from the appetizers.

CHAPTER FOUR

It was Saturday afternoon and Bryce had to wrap up some things at work before he could take the five days off for our wedding. Honey and I had already moved into Langdon Hall. That way I could oversee all of the wedding preparations. I was feeling as though I could use a change of scenery and drove my excited spaniel into town. Cambridge was a small city located at the confluence of the Grand and Speed rivers where beautiful walking paths flanked the waterfront. Instead of embarking on a riverside stroll I opted for the downtown scene to observe the ongoing activities and events already underway for the Christmas Winter Festival. The music and games occurred at night, as did the lightshow, which I hoped to take in with Bryce before our wedding day. The official tree-lighting event kicked off tonight and Bryce was scheduled to join me.

I led Honey prancing down a clear tree-lined street, darting between the numerous boutiques, bakeries, candy shops and bistros. Everything was trimmed in silver and gold, with ribbons and bows and multicolored Christmas lights. Each lamppost had a green wreath surrounding their tops with festive bits of red berries and silver-sprayed pinecones woven into the green stuff. The smells were divine: Christmas cookies, orange, ginger and cinnamon. And evergreen clippings. The sidewalks were mostly dry although there were low snow banks at the edge of the road and against the buildings that were slowly melting.

In front of a florist, I stopped. It was a sweet, quaint little shop with unique arrangements displayed in the windows. Most of these were holiday themed and they primed my creative juices. Sometimes, I thought, I would love to give up the rat race and just spend my days arranging ornamental flowers. I felt a hard tug at Honey's leash, then a ball of tricolored fur (black, white and rust) bounced into sight and Honey and Holly were doing their greeting dance. I looked up to see the teasing face of Jason Frost.

"If it isn't the Princess Bride," he said, his smile breaking into a grin. He dropped down to his haunches to pet Honey.

Scowl or smile. My reaction was always a mix of both when it came to Jason Frost. "Do you really think I'm a princess?" I demanded. "Because if you do, that's rather insulting. *If* I am spoilt—it's only because of your brother." I relented to his charm and ended up shaking my head with pleasure. "Regardless of what you've heard, I was not raised in the vulgar lap of luxury as the two of you were." He merely arched a brow.

As a matter of fact, my family was pretty ordinary, middle-class. My father owned a hardware store, my mom was an administrative assistant at the local university, and my brother and sister both had government jobs. The only one of my siblings who had attempted to enter the world of big business was me. I sighed. To avoid further confrontation on the subject, I crouched down to give Holly a good scratch behind the ears and on her rump.

I snuck a quick peek at him. I was not really vexed and he knew it. "Hi to you, too," he said as we simultaneously stood up. His eyes shot toward the florist window before he returned his mesmerizing gaze at me. "Looking for some pretty posies for your wedding?"

How little he knew of wedding planning. "The flowers were chosen months ago."

He shrugged. "It's just that you were staring so wistfully through the window. I thought you hadn't made up your mind."

My lips continued to curve in an upward trajectory. I knew what he meant, but my mind was putting a different spin on his words. He was so charismatic. "No," I repeated. "It's just that I was wondering what it would be like to run my own business. Like *you* do. But it would be taking a huge chance. And as a practicing professional—who gets paid the big bucks to advise other business owners how to manage risk—I know what the odds of success are."

He swept a mop of unruly hair from his eyes. "Risk analyst, huh? Is that what you do. Sounds like something I could use."

"Why? Is the business not doing so well?" That gesture for some reason made me conscious of my own hair, which was tucked under a white angora tuque.

"It's a horse-and-carriage service. How well could it do?"

"There *are* a few around I know, so you've got some competition, but surely you retain a sizeable clientele?"

He shrugged. "Let's not talk about me. What about you? So, being a risk analyst isn't your dream job?"

I giggled, and adjusted my matching angora mitts. "Of course not. But it pays the bills very nicely."

"I have to say, there is something to be said for running your own business. Why not try it and find out?"

"I'm not sure what Bryce would think of me quitting my job and taking such a big chance."

Jason huffed. "Are you going to let him control your life? Marriage shouldn't be about one person controlling another person's life. It should be equal." I remembered that *that* was exactly the reason Jason had given for breaking Melinda's heart. He had not wanted to control her life. Or so he had said. But really, wasn't the choice hers? In a way, he had made it for her by eliminating the choice. Now, both of them were alone.

"So, are you not happy with your business, Jason?" I asked. From what I'd gleaned from the family, that was *his* dream job.

"Oh, I'm delighted with it. I love horses. I love living on a ranch. I'm just not that great at making money."

I laughed. "This coming from someone who won a prestigious scholarship to go to business school."

"Theoretically, I understand all of the principles of how to make a business successful. I just find it tedious, and yes, I'll admit, a little boring. Sometimes what you're good at isn't what you want to do."

"So true," I said.

Holly and Honey were still performing the slow dance in tight circles around each other. They certainly seemed to have taken to one another. Their eyes were bright and inquisitive and their tails swished in unison. And I had to admit I was certainly surprised by Jason. He had a smile that could light up a whole house.

So fixated was I with Jason's charm that the squirrel sailing down from a tree bypassed me unnoticed. Not so with Honey. She jerked her leash out of my hand, sending one of my mittens flying, and charged down the sidewalk with me in a panic. I was close behind and so were Jason and Holly, who soon sped past me. Terrified Honey would dash across the street if the squirrel did, I prayed it wouldn't. Somehow my prayers were answered and the squirrel shot up another tree with Honey in its wake. Jason whistled. And Honey turned. She dropped her forepaws to the ground and trotted up to him. He grabbed her leash, and as I caught up, he handed it to me.

"Better hang on tight," he said. "That one's a runner."

"I can't thank you enough," I gasped. "How did you do that? How did you get her to stop and come to you?"

He shrugged. "Just have a way with animals, I guess." He grinned sheepishly. Then handed me the mitten that I had lost.

"Well, thank you. I can hardly breathe. I thought that was it and she was going to bolt straight into traffic."

"It's okay, you can breathe again. She's fine."

I slumped to my knees wanting to scold her, but I was too relieved and yelling at her would solve nothing. The fault was mine. I should have been paying attention and not let the leash go loose in my hand. Oh, what would I have done had she gone rocketing into traffic and got hit by a car? The thought was unbearable; I cringed. Thank God Jason was there. But then a horrific thought occurred to me: without Jason's presence the whole frightening episode probably would not have happened. I would still be holding the leash, casually strolling down the sidewalk. I kissed my dog on the head and rose. Holly approached and poked her nose into Honey's. Jason was watching me with an amused expression on his face.

"How old is Holly," I asked crushing my thoughts.

"About seven, I think."

"You think? You don't know?"

"I adopted her. How old is Honey?"

"Oh, I see. Honey is eight."

"Still acts like a puppy. Just like this little dickens here." He reached down to where Holly had leaped against his leg.

"Well, at least she doesn't chase squirrels."

"Oh, sure she does. Just not on busy streets. But on the farm she's their worst enemy." He chuckled. "I'm heading back this way. How about you?"

"I'll walk with you," I said, even though I knew I shouldn't.

We retraced our steps until we reached the flower shop again. My car was two blocks further down but I didn't feel like returning yet.

Jason hesitated then looked down at his dog and said, "Stay here, be a good girl," and handed me Holly's leash. "I'll just be a second."

Before I could even think of objecting, he vanished inside the florist's while I wrestled with Holly's leash. After that near disaster with my own dog it was a wonder he trusted me with his. Holly wanted to follow him, but no pets were allowed inside the store. I double wrapped the leashes securely around my hands and clenched my fists. No more chances. And no matter how Holly struggled to go indoors, I resisted. Who could blame the owners for not wanting dogs in their shop? These two would have all the vases toppled and crashing to the floor in two seconds flat.

My breathing had quieted by this time and so had my thoughts, and the feeling of panic had dissipated. I squinted through the window. Jason was at the counter paying for something. His body obscured the purchase. All I saw were multiple decorative arrangements on the countertop wrapped in silver and gold paper with shiny red bows.

He came outside and told me that he had brought Aunt Tessina to one of her favorite teashops in town. "Did you want to pop in and say hello?" he asked. "I can take Honey for a walk with Holly if you'd like to have tea with her. It's a rare treat for her to get out, so I took her for lunch. We had a nice visit—while Holly waited in the car—but she always ends a meal with tea. She's still there. I'm not much of a tea drinker so she told me to go walk Holly while she had her tea. She takes her time, so if you'd like to join her, I'm sure she'd appreciate the company."

"I'd love it," I said.

Together we strolled to the teashop, and I handed over Honey's leash. "Don't give Uncle Jason any trouble," I teased. I shot an upward glance at him. He could see the concern in my face, which was poorly masked by my joke.

"Don't worry, I won't let her chase any squirrels."

Honey turned her head immediately and attacked a stray leaf. I laughed. "Well, I guess she doesn't care if I'm gone for an hour. She seems to love you two." On a playful note as I left, I said, "Watch out for flying leaves!"

CHAPTER FIVE

Aunt Tessina was delighted to see me. She ordered more tea and scones and some delightful miniature cream cakes.

"How nice of you to join me, dear," she said.

"I ran into Jason."

"Yes, I saw you from across the street."

I smiled. My tea came and I helped myself to a light flaky scone.

"You're awfully quiet, Chelsea. Is something on your mind?"

"Not really," I answered, trying to boost my spirits. She was right; I was feeling strangely down. Maybe it was the crash after so much adrenaline pumping into my system when Honey slipped out of my grasp. But I *was* feeling oddly low. I was getting married in a few days. What was the matter with me?

"You're worried about the boys," she said.

Yes, that was it. Well…. Partly it.

Aunt Tessina did not prod me. I sipped tea and bit into the scone, before brushing crumbs from my chin with a cloth napkin.

"I've seen the way he looks at you," she said.

I glanced up, my pulse suddenly quickened. Who? What did she mean?

"Melinda had the same affect on them."

My gaze dropped to the ring on my hand resting on the tabletop, heat rising from my collar. Jason was nice. Everyone liked him. Why did I have to feel so hot around the collar every time his name was mentioned? Slowly my eyelashes lifted, and I gave her a cautious glance. Her expression was well meaning—without an ounce of malice in it. I ventured what I hoped was an innocent question. "Do you think Bryce has any feelings left for Melinda?"

"No," she said quickly.

If the tone of her voice was anything to measure by, she was quite certain. "Jason, then."

Her silence was a little disturbing. It was as though she were weighing the meaning of my words. I meant nothing by them. It was none of my affair how Jason and Melinda felt about one another. "I've seen the way *he* looks at you," she repeated. "That should count for something."

Had her eyes hardened somewhat? Did she suspect what I was feeling? Who was she talking about? A burden weighed on my heart. I hoped to God, she was talking about Bryce.

"Do you believe in true love?" she asked me.

I had not meant to hesitate. How had the conversation taken this turn? I thought I did. I honestly thought I did believe in true love, destiny, finding Mr. Right. I had always believed in that. So why did I keep wanting to run into Jason? Why did his smile and his clever jibes amuse me so much? What was wrong with me?

"*Do* you?" she repeated.

This time I gathered my wits and answered swiftly. "Yes, I think I do."

"But you're having doubts?"

"No. Not exactly." I was flustered. I wasn't having doubts. I was just having unexpected feelings for my fiancé's brother. Was that unusual? Should I be worried? My mind was running a mile a minute. I resented having these feelings. It was disconcerting to receive a thrill whenever Jason Frost appeared on my horizon. No, no I couldn't possibly be having doubts. It was just—how do you know when you've found your one and only? Do your eyes simply never stray again? The questions froze on my tongue. They were incriminating, and they were absurd.

The old lady's lips twitched. "You're worried about

Melinda and Bryce. Because they were engaged and you think that he might not be over her."

I exhaled with relief. The secret remained my own. Aunt Tessina's thoughts were on a different tangent. Bryce was loyal. If anyone's loyalty should be questioned it was mine. After I reclaimed Honey from Jason, I must not see Jason alone again. Ever. I was not to be trusted.

"He thought she was *the* one at the time," Jason's aunt said. "He changed his mind."

Aunt Tessina's eyes were earnest and sincere, but behind the understanding was a level of wisdom that was quite unfathomable. Was she saying what she meant or did she mean something else? I answered honestly, "That's the thing that troubles me. How do you know when love is forever?"

She smiled and shook her head, breathed shallowly and sighed. "You don't, dear. When I was a girl I married Bryce and Jason's Uncle Ken. I loved him more than anything. He was tall and handsome and strong. And so kind. So very kind. And brave. Like Jason he loved dogs. Like Bryce he knew how to make money. He left me financially very secure, but money isn't everything. I would have given up all our riches to have him come home—and see his son grow up. You see, my dear, I was pregnant when he went away to war. He never came back. I didn't get the chance to know if our love would have been forever. But maybe *you* do. From what you've told me your parents have been married a long time."

"Yes, but my brother lives with his girlfriend, and my sister is onto her second marriage."

"Sometimes it takes more than one relationship to know. I never remarried. I never found anyone else I *wanted* to marry. I never felt that spark again. I think you are worrying over nothing." I could not bring myself to tell her that it wasn't Bryce's past relationship with Melinda that troubled me.

I was having problems staying focused on her words. My eyes kept drifting to the window, hoping to catch a glimpse of Jason's tall, broad-shouldered form. Seconds passed and I became aware of total silence. I jerked my eyes from the frosty street and met Aunt Tessina's gaze. As I observed her now, her makeup appeared impeccable. Sometime between my speaking and her answering, she had brought out her compact and touched up her lipstick. Her skin was carefully powered and blushed in just the right places, and her lips were contoured in soft pink. I knew she had to be close to ninety and that she had been ten years younger than her deceased husband. But she didn't look a day over seventy-five.

"Are you sure you're all right dear? I shouldn't have said anything about Bryce's past. I was concerned about the bad feelings between the boys, and I was hoping your presence could help mend their relationship."

My phone suddenly chimed, startling me, and I fumbled for my mitts as they spilled from my lap onto the floor. "I'll do what I can," I promised.

I couldn't linger as a text indicated that Bryce had arrived at Langdon Hall and had checked in. The text said that he was about to have a shower and that he would see me for dinner. As luck would have it Jason was back with the dogs, waiting outside the restaurant and grinning at us through the window. I tried to squash the warm feeling his twinkling eyes evoked inside me and thanked Aunt Tessina for her advice and the tea. Then I fetched Honey from Jason, avoiding further conversation with him, except for a swift and superficially pleasant 'thanks' and 'goodbye', and I drove back to Langdon Hall and to my luxury suite at the Cloisters.

Bryce and I had decided to book separate rooms until the wedding night, where we would move into the Stable Suite with its large living room inclusive of entertainment center and wood burning fireplace. It had beautiful glass doors that looked outside over the frozen lily pond and the ice encrusted apple orchard. I couldn't wait. My sister, when she arrived from Montreal in a few days, would stay with Honey in my current room. And Bryce would be giving up his present accommodation in the Main House to his parents.

***

Back at Langdon Hall, I chased Honey into our room and as I dropped my purse onto the sofa I noticed an exquisite flower arrangement on the coffee table. I removed the giant multi-colored bow and decorative outer paper from its base, and the green cellophane from the top, and was delighted to see a bouquet of white Oriental Lilies, red tulips, lush greens, and a classic red glass vase burst out of the wrappings. It was simple, but elegant. What a darling Bryce was I thought. I opened the card eagerly, pleased that all thoughts of his brother were a cozy but distant memory, and read:

For the Princess Bride,
May the honeymoon last as long as the love?

Jason

P.S. I have inside information that this florist is going to be for sale after Christmas. Opportunity knocks!

I cannot describe how I felt. I was thrilled beyond explanation… but horribly, wickedly guilty. It was innocent enough of him to send me flowers and there was nothing incriminating in the message. So why did I feel like I had just left my secret lover's bed?

I knew what it was. It was the question mark after the word 'love'. Why had he placed a question mark there? Did he not think my love for Bryce would last?

I placed the card on the table, before quickly lifting it again, and slipped it inside a side slot of my purse. I clasped my hands together. How did he know that I was partial to white lilies and red tulips, and that red was my favorite color?

This was obviously what Jason was doing in the florist

shop as I waited outside with the dogs. I pressed my face into the elegant blooms and got a nose full of wonderful fragrances. I should never have told him about my dream to operate my own floral boutique. That was a mistake. If he knew me at all he would know that I was hardly serious about giving up my big city job to enter the flower business. But then I realized that *that* was the issue. We were practically strangers. We had barely met.

My hands felt icy and I paced the room, Honey staring at me, puzzled. She whined and I approached where she lay curled up on the sofa in front of the cold fireplace. I petted her sleek toffee-colored fur and she settled down to sleep. Then I decided to call Bryce's room in the main house to see if he was out of the shower. A woman's voice answered.

At first I was too stunned to respond. My first thought was why would the maid answer the phone. There was voicemail for that. Then it dawned on me that I recognized the voice. "Melinda?" I said.

"Oh, hi Chelsea. I couldn't find you, and Bryce was in his room so I came up to see him instead."

That was a lie. I shook my head.

"Is he out of the shower?"

"Uh, no. Oh, wait a minute. I just heard the water turn off."

I hesitated. Why would she be in his room while he was in the shower? Something about this stunk to high heaven. "Who let you in?"

"He did."

"And then he went to take a shower?"

There was silence at the end of the phone. "Yes. He was tired from the drive in. He wanted to freshen up for you."

"Tell him I'm coming up."

"Will do," she said in a cheerful tone.

I was about to hang up, when it occurred to me that she hadn't mentioned what she'd wanted to consult me on. "Was there something about the wedding that you needed to tell me?"

"Oh, yeah." The fact that she hesitated made me suspect she was thinking on her feet. "Chef wants to know if you still want fresh flowers on the top of your cake or if you had a wedding topper for it."

The bakery was taking care of that. Why would he want to know? "Fresh flowers," I said.

I hung up and told Honey I had to go out for a while. She gave me a yearning look, then jumped off the sofa and went to her bed and curled up. I really wished that dogs were allowed in the main house. I wanted Honey to be part of my wedding party. That was the one thing I regretted about having a winter wedding. Otherwise we could have had the ceremony outdoors. "Be back soon, Honey Bear."

I touched up my hair in the wall mirror and noticed a look of strain on my usually smooth features. That wouldn't do. I would have to try to get more sleep.

I grabbed my jacket and walked across the courtyard to the main house. I hoped Melinda would have the sense to leave. I wanted to see Bryce alone. As I reached Bryce's room Melinda was at that moment leaving. "Oh, Chelsea, I was just talking to Bryce about Jason." She closed the door behind her and beckoned me away so that no one was in earshot of what she had to say.

"What is it?" I asked.

"He doesn't want Jason at the wedding."

"What? But they're brothers."

"I know. He thinks he might be hitting on you."

"What? That's absolutely ridiculous." I lowered my eyes slightly and hoped the discomfort in my demeanor was undetectable. "Let me go in and talk to him."

"Oh, I wouldn't do that right now."

"Why not?"

She paused, then said, "He saw the flowers Jason bought you."

CHAPTER SIX

Oh no. Had the hotel people sent the floral arrangement up to Bryce's room first? Melinda relished the distraught look on my face and took my arm. "He's in a tiff right now. I think you should wait before you talk to him."

"There's nothing going on between me and Jason."

Melinda's eyes were sympathetic. She of all people understood the magic of the Frost brothers. "I saw the bouquet, too."

"You were both in my room?" I was outraged. I would have to reprimand the hotel staff for violation of my privacy! But as my mouth opened to lambast Melinda for her unfounded presumptions and blatant intrusion, I realized I was acting like a guilty lover. I also realized if I spoke now everything would come out malicious and fumbled.

"I was in the lobby when the delivery man arrived. Bryce was at the front desk checking in."

And they read the card? How dare they? What was the world coming to when no one respected another person's property—or privacy?

"He didn't mean to read the card," Melinda explained. "It fell out of the package. It wasn't inside an envelope. And he knew it was meant for you because he overheard the delivery guy explain that they were for you. He thought it was okay to read it because...well...he *is* your fiancé...and he didn't expect you to have any secrets from him. Besides, I think he believed the flowers were for the both of you. After all you *are* going to be married in a few days."

He didn't expect me to have any secrets from him? Did she know what that sounded like? I *didn't* have any secrets. I did NOT. I was at a loss at what to say. I was certain my mouth was open but no words were emerging. What must he think? What must *she* think? My head felt like it was going to implode. I was acting like I had something to hide.

"So... you want to be a florist?"

Her voice was subtle but somehow she made my dream seem demeaning and stupid. I detected a sudden total loss of respect for me in her manner. Her smile was almost... *pitying.*

"A floral designer," I said, defensively. Why was I being defensive? I had nothing to defend. And what was wrong with being a florist? They did beautiful work and made people feel good. And yet I failed to keep myself from retorting: "It's just a hobby. I'm a risk analyst." I wanted to throw how much money I made in her face. But that would be boorish, not to mention petty and juvenile.

She nodded, her chin tilted at a superior angle. "I'll tell Jason you got the flowers."

She let go of my arm. I spun towards Bryce's room. What had just happened here? I turned back to confront Melinda again. I should fire her for her insinuations. But the moment had passed. She was gone.

I knocked on Bryce's door, my nerves jangling. But when he opened the door I knew I had no need to be fearful. His warm smile and sparkling eyes said it all. He suspected nothing. He drew me into his room and held me in his arms. Then he kissed me and I felt safe. I hugged him back with all my heart.

Later, after I had fetched Honey to join us, and we were snuggled up by the fireside, we decided to order room service for dinner rather than go out. That was perfectly fine with my little cavalier. We started with Roasted Squash and Saffron Soup, which had a swirl of maple cream and was topped with toasted almond croutons. The soup was followed by pan roasted Mediterranean Sea Bass, fingerling potatoes, market vegetables, and warm grape tomato and kalamata olive relish. Delicious. By the time I dug into my dessert, hazelnut crème brulée, and was settled with a hot cup of coffee, I was feeling so contented and secure that I finally dared bring up the subject of Jason. During our entire meal I had said nothing about Jason's flowers, and when Bryce failed to mention them, I suspected Melinda was lying.

"Bryce," I said, cautiously. "You're not upset about the flowers?"

"Which ones?" he asked. "The ones we ordered for our wedding, or the floral arrangement you crafted for Aunt Tessina?"

For a second I wondered if Melinda had lied about Bryce even seeing Jason's bouquet.

His eyes gleamed and I saw the mischief in them. "I don't care about Jason sending you flowers. That's Jason. That's what he does. He thinks its charming and sweet. And maybe it is. I've had time to think about things, now that you've met him."

"Sooo…" I frowned. "You're not upset about what he wrote in the card?"

"Hmm. Melinda told you. I'm sorry, I wouldn't have read it if I had known the bouquet was meant just for you."

"So, it's okay for him to attend the wedding?"

"He's my brother."

It was my turn to mutter, hmm. "What happened, Bryce? You were so angry earlier this week. I saw how you two greeted each other."

Bryce laid down the iron poker, and came over from where he had been tending the fire. He sat down on the edge of the coffee table, in front of where I lounged on the sofa with Honey's head on my lap. "Like I said, I've had time to think about it. Who am I to judge how he lives his life? I have to admit I was pretty ticked off by him dropping out of school. I don't know if he understands what a privilege it was to have been picked for a scholarship that I would have given my eyeteeth for. And to be the youngest recipient of such a prestigious award. He wasn't even finished high school yet. But like Aunt Tessina says, it's ancient history. I'm fine with it."

"Are you sure? Melinda said you wanted him off the guest list."

"What kind of a brother would I be if I didn't want him at my wedding?"

"You're amazing," I said.

"Well, we'll see if you still think that in ten years." He laughed.

I was no longer torn. What had I been thinking? Must be wedding jitters. I remembered my sister had told me that she had burst into tears the night before her second wedding. Our mom had asked: "Don't you want to get married?" She had replied through her tears: "Yesss." It was only the stress of making everything perfect Mom had said. "Everyone goes through it." And I thought it was only men who suffered cold feet. I smiled.

Despite the fact that I had vowed not to spend the night with Bryce until our wedding night, Honey and I stayed. I know it's old fashioned especially since we had been living together for a year, but I thought it would just be so exciting to spend those five days apart in the hotel before we got married.

In the morning, Bryce got a call to deal with some financial emergency at the office, so after he apologized profusely we kissed and he promised to return as soon as possible. Just as I was leaving his room Melinda called on my cell phone.

"Chelsea," she said. "I just want to apologize."

I was floored by the unexpected solicitousness.

"For what are you apologizing," I asked coldly.

"Bryce really seemed angry when he saw the flowers and the card from Jay. I just felt I should warn you. He's the jealous type."

I guess she would know.

"He wasn't mad. And he wants Jason to attend our wedding."

"Oh?" She sounded unconvinced.

"Anything else?"

"Yes. I hope you didn't think I was being rude yesterday. I am just so stressed out with doing two winter weddings, and a spring one down the line. And it *is* the Christmas season so everything is doubly hectic. I just want you and Bryce to have the most perfect day. And I know with the last minute scheduling things have probably been stressful for you, too. I'm an old family friend, Chelsea. I know I should have mentioned it, but I figured if Bryce hadn't, then it wasn't my place to spring it on you."

"I appreciate that," I said, cautiously.

"Anyway, I know Jay—Jason—is smitten with you—in an innocent way of course—so I was maybe a bit jealous. The brothers mean a lot to me. I cared for them a lot—once upon a time."

I know it was blunt of me but I had to know. "Do you *still*?"

There was barely a second of silence before she replied, "Well, obviously Bryce is out of the picture for me, but there's no reason we—he and I—can't be friends, is there?"

It was my turn to be silent. Animosity was not a nice feeling, but like I said earlier, something had changed. "And Jason? Are you interested in Jason?"

"Does it matter? After all, *you're* taken."

She was right, of course. It was none of my business who Jason dated. Why was I even asking? If I was to be absolutely honest, it was true that a revival of Melinda's relationship with Jason disturbed me. Her sudden about-face made me suspicious. She was up to something—but what was it? Was I being fair to her? After her remarks yesterday I would say, yes. But she had apologized and I had accepted it. So the whole thing should be laid to rest. And this feeling of duplicity, well that was something I would have to deal with. It was too late to fire Melinda for whatever reasons. Really, what had she done? Except point out to me what I already knew. That I had succumbed to Jason's charms, resulting in a ridiculous crush on my fiancé's baby brother, and possibly making a fool of myself.

***

I decided to go and see him to thank him personally for the flowers and to ensure that I had not sent him any inappropriate signals. I pulled up at his ranch and parked. There was a sign on the fence that read:

Dashing Through The Snow (or Sun)
All-weather Horse and Carriage Service
For that Touch of the Past

I felt shivers run throughout my entire body. The name of his business made me feel warm. It was such a dynamic name. His logo was that of a stylized horse and sleigh in midflight. The colors he had chosen were primarily black, red and white. I heartily approved.

I turned to look for the house. To my left I saw a flagstone path lined with three near life-size natural fiber reindeer. They looked to be made from bark and dried vines. The path led to a low, long building with remnants of snow on the roof. Icicles hung from the eaves in long glittering spears.

It was a nice place but on closer scrutiny I could see it needed some repairs. The railing on the front veranda was grey with age and the wood feathered in places. The deck boards were stripped and spotted with encroaching moss around a very nice welcome mat. There was something about the way nature had added its own touches that made the structure seem homey rather than rundown.

The house itself was ranch style with log siding and a beautiful antique wooden door with a stained-glass window. Just below the window was a natural, mixed cedar and pine wreath with cones and red ribbons. The creative half of my mind longed to fiddle with the wreath to make it less plain, my fingers going so far as to twist the drooping bows into stiffer shapes, and I almost laughed aloud at my audacity.

Bryce had never been one for public displays at Christmas, so it didn't surprise me that his brother was the exact opposite.

I had texted Jason to announce my imminent arrival, and he had texted back to inform me that he would be delighted with my visit. Just before I left I had played with the idea of returning the bouquet to him, but if I did that, wouldn't that be an admission of guilt? I did not want him to think I had any romantic feelings for him—because I didn't.

When he answered the door, he looked so cavalier, so handsome in his jeans and shirtsleeves that I caught my breath—and had to ball my fists to control the unwanted sensations coursing through my body. "Hi Jason," I said.

"Nice to see you again, Princess Bride."

Please stop calling me that.

Honey jerked free of my hold and galloped through the door as she greeted Holly. "Those two really love each other," I commented in an attempt to normalize the situation.

"Sure and why not?" he said. "It's all in the family. So what brings you to my humble abode?"

Now that I was here I realized that nothing overt had ever happened between us. I had never shown him how I felt (I hope), and nothing inappropriate had been done on his part. That connection I thought I felt with him was probably just because he loved dogs. And now that I was here, I felt rather stupid. *Because really: what if I am just making it all up?* He didn't exactly hit on me.

But then Melinda had noticed, hadn't she? She had said that Jason was smitten with me. Those were her exact words.

"Did you want a tour of the facility? Afterwards, maybe I can take you for a ride in the carriage that Mel hired for your wedding day."

Yes, I thought. That was exactly what I wanted. But why did his mention of Melinda and his nickname for her prick so uncomfortably? Mel. Mel and Jay. I crushed the involuntary flinch, and filed away the intimate image of them for a future day to analyze.

"I'll introduce you to the gang first."

I told him I had been thinking about what he'd said about needing my services. As a risk analyst I could help him to better manage his business. I wondered briefly if he knew he was just giving me an out for my bold and spontaneous visit, but so what? I was going with it.

He grabbed a jacket off a hook on the wall and whistled for Holly. My dog came running as well and we all went outside, me making a mad dash for Honey's leash. Holly was so well trained and so attached to Jason that she never left his side, and needed no leash.

CHAPTER SEVEN

Jason introduced me to his trainer and one of the team drivers, Joe, whose passion for horses was obvious. He also had a wagonette designer and a carpenter named Vern to do the building construction of the custom horse-drawn vehicles. There was also a young woman, Barbara, an equine specialist who did just about everything from driving the teams to grooming, care and nutrition of the animals and working the farm. She was the one that Melinda had coordinated the details of the horse-drawn service with: i.e., she was responsible for the ribbons in the horse's manes and the jingle bells on their bridles.

Most of the horses were out on the open pasture, grazing at the tufts of winter grass that poked through the clumps of shallow, melting snow. There were no scheduled events for today so Jason pointed out some of his animals. The handsome dark brown quarter-horse with a black mane and tail that trotted over to his outstretched fingers was called Mac. At the far end of the field was Saffron, a beautiful golden palomino with a flowing white mane. Sheena and Deirdre were Belgian horses, weighing in at fifteen hundred pounds each. The girls he said were gentle giants and were used most often to pull the larger wagons for corporate and private parties.

"And Snowflake, you've met," he said, extending a hand to pat the white mare that sauntered over at his beckoning. "She will be pulling your one-horse-open-sleigh. Or wagon—depending on the weather."

"What a wonderful place," I exclaimed, turning shining eyes up at Jason.

"The world is as wonderful a place as we make it," he cheerfully replied.

At the time I did not realize how profound a remark that was. It had never occurred to me that I had any control over the wonder of the world. My response was: "You're happy here." It was a statement and not a question.

"Yeah, it's pretty cool." His eyes were lit up like a schoolboy with his first bike. Then he turned away to open the gate and led Snowflake back to the stables to be harnessed. "But like I said it's losing me money."

One of his employees, I think his name was Joe, hitched Snowflake to the beautiful carriage that was to be my wedding conveyance. Jason boarded first and then lowered a hand to help me up to the cushioned seat beside him. The dogs also wanted to come; both of them were bouncing around, Honey straining on her leash where Joe was holding her. He lifted her up onto my lap and Holly leaped up by herself like an acrobat, climbed up on the seat and wiggled between us.

I laughed. "I can see she's use to coming with you."

He shrugged. He snapped the reins and the horse started off at a trot. We took the scenic route through the woods where there was a wide trail. "Are you warm enough?" he asked. He grabbed a blanket from the backseat and gave it to me. I maneuvered it under my dog onto my lap.

The sun was bright and slanted through beech and elm trees that provided just enough shade to keep me from squinting. There was a beautiful cluster of slender birches, their plain branches almost glowing against the darker trunks of the maples and oaks. I glanced sideways at the thin layer of trampled slush, the horse's *clop clop* making a rhythmic sound to the gentle vibration of the wagon wheels. Through white clumps of soft snow the green of wilted trillium tried to poke their leaves into the dappled sunshine, and the remains of dried huckleberries scarred the edges of the path. I turned back to Jason, unsure how to broach the subject of his gift but I knew I had to try.

"By the way, thanks for the flowers," I said.

"You're welcome." He glanced sideways at me and said, "I know the owner of that shop. It's going up for sale. You should seriously consider buying it."

"I *have* a good job."

"Of course you do. But you're not happy."

"Why would you say that? You don't know anything about me *or* my job."

"I know that you wouldn't get so annoyed—*if* you were content with that job."

I fell silent. "I have a degree in Business Management and Risk Analysis."

"Doesn't mean that that's what you want to do. It's not exactly creative."

"It is in a way. I have to solve other people's problems to make sure their businesses are financially viable and more likely to succeed. I've even saved a few companies from bankruptcy."

"Good for you." It was his turn to go silent, before he said, "What's wrong with running a flower shop?"

"My parents would never understand. Not after all the money they spent sending me to university."

"Like *my* parents?"

Oh dear, major *faux pas*. Aunt Tessina's snap rundown on Jason's history returned to me in a flash. I had forgotten. It was no fun to be considered the Black Sheep of the family. I turned apologetic eyes at him.

"It's okay. I'm used to it. Doesn't faze me a bit." He grinned. "I think you'd be fantastic as a floral designer."

Why would he think that? I frowned.

"How you earn your living doesn't make you who you are, Chelsea. It's what you do with your life, how you treat other people that makes you who you are. All I'm saying is that, why not be happy at what you do?"

I had a highly sought after, prestigious position at a top company. I was an indispensable pillar of the finance world. It was up to professionals like me to prevent or mitigate losses and damages to firms, and therefore the economy, as well as overall integrity within business and the finance industry. It took brains and the ability to think outside the box to do what I did!

"I'm not arguing with you," he said.

"Yes you are. You said my job wasn't interesting. It *is* interesting. Risk managers deal with all sorts of different areas of risk, spotting the dangers through a mixture of investigations, industry and market research, data analysis and calculations and developing ways to best manage it all. We constantly have to adapt to new challenges posed by changes in industries, new regulations and government legislations and the individual needs of clients. So yes, it *is* interesting *and* challenging," I ended breathlessly.

"I didn't say your job wasn't challenging. I said it wasn't creative. And if it's such a great job why are you being so defensive?"

I scowled. "I know people who would give an arm and a leg to have my job. I *am* happy."

He shrugged. "It's *your* life."

He stopped at a clearing in the woods. The snow here was deeper, flat and totally untouched. We both stared at it, and I caught the mischief in his eyes as he smiled at me. "Are you thinking what I'm thinking?"

I have no idea why I thought that I was. I nodded and made to leap from the carriage. "Hold on," he said. "Let me get Honey down first."

She was eager to mess up the pristine snow. But not before I could.

Jason lowered Honey to the ground keeping her leash looped around his wrist and handed me out of the carriage. He was so strong. I forced that thought out of my head and beat him to the clearing. "Will the horse be alright," I gasped.

"Don't worry, she won't leave. I tied her to the trunk of that tree." He shoved a finger in the appropriate direction.

"Good." I ran into the middle of the clearing and dropped onto my back. Honey pranced around me while

Jason flopped down beside me a few paces away and Holly danced around him in circles. Fortunately, I was in jeans and parka today. Jason began to wave his arms and legs repetitively, creating a giant snow angel. I giggled like a girl and did likewise.

Why did I feel so free with him? I have never done anything like this with Bryce. At the thought of Bryce, I opened my eyes and stopped moving. I sat up. What was I doing? Honey was digging furiously in the snow, and then raised a snow-encrusted snout. "Okay, Honey," I said. "That's enough. We'd better go."

Jason was puzzled at my sudden change in mood, but I refused to explain. I refused to explain anything to him. He wasn't my boyfriend.

***

The return trip felt shorter than the outward journey and after an awkward few moments of silence we resumed our conversation of earlier. Jason really thought I should pursue my dreams. And I had trouble convincing him that dreams were dead ends. "For someone who studies financial risk," he said, "You're unusually cautious... Even afraid?"

It felt more than a little annoying to be analyzed by Bryce's little brother. How old was he anyway? I did a quick calculation in my head. Bryce was a couple of years my senior. That made Jason about the same age as me.

I was glad when we turned up the trail to the ranch. I declined to discuss my future prospects with him anymore. Why was it so upsetting? Could it be because he had managed to hit on the truth? But that was absurd. I made a pile of money. He was the one who should be coming to *me* for advice.

We wheeled into the drive and he stopped. Snowflake snorted and a puff of steam rose from her nostrils. Joe came out from the stables and helped Honey and me down from the carriage. "Enjoy the ride?" he asked with a big smile.

Mostly. I squirmed. "Yes." And returned his smile. I

placed Honey on the ground and looped her leash around my wrist. "Well, thanks for letting me try out the carriage," I said to Jason.

"Anytime."

I looked around. Joe had gone inside the barn, and no one else was around. I was still a little perturbed by the fact that Jason could make me feel so happy one moment, and so annoyed the next. I had to get to the bottom of these feelings. It made no sense. I glanced around at the ranch. "So, you said you're not making much money with this enterprise?" I assumed my professional Risk Analyst persona and continued. "Well, maybe I can help you with that. Call me and we can set up an appointment."

My tone was deliberately stern, but he saw through my tough act. It was true that with Jason, nothing fazed him. He observed me with heavy lids and smiled. "You are so sweet. Why would you do that?"

"We're going to be family. Why wouldn't I want to help you?"

He placed a hand under my chin and tilted my head up. "Sure you think that's a good idea?"

I pulled away. "Jason—"

"Yeah," he said.

"What did you mean by sending me those flowers?"

He shrugged. "I thought you might like them."

"And the card. It was rather cryptic."

"Was it?"

I knew I wasn't going to get any cooperation out of him this way. The card was not only cryptic it was insinuating that love, the love between me and his brother, was finite. I had to be blunt. "Are you flirting with me?"

He laughed. Darted his eyes up at the sky then down the trail. "You tell me. What was that business in the woods, in the snow, back there?"

Why did he have to be so handsome?

"Hey, I'm sorry Chelsea. Am I making you uncomfortable?"

I scowled. "You know you are."

"I think you're really.... I think you're really great."

"Thanks, but—"

The dogs started barking and I saw a car roll up the long gravel drive and park beside mine, a blue Lexus. Bryce exited and on the passenger side, Melinda followed.

I could see in Bryce's eyes that he was trying really hard to contain his emotions. I forced myself to imagine what this must look like to him. I pushed away from the fence where I had been leaning, lost my footing, and almost went chest first into Jason.

"Bryce," I said. "What are you doing here?"

"What are *you* doing here?" Melinda asked. "Was the horse and carriage I chose not to your liking?"

"No. I mean yes. It was perfect. I was just... I came here to give Jason some free advice regarding his business."

"Oh?"

We both sounded awkwardly formal. Why was Melinda being such a jerk? And what was she doing with Bryce? I glanced up at him for an explanation and he returned my glance equally demanding of answers.

"I was looking for you at the hotel," she said.

"Why didn't you call my cellphone?"

"I did. There was no answer."

I yanked out my phone from my handbag and saw that the battery was dead.

"How did you know I was here?"

"Just a guess."

What would make her guess that I would be at Jason's ranch?

"I ran into Bryce in the hotel parking lot. Told him I couldn't find you. So we came out here to look for you."

All this time Bryce had not said a word. Now his eyes took in his surroundings and I noted a slight frown. Yes, the place needed some work. Had Jason been neglecting it?

"What did you want to talk to me about?" I asked Melinda.

"Oh, right. I was trying to get permission to have the dogs be part of your wedding party. But Langdon Hall is firm on that. They apologized and wished they could accommodate your request, but they can't have dogs indoors where there is food being served. It would violate health regulations."

"Oh." My face fell. I always ate food with my dog. "Well, thanks for trying."

"Of course."

I still could not figure out Melinda. One moment she was as sweet as sugar, trying to please me, and then the next she looked like she wanted to get her hooks into my fiancé. *And* his brother. Well, what Jason did was not my concern.

"Jason," Bryce said. "We need to talk."

"Sure, anytime, Big Brother."

"I'll call you."

Jason nodded. It was hard to tell if Bryce was upset or not. He had nothing to be upset about. At least not where I was concerned.

CHAPTER EIGHT

Next day Bryce went into Toronto to pick up his parents for the wedding. Which was to take place in four days. They had decided to arrive early and make a mini holiday of it. Melinda called for me to join her in the lobby of Langdon Hall. "I've had an idea," she said.

Trusting her had become a major issue for me, but I answered, "Okay. What is it?"

"I know how much you want Honey at your wedding, so I've been trying to convince the owners to allow us to perform the ceremony here instead of at the church."

"But I thought you said she wasn't allowed indoors, except for the specified rooms allocated to guests with pets."

"I said you couldn't bring a dog into any place where they are serving food. If we have the ceremony in one of the smaller rooms it should be okay. The Orchard room, as far as I know, is still available since we've moved the reception to the larger venue. It's just a matter of setting up an altar and rearranging the furniture to create a chapel. I have a friend who can do all of that on short notice. We'll simply have the flowers shipped here instead of the church. What do you think? This way Honey can be in your wedding party. She just won't be allowed inside the Firshade room for the wedding feast."

"Really?" My mood brightened at the thought of my Honey at the ceremony.

"Shall I go ahead and make the arrangements? I don't know what the church will do. They'll probably still charge you for the cancellation."

"No matter," I said. "I will gladly pay all the fees, plus

offer a donation to make up for the inconvenience and loss of revenue, oh anything to have my Honey Bear at the ceremony!"

Melinda smiled. I stopped thinking badly of her. She was certainly making up for her unpleasant behavior of a couple of days ago, so I decided to trust her and returned the pleasantries.

"I know you and Bryce will probably want to have dinner with his parents tonight so if you need someone to puppy-sit I'm available."

That was so nice of her. I had been considering using one of the hotel's pet sitters. We had been living at Langdon Hall for three days now and Honey was getting used to being alone in the room. But if she got bored she might bark and I couldn't risk disturbing any of the other guests.

"You really wouldn't mind?"

"Not at all."

That evening after I was dressed for dinner I received an unexpected email from my boss. It said:

Chelsea, great news. Just heard from Corporate. You've been promoted. You are now senior risk consultant. That means a big jump in pay. How's that for a nice wedding gift? I know you're busy with wedding preparations. But congrats! See you at the ceremony.

I was floored. What an amazing piece of news. I would be the youngest Senior Risk Manager my company had. Why didn't I feel more excited? Bryce would be so proud. And Jason. What would *he* think? That whole conversation at the ranch suddenly repeated itself in my head. Oh, why did I even care what he thought?

This was a great promotion. I would be head, the *head*, of the Risk Management Department. I would be responsible for forming advisory and professional services specializing in operational and financial risk. I would no longer be stuck in the office but would work on site on certain projects and have the opportunity to travel Business Class, all expenses paid, and stay in the ritziest hotels in the most fabulous cities in the world.

Why wasn't I happy? Why hadn't I called Bryce to tell him the awesome news?

Honey barked at me to draw me out of my thoughts. Did *she* have something to do with it? I would have to leave her alone. A lot. A soft knock came from outside. Someone was at the door.

I let Melinda in to sit with Honey. I told her that if she needed to let Honey outside, to use the entrance onto the private patio that led through an archway onto the croquet lawn. The lawn was currently blanketed with a light coating of snow and the lily pond was frozen over. I insisted she keep Honey on a leash if they went outside. I made her promise, and she did.

As I finished putting the last touches to my makeup and hair, I heard on the TV that there was a forecast for more snow. In fact, the meteorologist was predicting a blizzard and warned people to stay off the roads and remain at home. Feeling cozy and safe in my luxurious room I was grateful that we planned to eat in the hotel's dining room tonight. Outside my windows however there was no sign of a single snowflake.

But then I got the phone call that was going to change my life.

The post office in Cambridge was holding a parcel for me. I knew what it was. It was the Christmas gift that I had ordered online for Bryce. They were supposed to deliver it to the hotel, but there was some sort of mix-up and because of the impending storm they were suspending deliveries until further notice. That meant I would have to pick it up myself if I wanted to have it by Christmas Day. I glanced outside. It had not started snowing in earnest yet, only a gentle sprinkling, like dust. Downtown Cambridge was a mere few minute's drive from here. The post office closed at 7:00 pm.

Dinner was at seven-thirty. I had time to make a quick trip into town and claim the parcel.

On reflection it was a mistake not to tell anyone where I was going, but I thought I would be back in twenty minutes.

***

I drove my Honda into town and parked by the side of the road. There was little traffic now that rush hour was almost past. The snow was falling heavily but I still wasn't worried. I went into the post office and showed my ID. When I returned outdoors with the small parcel, the wind had picked up and snow was swirling. The post office put up its closed sign. Lucky for me they hadn't closed before I arrived. I ducked my head, hugged my fur collar to my throat and dove shoulder first into the squall. I could not believe how hard it was blowing. I jerked open the car door and jumped in, bringing all sorts of snowflakes with me. I dusted myself off and fastened my seatbelt.

By now the streets were practically empty. Nobody in her right mind would be braving this blizzard. Had I known it would catch up to me so fast I wouldn't have bothered to head out, but I did so want to have Bryce's gift with us for Christmas Day.

I headed up the road, the white glazed forest appearing out of the whiteness. I could barely see my way as I wound through the faint trees. My wipers were swishing back and forth at full speed, but the snow was falling just as quickly as the blades could sweep it aside.

It was piling up on the road too. I could hear my tires laboring, churning the heavy stuff into thick slush. Then it thickened to the point where it felt like I was plowing through bread dough. Only another few kilometers and I'd be safely back at the hotel. I saw the lane that turned off toward Jason's ranch. If worse came to worse I could stop there to wait out the storm. I could even abandon my car and go the rest of the way on foot—if I had to. But then I glanced down at my spike-heeled designer boots. These boots were not made for walking—no less slogging through two feet of powder.

Suddenly the tires seemed to slide out from under me. I lost control and slammed into a snow bank. A clot of snow landed from the tree branches overhead onto the hood of my car. A double thud struck my ears as another clot followed, then another. I stepped on the gas, starting to panic. I tried again, and again. The wheels spun in place, churning up pellets, the hard metallic pings warning that my efforts were futile. The engine choked, the tires ground on ice beneath the snow. I wasn't moving. The car was stuck.

I shut off the engine and scowled. It was dark except for the brilliant white of the snow. If I sat here much longer the car door would be blocked. I would be buried alive.

I got out and trudged to the rear of the car. Maybe if I pushed I could get it dislodged, but then I realized as I stared at the car's rear bumper that it would only make things worse. The snowdrift obstructed the front end.

Well, what about shoving at the hood? If I could wedge myself in between the snow and the front bumper, could I budge it even a few inches and get it unstuck? I glanced around me, then up at the sky. White flakes were dropping down on me fast. Two more inches had piled up in the time it took me to realize my vehicle was hopelessly trapped, and the interior seats were no longer visible through the windshield.

I could not wait around for someone to dig me out. I had to make my way on my own. I futilely shook myself free of the relentless flurry, and tucked in my newly curled hair, which was now uncurling and dragging around my shoulders. I pulled my fur collar up as high as it would go and made sure all of my buttons were fastened. My brand new lambskin gloves were not made for inclement weather. Already my fingers were cold. Soon they would be icy. The thin leather was all there was between frostbite and me.

Time to move. I knew where I was. The hotel was less than two kilometers from here. Could I make it? These boots would be ruined. But it was either that or die here in the snow.

I started to walk, tears blurring my vision and freezing on my cheeks. I was already knee-deep in the white stuff. If I didn't hurry it would be up to my thighs before I ever reached the hotel, and I was pretty certain that I didn't have the strength to plow through that. This had to be one of the stupidest things I have ever done. And for that reason alone, I was going to have to make it out of this storm.

The swiftly falling snow muffled all sounds. Only the whining of the wind penetrated my ears. I could no longer see the road. The only way I could tell that I might still be on it was the parallel row of trees on either side. I had only made it a half a block up the road when I heard something—or thought I heard something. The drumming of hooves in the snow. I turned and what to my amazement should I see but Jason in a fleece-lined leather jacket astride a white horse. I swear at first I thought I was dreaming. But when he appeared through the blur of white, slowed to a halt and dropped to the ground and came to me, I knew the nightmare was over.

"Chelsea," he shouted, "what are you doing out here? I saw your car back at the turnoff. Are you hurt?"

"No." But I was freezing cold, and loose strands of my hair were wind-whipped against my cheeks.

He grabbed me by the arm. "We have to get you inside and warm before you get hypothermia." He lifted me up onto the back of his horse, and then got on behind me and thrust his boots into the stirrups. He glanced around, sizing up our options. "We can't make it to the hotel. Weather's too bad. Hang on. We're going to have to outrun this storm!"

I had never ridden a horse before and all I could think to do was hang on to the saddle horn. And that was exactly what he advised me to do. He had one hand on the reins and the other around my waist so that I wouldn't fall off.

I clenched the saddle horn like my life depended on it.

Flurries plastered against my face, wind whipped my

hair.

I hung on.

CHAPTER NINE

By the time we got to Jason's ranch I was covered in snow. He leaped off the horse and helped me down then tied the animal up to a post. I shook myself like a dog, white stuff showering down like sand, and slapped loose white clumps from my shoulders. My hair was streaming wet and just as quickly starting to freeze. I demanded he take the horse to the stable first, but he insisted just as firmly that I go inside the house. He unlocked the door and Holly came charging out to greet us. I welcomed her warm tongue on my hands and cheeks. "Get those wet things off," he ordered me. "I'll be right back as soon as I get Snowflake settled in the barn."

I began to peel my gloves off like an obedient child. My fingers were so frozen that they refused to obey. The leather was sodden and would be stained and brittle upon drying. Then came my coat. The fur around my neck was soaked and flattened to my skin like a newly bathed puppy. The coat was no easier to unbutton than removing my gloves had been. Eventually I got it off, shook out the excess moisture, and hung it up on one of the hooks by the door. I had nothing to dry myself with and let the meltwater drip down my face and onto my dress. My boots were next, and yes, they were ruined, but at least *I* was all in one piece. My wet things had made a puddle on the floor and I went into the kitchen to locate some paper towels.

Jason was gone for about twenty minutes, but when he returned he was breathless and coated with snow. Without thinking I helped brush him off, before I realized what I was doing and stopped. He sent me away laughing. "You're going to ruin your dress if you do that."

I glanced down. I was clad in an emerald silk evening dress. My wet hair was dripping all over it. I grabbed a handful with stiff fingers and tried to squeeze out the excess moisture onto the already sodden doormat, but only succeeded in dampening my dress more.

He smiled at me. "Do you want to get out of that wet stuff?"

I shrugged helplessly. "I'm supposed to be up at the main house having dinner with Bryce and your parents."

"Well, *that's* not gonna happen." He glanced briefly out the window. "Not tonight." He returned his attention to me, his brow creasing like a scolding brother and said, "Now... would you mind telling me what you were doing in that whiteout?"

At first I was annoyed at the tone of his voice. But then I realized that he was teasing me. I felt foolish for what I had done, so naturally I was taking him seriously. I relented at the glimmer in his eyes. "I drove down to the post office to pick up—" I clapped my hand to my lips in utter exasperation. After all that fuss, inconvenience and excitement I had left the parcel inside the car! "I went to pick up Bryce's Christmas present at the post office." I shut my eyes briefly before I added, albeit lamely, "It wasn't snowing much when I left the hotel."

"Didn't you hear the storm warning?"

I sighed. Of course I had. I had heard and seen every evidence of it on the weather map on TV and could now imagine the meteorologist shaking his fist in a nonverbal but equally effective gesture of 'I told you so.'

"There's no point in yelling at me, Jason. It's done."

His eyes softened as he spoke. "Jeez, I'm sorry Chelsea. I was just thinking what could have happened to you if I hadn't come by."

So was I, and I was so grateful to him I could have thrown myself into his arms. Instead I stepped backwards and asked, "So, what were *you* doing out in the blizzard?"

"I was making the rounds to ensure all the animals were

indoors. I thought I saw a car stuck in the road when I looked through the woods, so I rode up to investigate. Why didn't you just come up to the ranch? It was a heck of a lot closer."

I realized I was staring at him. He still had his coat and boots on and his hair was plastered to his skull. For some reason that made the color of his eyes stand out. He shrugged out of his jacket and scraped off his boots, before he glanced toward the main bathroom. We were both dripping on the floor. "I'll go get us some towels."

I nodded, remaining where I was, shivering.

When he returned with two fluffy grey towels, I took one, my hands barely controllable from shivering, and mopped my hair, certain that I must look like a bird's nest—a drowned bird's nest at that.

Jason didn't seem cold at all. He tossed his towel onto a sofa and went to the landline and lifted the receiver. "Line's down, just as I expected. You should probably call my brother. Do you have your cellphone on you?"

With dead fingers I dug inside my beaded evening bag, which was also ruined by the snow, and took it out. I felt stupidly nervous. And my nerves could be mistaken for just being cold. How was I going to explain to Bryce what had happened, and how I had ended up here? Good thing I had remembered to recharge the thing. Although I have to admit I almost wished that I hadn't. A dead battery was always a good excuse for doing nothing.

I waited, my fingers tingling as the blood returned. Hesitantly, I tapped his number, but no amount of hedging was going to make this any easier.

He answered almost immediately. "Chelsea, where the devil are you?"

I exhaled before I spoke. Why was it so hard to breathe when you were anxious? "I'm so sorry, Bryce," I managed to say. "I had to go into town to pick up something. I got caught in the storm."

"Where are you? Are you okay?"

"I'm fine...I'm—" Why didn't I want to tell him where I

was. I clenched the fist of my free hand, which was beginning to feel cold again (this time due to nerves) to get the feeling back into it. The situation was innocent, and yet I could imagine how it would appear to him, and especially to Melinda when she learned the truth. Then it occurred to me that I had left Honey in her care. All concern over my predicament vanished. I had to get back to the hotel.

"Where *are* you?" he repeated.

"I'm… I'm at… Look, I got stuck in the snow driving home. Jason was out horseback riding. He found me."

"Oh, thank God," he said.

A weight like a rock lifted from my chest.

"So, you're at the ranch?"

"Yes, we couldn't get any further than his place without injuring the horse and getting all three of us stranded in the storm. But I did try. I was trudging up the road to Langdon Hall when he saw me."

"It was the right decision. It would have been suicide for you to try to make it to the hotel in this weather." He went quiet for a moment. "I'd come and get you, but I'm just looking out the window here in the dining room, and it's a massive whiteout. Will you be okay there until tomorrow? I'll drive down to get you when the storm's over, and the roads are cleared."

"Yes. Thanks, Bryce," I said.

"See you tomorrow, sweetheart."

"Tell your parents I'm so sorry—"

"Don't worry about it. They'll understand."

"Oh, and Bryce, can you please check on Honey. She's in my room. Melinda's pet-sitting."

When I hung up I realized that I had forgotten to mention the promotion. I shrugged; it could wait. Jason already had a roaring blaze going in the fireplace. His dog Holly was curled up on the rug in front of it and Jason was now in the kitchen making the clanking sounds of food preparation. I waited a few minutes to let my nerves settle down, and to absorb the wonderful ambience of the room.

"It's not much," he said as I peeked into the kitchen to check on his progress. "Just tomato soup and saltines. And frozen pizza."

"Sounds delicious."

"Do you want to get out of that dress?" he asked. "I don't have anything you would fit, but maybe you could improvise."

It was a perfectly innocent query and I did want to peel out of it because the shoulders were soaked from my wet hair and beginning to itch unbearably—but I felt guilty for wanting to do so.

"It's all right, Chelsea," he said. "I won't try anything."

"I don't know what you're talking about," I mumbled.

"Don't you? You've been avoiding me like I had the plaque ever since we got here."

"I have not."

"Then why are you hovering in the doorway, twisting your hands like that?"

I dropped my hands and stepped into the kitchen.

"Do you want to have a hot bath? Warm up first? Before we eat?"

"NO," I said. My voice came out a little too loudly and even more shrilly.

He arched an eyebrow. "And you're not bothered by being alone with me?"

"No," I said more calmly.

He brushed past me, grabbing me by the wrist and dragged me towards his bedroom. I resisted and he turned around and snickered. "My God, you would think we were in high school. I just wanted to give you something to change into." He let go of my arm and entered the bedroom and went to his closet. He found a large red and black flannel shirt and tossed it at me. "Here, this will probably work as a dress on you." He handed me a black necktie. "Use that for a sash."

I looked down, then up. He was right. I was acting silly. He closed the door behind me and I was face-to-face with my reflection in a door-length mirror. I was a sad sight.

Bedraggled hair, which did nothing for the fresh highlights I'd had put in earlier that week, and the damp spots on the shoulders of my dress were dark, as was the hem of the skirt where the wind had blown snow under my coat. The main reason I wanted to get out of the dress was not because it was damp, but because it was sleeveless, made of thin silk, and I was chilled-to-the-bone cold.

A knock came at the door and I jumped.

It slowly opened and a masculine arm holding a towel punched through the gap. "Still decent? Thought you might want this if you change your mind about a bath." His face remained hidden behind the door, and after I had taken the towel he withdrew his arm and shut it.

I would have loved to have had a bath, but that was out of the question. I peeled out of my wet clothes and toweled myself dry. My skin was red and chafed at the shoulders and thighs from the wet silk, and it was a relief to get the damp thing off. When I was sufficiently dry I put on his shirt.

The warm flannel was divine. It smelled like him, kind of like the forest. I knotted the tie around my waist karate suit style. He'd also left me a pair of clean, black wool socks to use as slippers. I rolled them down to my ankles because they wouldn't stay up.

I combed my fingers through my hair. It was starting to dry. There was a brush on his dresser. Should I use it? At home, I wouldn't presume to use Bryce's brush, but the idea of running Jason's through my hair didn't even cause a flinch.

I finally looked decent, cheeks slightly flushed and skin glowing from the recent exercise, and opened the bedroom door. The smells of tomato soup and pizza filled my lungs. I was starving.

CHAPTER TEN

I found him in the living room with the pizza cut into thick wedges and the soup steamy hot in large ceramic mugs on the wooden coffee table. Everything in this room looked rustic, and so Jason. I liked it. It made me feel warm and fuzzy.

Holly went to sniff at the food and Jason shooed her away. She came to greet me and I squatted to cuddle with her. She had a raw bone on the mat and before returning to gnaw on it she gave the food-laden coffee table a mischievous glance. As I raised my head I noticed a fresh Christmas tree in the corner, decorated with old-fashioned ornaments. I went over to look at them. They reminded me of the type of decorations my grandparents use to have.

"Are these your great aunt Tessina's?" I asked.

"Yeah, how did you know?" Jason said, joining me. He plucked a fabric Santa Claus off a fir scented branch and pointed out its red velvet suit, and its cotton wool beard and hair. "I think these were handcrafted."

"Lovely, I wonder if your great aunt Tessina made them."

He chuckled. "I doubt it. More likely she bought them from some craftsperson and passed them down from generation to generation. And that generation ended with me. My folks are more into modern stuff. You must have seen their aquamarine and pearly white Christmas decorations. Looks like something that just stepped out of Martha Stewart Living."

I laughed. "It's too bad that nobody makes ornaments like these anymore. I would love to use these Victorian and cottagey elements in my floral arrangements."

I almost clapped a hand over my mouth. I shouldn't have said that. I didn't want him to think that I was serious about owning a flower boutique.

"And why not?" he asked breaking the sudden silence. "Why not open up your own florist shop?"

Oh dear lord, he could read my mind!

I pivoted on my heel to return to the sofa. My brows shot up as I caught sight of what was happening there, and I started to laugh. Jason swung about from where he had been replacing the Santa ornament and broke out into peals of laughter. Holly was scarfing down our pizza!

He dove at her and pried the wedge of cheesy crust from her mouth.

"Oh let her have it, Jason," I said. "*I'm* not going to eat that, are *you*?"

He guffawed and dropped his hand, at the same time releasing Holly's collar. "So much for the raw food diet."

He slumped onto the sofa watching her gulp down her loot. "You are a little dickens aren't you? Okay, that's the last piece. Go chew your bone." He glanced up to where I was still standing, observing Holly. "You know, she's actually a very well trained little girl. Except when it comes to pizza. I don't know why—but she just loves it. She snatched a piece when she was a puppy and ever since then, she'll grab a bite any chance she gets. I should have known she'd go for it. I'd completely forgotten her penchant for Italian cuisine; it hasn't happened in so long."

"It's okay, there's plenty left and she didn't touch the soup or the saltines."

My gaze skimmed over the coffee table, then bounced off the four walls, before I realized I had no option except to sit down beside Jason. There were no other chairs—otherwise I would have sat as far away from him as I could.

"Hey, you look nice," he said after he'd taken a mouthful of pepperoni and cheese. "You can keep that shirt if you like. I never wear it."

Although the offer was tempting I knew I could never accept it. When I left, this shirt was going back into his dresser drawer. He offered me a glass of Chianti and *that* I could accept. We sipped wine and ate what was left of our dinner while Zooey Deschanel's silky voice crooning "Baby it's Cold Outside," streamed from his computer tablet.

It was the best pizza I had ever tasted and I told him so. He explained that he had picked it up from a place in town and frozen the leftovers. His only claim to culinary excellence was that he had reheated it. He had to admit it was superior pizza, and even his dog could attest to it.

The fire was dying and I was beginning to feel a little awkward. Jason got up and put another log on the grate. It wasn't very late, only nine-thirty or so. Too early to go to bed. "Do you want to watch *Elf*?" he asked. "It's one of my favorite Christmas movies."

Mine too, but I didn't say so. "Sure," I said, trying to express indifference rather than the thrill I actually felt.

Will Ferrell was hilarious and touching as the boy raised in the North Pole who thought he was an elf and goes to New York City in search of his human father. This was a safe movie that Jason and I could watch together. He turned on the flat screen TV that hung above the mantel. Because it was mounted so high we had to almost lie down on the sofa to watch. Jason threw a soft blanket over me, being careful not to cover any part of himself with it. I was warm by now and Holly had climbed into my lap to sleep. I didn't mind as she was an angel and kept me from missing my Honey Bear too much. The fire was dying again. The shadows danced against the walls. Outside, the snow slapped against the windows, and when I glanced over I saw the fluffy white stuff piling up against the glass.

I turned back to the movie. Out of the corner of my eye I glimpsed Jason, an amused expression on his face, as he watched Buddy eating spaghetti with maple syrup to the discomfiture of his newfound family. I stroked Holly's head, listening to her soft snores and found myself wishing Honey were with us.

I never saw the end of the movie. The next thing I knew, a tremendous pounding was coming from the door. I awoke with a start and felt a body, muscular and warm, flex from beneath my shoulders. At first I thought it was Bryce, then as my bleary eyes focused on their surroundings I saw oak walls and a vaulted ceiling, and a cold fireplace off to the side. Holly was on the floor barking at the door and I realized where I was. I had fallen asleep on top of Jason on the sofa. As I jerked myself upright at the realization, my vision landed on two figures peering through the semi-frosted window. Bryce and Melinda. Bryce had a look of disbelief on his face, while Melinda's expression was one of pure triumph.

I got up with a start. Jason moved me aside as he went towards the door. The two figures had left the window and were now knocking at the front entrance. I ran a useless hand through my tousled hair, the expressions of the two observers sharp in my mind.

When Jason let them in I thought for sure that Bryce was going to sock his brother in the face. But I should have known better. Bryce was too much the gentleman, too well brought up and decent. No matter what he felt he would never react physically.

"Oh, Bryce," I said, my voice light and innocent. "I'm so glad to see you. Did you bring Honey?"

"She's in your room," he said. "I didn't think to bring her."

Of course not. How could I be so self-centered? But I was trying to avoid an altercation. "What time is it? We were watching a movie last night. We must have fallen asleep."

"Yes, you *must* have," Melinda said.

Her intonation spoke volumes. I could have slapped her. Nothing had happened between me and Jason. We had fallen asleep.

Bryce's eyes swept the room, briefly landing on the two wine glasses and the remains of our evening meal. The TV thankfully was still on with some quiet drama playing in muted colors. So *that* at least propped up our alibi.

"Come inside," Jason said. "What's it like out there?"

"Cold," Bryce said curtly.

I shot him a look and he said, "Are you ready to go?"

It was obvious I wasn't. "Just a minute while I change back into my dress." I was about to explain why I was wearing Jason's shirt but I realized that would only make things worse. If I had nothing to feel guilty about, then I had nothing to explain.

"Do you want me to help you clean up here?" Melinda asked Jason, drawing everyone's eyes to the wine bottle. She had gone over to the coffee table and was examining the vintage with an experienced eye.

Jason shrugged. "Leave it. I'll clean up later."

She set the bottle down and glanced at the rumpled blanket on the sofa. "Cozy. Pizza and Chianti. What movie did you watch?"

"*Elf,*" he said.

She nodded. By this time I was in the bedroom hurrying out of the flannel shirt. I went into the adjoining bathroom and washed my face and fingered the tangles out of my hair. I rinsed my mouth and spat, then dug some cosmetics out of my purse and fixed up my face. Why did I feel so wretched? I had done nothing wrong. And why was Melinda always tagging along with Bryce? I slipped on my green silk dress, which had dried nicely overnight and didn't look too bad, and pulled on my spike-heeled boots. Where was my coat? It was there, flung over a chair in the corner at the foot of the queen-sized bed. Jason must have put it there sometime last night to keep it from getting any wetter or soiled from his outdoor gear on the hall hooks. It appeared as though he had been planning to let me use his room as a guestroom.

I lifted my coat by the fur collar and carefully replaced it with the folded red-and-black flannel shirt. I laid the black tie overtop it and grabbed my beaded handbag. Then I took one last look around to make sure I hadn't left anything behind, and opened the door.

At the threshold I struggled into my coat, balancing my handbag from one hand to the other. They were all standing in the foyer, Melinda chatting cheerfully like nothing was wrong. Nothing *should* have been wrong except the tension between the two brothers was so thick you could slice it with a shovel. Bryce caught my eye. It was clear he had no intention of lingering any longer than was necessary. His voice was stiff and formal. Cold. "See you at the wedding," he said, hoarsely to Jason. "Come on, Chelsea. Let's go. We have a lot to do."

Jason grunted a brief farewell, and Melinda smiled beatifically. She left, and I was about to follow her after giving Holly an affectionate pat on the head when I felt a hand on my shoulder.

"Chelsea," he said.

I turned.

"Tell Bryce I'm sorry."

"For what?" My heart was beginning to thump.

"I won't be coming to your wedding. I was sending one of my guys to drive the carriage anyway, so that won't change. But I can't go to your wedding."

My heart was thudding painfully now. He *had* to come. If he didn't come…

"Why not?" I whispered.

"You *know* why not."

No, I don't, I wanted to scream.

"It's better this way. I'm tired of Bryce being mad at me."

"He isn't mad at you. Not anymore. He told me so."

"That was before this."

"*This?* This what? You didn't do anything. You just rescued me from freezing to death in a blizzard. He's grateful." Although, come to think of it he had not overtly expressed any gratitude.

He sighed. "I still don't think he wants me to go."

"But what will your parents think? And Aunt Tessina?"

"They'll understand."

No, they wouldn't. *I* didn't understand. "Please Jason. You have to come. If you don't come people will talk..."

"So let them talk. What's there to talk about anyway?"

"They'll think there's something between us. Melinda already thinks that. Did you see the smirk on her face?"

"Don't worry about her. I won't let her rumor-mongering hurt you."

"You won't be able to do anything about it."

"Is that all you care about?"

I lowered my head. "Of course not."

"Then don't worry. I have more influence over her than you think. You'd better go. I can see Bryce watching us."

I turned to look, and saw that he was. I couldn't detect his expression but I knew it wasn't happy.

"Oh what the hell—" Jason grabbed me with his other hand and pulled me out of sight. "They already think it. I might as well give them something to fuel that thought." His lips landed on mine before I could object.

I didn't object, didn't want to. I wanted the kiss to go on and on...

But it couldn't and we both knew it.

He raised his head, his voice a hoarse whisper. "Honey's waiting for you." He squeezed my hand, a look of utter surrender in his eyes. "Hey, it was nice knowing you."

What was he talking about? We would see each other again. Day after tomorrow we would be family.

His voice was almost inaudible as he added, "I'm sorry, Chelsea. I shouldn't have done that. Don't feel guilty. You did nothing wrong. It was all me...I've decided I have to move back to California. I just wanted something to remember you by."

Tears were threatening to spill. I had to go. I bit my lip—put my game face on—and turned. Melinda was halfway down the path returning to fetch me.

CHAPTER ELEVEN

"Hey, what's going on?" she whispered conspiratorially. As if she didn't know.

How had I gotten myself into this fix? I glared at her, tears sitting unspilled in my eyes. It was her fault. If she hadn't introduced me to Jason, none of this would have happened. But then the look of comprehension on her face made me realize it would have happened anyways. I would have met Jason at some point in our marriage, and I would have felt the same—even if he hadn't been hired for the horse-and-carriage service. He was Bryce's brother.

Bryce was unusually quiet all morning and I didn't blame him. I hadn't had breakfast yet and after I had showered and prettied myself up, he offered to take me for brunch. We still didn't dare test the roads into town. They were mostly blocked, but the snowplows were on the move and in another day—our wedding day—all would be cleared and the guests could arrive.

We sat in the hotel's crowded dining room and sipped mimosas. Bryce's eggs benedict were getting cold. His attention was fully fixed on his phone. He was texting someone. I hoped it wasn't Melinda.

"You've been seeing a lot of Melinda lately," I commented.

He looked up. "No more than you have been seeing Jason. Melinda is our wedding planner. What is Jason to you?"

I flinched. If I had wanted it blunt I was getting what I deserved. "My brother-in-law-to-be."

"I should have driven over to get you last night when

you called. Blizzard or no blizzard."

"You would have got stuck in the storm and probably ended up spending the night at Jason's ranch like me." I giggled, trying to make light of the conversation and dampen the hovering guilt.

"My point exactly. It seems you two need a chaperone."

I reached over the table. "It's not like that, Bryce. Nothing happened. Honestly. He just gave me a shirt to wear while my dress dried. It was dripping wet from my hair and the snow flying up under my skirt when I was trying to walk through the snowstorm after my engine stalled. Not to mention the flight on horseback. My coat was flying up practically over my face. It was no wonder my dress got soaked. He fed me and we watched a movie. We fell asleep." It was all true—until that irreversible kiss behind the door.

"You looked pretty comfortable lying there in his arms."

"I *wasn't* in his arms. Neither of us was aware of the other when we fell asleep."

"What about when you were *awake*?"

"Are you sure you want to go there?" I asked.

"Are you sure you want to go through with *this?*" He raised his hands to take in the lovely dining room. "It's not too late to back out."

My eyes were filling with tears. I was so unhappy, so confused. My fairytale wedding could disappear in a puff of mist with one word. All I had to do was say it.

"Are you going to marry me, Chels? Yes or no."

I swallowed the hard lump in my throat. It wouldn't go away. I fiddled with my fork. "Why are you even asking me? Everything is set: the food, the flowers, the venue, the band... the guests. Everyone will be here day after tomorrow."

"That's *exactly* why I'm asking you."

"What did Melinda accuse me of?" I demanded angrily.

"She didn't say anything. I love you, Chelsea. Do you love me? You haven't answered my question."

The way he said 'I love you' sounded so flippant, so

often used, that it seemed to have lost its magic. "Of course, I'm going to marry you."

He looked down at his phone. He flipped it around and pushed it across the table under my nose. On the screen was a text from Jason explaining that he wouldn't be able to make it to the wedding.

Apologies, Bro'. Got a business thing I forgot about. Can't make it to the nuptials. I know you understand as you've always put business first. Congrats. You have a beautiful girl there in Chelsea, a real Princess Bride. Take care of her, she's one in a million. Have a great honeymoon— J.

He raised his eyes to capture mine. "There's only one reason he isn't coming to the wedding."

I was quick with my response, and swallowed the guilt. "He has a business opportunity. Obviously, it can't wait. Wasn't it you who always insisted on putting business first?"

"Yes, and the first thing you have to learn when you go into business for yourself is that things don't *always* turn out the way you want them to. The trick is to turn the outcome into an advantage."

If I weren't so distraught I wouldn't have thought that this piece of business advice was my fiancé suggesting that— I leave him. My eyes sought his, thoroughly troubled. He had just thrust a double-edged sword into my heart. Those words had two meanings and he knew that I recognized it. I decided to comment on the second meaning—the meaning that was less painful. "I never mentioned that I wanted to go into business for myself."

"You didn't have to. It seems someone else has a direct line into your dreams."

I poked at my smoked salmon omelet, my appetite completely soured. His voice softened. "Why don't you take Honey for a walk. The trails into the woods have been plowed by the hotel."

I missed my dog. I nodded and rose, dropping my linen napkin on the tablecloth. He was right. Who was I fooling? I needed to think.

Outside the sun was shining, it was still bitterly cold, but the warmth of the sun made a difference. The shadows were long and cast dark indigo shapes on the white ground. My footsteps crunched, while Honey's sounded like a small galloping horse. Crystalized mist blew in tufts sparkling in the air. The sky was clear and shockingly blue but with that unmistakable hue that reminded you it was winter. Honey was having a wonderful time romping through the snow. A small tractor had cleared the trail leaving the ground packed and shallow. This time I was wearing proper winter boots, a puffy red parka and mitts. Honey wore a green sweater with white trim. A cardinal sang from a treetop and I stopped to listen to it. Honey wasn't interested in the bird, there were rustlings coming from the bushes. "Stop pulling, Honey," I said.

My face was beginning to get cold, and we had only been out for about a half hour. We were on our way back and she was chasing something under a leafless bunch of branches and sticks. She wound in and out until her six-foot leash was totally twisted and snagged. "Oh, great. Now look what you've done. How am I going to get you out of this?"

She was firmly entwined in the brambles so I wasn't worried about letting go. There was no way she could dash off with her leash so utterly tangled. I removed my mitts and allowed the loop to slip out of my right hand. Then I went to work on unwinding the cord. Honey was still trying to locate the varmint that had got her attention in the first place, and now the leash near her collar was covered in burrs. She whined and squeaked in objection as I tackled the thistles and brambles. I finally got most of the cord unraveled, but she still had all the burrs on her neck, and they were preventing me from freeing her completely. "Hold still, sweetie," I said. "I can't get these buggers off with you wiggling like that."

Eventually, I realized I would have to detach her leash

from her collar because the burrs and her pulling were choking her. In order to free the thing I had to stop her from tugging it tighter. I put three fingers under her collar to hold her while I unhooked the snap. She jerked forward but I was ready for it. "Sit," I ordered. She sat, but her tail was swishing to and fro, waiting for a chance to chase the creature that had burrowed under the bushes.

Finally, I got the leash free. It still had a few burrs attached to it but they would have to wait until we got home. "Okay, enough of the great outdoors," I said. "Let's go."

I squeezed the spring to reattach the hook when suddenly something black went shooting out from under us, and went headlong down the path. Honey bolted out of my arms before I could release the snap to rehook her leash, and dashed snout first after it. Squirrels!

I lunged after her but wasn't too worried because we were almost out of the trail. I could see the gardens of Langdon hall and the apple and beech trees there. The squirrel would dart up a tree and Honey would stop. She always did.

I broke out of the woods in Honey's wake. The garden was a vast white wonderland. The gnarly branches of the trees were heavy with snow and even the trunks had been lapped white like frosting.

The squirrel scampered over the lawn, white crystals flying. Honey pounced after it and I laughed as she fell flat on her face before regaining her balance and catapulted in its wake. It had stopped briefly to chatter at her as though daring her to catch it, and then it raced across a smooth flat plain of snow. I stopped laughing as horror struck. Oh, no! The pond. I prayed that it would be frozen solid. The squirrel was light and slithered across and up a tree on the opposite side. "Honey!" I shouted. "Come back!"

It was too late. She was on the pond and it wasn't solid. She went crashing through the snow and ice, and into the freezing water. I raced to the edge and was ready to dive in when I heard a voice shout.

"Chelsea, stay where you are! I'll get her."

Jason was coming across the lawn from the other side. He had a parcel in his arms. He dropped it in the snow and dashed to the rim of the pond. Honey was splashing, but if she didn't get out of there in another few minutes she would freeze. Jason strode into the pond the sounds of cracking ice sending my heart into my throat with each cautious step. The ice was thin and wouldn't hold him and he knew it. But he was ready as he braced himself and sank into the icy pool. I knew the pond wasn't more than three feet deep, but even so, he was up to his thighs in freezing water. Honey was in the middle of the pond splashing frantically, the jagged edges of ice circling her and thwarting her attempts to find dry land. I only hoped that she would keep her head up until Jason reached her.

"Come here, girl," he said, calmly. She stopped panicking and paddled toward him, while he struggled through the icy pond to meet her. He lifted her out of the water and called to me. "She's okay, I've got her."

He reached me and laid her into my arms. I didn't care about the water or the mud or anything spattering all over my face and clothes. I was just so grateful to have my little dog back. Jason stripped out of his jacket and wrapped it around her. It was then that other guests, who saw what was happening from the hotel's windows, came out to help. Bryce and Melinda were there. "We have to get her inside and dried," Jason said, the wind reminding us of just how cold it was.

Bryce took Honey from me, wrapped in Jason's jacket, and brought her to my room. I was crying uncontrollably by now. Tears of joy and terror, and gratitude all mixed together. "Are you okay?" Bryce asked me, once we had Honey warm and dry by the fireplace.

"I nodded."

"Do you want me to take her to the vet?"

I looked down at her. We had been inside for fifteen minutes and I had dried her with my hair dryer. She felt warm when I stroked her body. She looked up, her eyes bright, and then stood up, her tail wagging. "I think she's okay."

"What happened?" he asked.

"It was my fault. I shouldn't have let her go into the bushes. She got tangled and I had to unleash her—"

"And she saw a squirrel."

I nodded.

"Well, she seems fine now."

"She's normally so well-behaved. It's just when it comes to squirrels..."

"It's a dog thing," he said and smiled. "Hey look, I have to go out for a bit. Will you be all right?"

"Yes. I think I'll take a hot bath."

"Make sure the veranda door is locked." He went to make certain of it himself, then let himself out.

A few moments later, a knock came at the door. I was in bathrobe and slippers, my hair wound up on the top of my head. I was so wired myself that for a second I was inclined to leave it unanswered. But it could be Jason. I was hoping it *was* Jason. I wanted to thank him properly for saving Honey from the icy pond. But it wasn't Bryce's brother at the door. It was his great aunt. She waved away the hotel staff member who had accompanied her and asked him to return in fifteen minutes. She must have had something important to say to leave her comfortable suite and come all the way here on her own. And with my wedding day so close.

"I'm sorry, dear, I can see I've come at an inconvenient time. I heard about the accident. Are you and your dog all right?"

"We're fine, thanks to your great nephew."

Her face changed. I'm not sure how much she knew or what she thought about the whole thing, or whether she even understood which great nephew I was talking about, but I asked her in. I only knew that I had grown impossibly fond of her and if it was within my power at all I did not want to disappoint her. I helped her to my sofa where Honey lay curled up on the floor at one corner. "Jason wanted me to give you this," she said.

I took the package from her. It was my Christmas gift to Bryce, the object that had started the whole mishap and ended so disastrously. I fingered it nervously; then placed it on the coffee table. Where were my manners? I should order up tea from Room Service. But I suddenly just wanted her to leave. "Where is he?" I asked quietly. But what I really wanted to say was: why didn't he come himself?

She smiled, an attempt to lighten the mood. "I heard about your promotion. Congratulations. Bryce is most thrilled for you. Your family must be very proud of you, as is ours."

Right now I couldn't care less about my job. When I remained speechless, and just nodded with a weak smile, she said, "He's gone home."

I was dead silent and Aunt Tessina noticed that silence. "He drove your car up after the snowstorm to return *that*"— she indicated the package on the coffee table—"and your vehicle to you. He said to tell you there was no damage to the car."

So that was why he had been here at the exact moment of the accident. What would I have done had he not appeared? I was ready to dive into the pond to save my Honey Bear. And would have. He knew that. And he had rescued her for me.

"Why didn't he drop off the parcel himself?"

"You probably know better than I do."

Her response was loaded with meaning. And I was the only one in this room who refused to acknowledge the meaning. "What did he tell you?" I asked. "I mean other than to give me the parcel."

"He said I would not see him at the wedding."

So he was adamant on that.

Nervously I continued: "Did you ask him why not?"

Aunt Tessina sighed. "I didn't have to. I've seen this story play out before—but this time the ending will be different. You are not nineteen and you are not Melinda."

Some part of me wondered if this was a threat. But the look on Aunt Tessina's face was nothing but kindness and deep concern.

"Melinda is still in love with Bryce," I said.

She nodded. "That is inconsequential. Melly may at times seem like a conniving selfish brat with only her best interests at heart, but she has one thing that so many people lack today—and that is loyalty. And I believe at some level she is able to put the needs of the ones she loves above her own. Yes, I know how attached she is to the family and especially to Bryce. The boys did not treat her right. They were young and foolhardy, and competitive, and had a destructive kind of sibling rivalry, but beneath that childish jealously was always love. My hope is that today all is resolved. Melly is strong, she always was. Her love for the Frost brothers will survive. The question is—will yours?"

I felt the color rush up my cheeks and I hugged the collar of my fluffy robe to my throat. Why would she say that? And to which brother was she referring? It brought to mind the cryptic card Jason had sent along with the flowers—and that now seemed an eternity ago. He had placed a question mark at the end of his message:

For the Princess Bride,
May the honeymoon last as long as the love?

"What are you telling me, Aunt Tessina?"

"One way or another, you will become family. I can't *tell* you anything. I can't pretend to know your heart. But your heart is the only thing that will tell you what is right. Trust it."

I made my choice a long time ago, before I met Jason.

"People don't choose to fall in love with whom they do, or when. Not everyone is so lucky as to have a choice. And some peoples' choices are taken away from them."

She was refusing to be blunt with me. I couldn't really

know what she meant unless she said it quite clearly. Why did she resist saying what she meant? Just how much did she know?

"I have a front stage view from my top story window, dear, as you know. My suite runs the entire length of the manor from front to back. I have a lovely view of the croquet lawn from my bedroom, and the lily pond. My eyes are weak, but they are not *that* weak. Some things cannot be hidden even though their faces are."

Then she knew.

"There's one more thing. I almost kept this to myself, but my conscience told me that I would never be able to live with myself—whatever little time I have left—if you didn't see it."

It was a note in Jason's handwriting:

**To ease another's heartache
is to forget one's own**

I recognized the Abraham Lincoln quote. That was why he was skipping the wedding and returning to California.

Aunt Tessina's hand reached out and touched mine. "I didn't come here to chastise you or to give you advice, Chelsea. I came here to give you my blessing."

CHAPTER TWELVE

The world is as wonderful a place as you make it. Jason had said that, and I was determined to make my world as wonderful a place as I could. I was determined to do the right thing. I intended to get married. It was Christmas Eve. I was committed to making my marriage a wonderful thing and my future life with my husband a wonderful journey. My fairytale wedding was waiting for me outside those doors. All I had to do was walk down the aisle with my father to my groom. But I felt miserable.

I lifted my off-white Simon Carvalli dress and slipped it on over my up-do. It was a slim, silk crepe floor-length wedding gown featuring a tulle bateau neckline over a V-shaped bodice, with pearl beading. The sheer jeweled cap sleeves fit snugly over my slim winter-pale shoulders. I turned to admire the flowered back and chapel length train. My sister gasped and my mother smiled. "You look stunning, Chelsea," she said.

My sister agreed. She and several of my cousins were bridesmaids. "Please," I said, "Could you all go out now. I'd just like to finish up alone."

"Are you okay?" my sister asked.

I nodded. "I'm fine."

"Don't worry. I went through the exact same thing when Mike and I got married."

Not exactly the same, but I did not say so out loud. Back then, Madeleine, my only sister, was marrying for the second time. It was normal to have doubts after a failed first marriage.

"Everything will be just fine," she said. "Bryce is a

gorgeous groom. I have to say—you know how to pick 'em."

For some reason that comment sounded disturbingly familiar. When my mother and sister had left and I was alone, I stared at myself in the full-length mirror. This really was a beautiful dress. With my hair done up and highlighted in golds and coppers, I looked like something out of a magazine. Of course, anyone could look like this if you were willing to spend the money. But was this happiness? Was this what made me happy?

A knock came at the door. "Hey, Maddie," I said, forcing my voice to sound even. "Just a few more minutes, please."

"It's not Madeleine," a voice said.

I froze. It was Bryce standing outside my door.

"What are you doing here? It's bad luck for the groom to see the bride before the wedding." I tried to make my voice light and teasing. But Bryce could always see through me.

"I don't think my seeing you now is going to make our luck any better."

What did he mean?

I opened the door a crack so that only part of my face was visible to him. "What happened?"

He pushed the door wider and he gazed at me. "You look beautiful, Chelsea."

"Thanks."

He nudged me inside and stepped into my room. My brother had earlier taken Honey to his room so she wasn't here to be in my way while I was dressing. Bryce's face was serious. I knew that look. It was the look on his face when he was about to close a deal. "What's wrong, Bryce?" I was worried now. "It's not Honey, is it? She hasn't had a relapse or anything?"

"No, your dog's fine."

"Then why are you here? Shouldn't you be in the chapel?" Melinda had managed to convince the hotel to turn the Orchard room into a chapel for our service.

"Come here, sit down for a minute."

I glanced at the digital clock on my nightstand. If we didn't leave in a few minutes we would be late.

His eyes were on the French doors leading to the snow-covered croquet lawn. There was some activity going on out there but I wasn't paying attention. I turned back to him really aggravated.

"Why are you marrying me?" he asked.

The question should not have surprised me, but it did. Some sort of time lapse happened between the moment I heard the question and the point at which I returned an answer. It seemed like forever but it was only a few seconds before I parted my lips to speak. *Because I...love you.*

He continued to observe me, the same way he studied the figures on the stock market. Only with *this* there was no thrill of buying and selling, winning and losing. Almost no emotion at all, except an underlying sadness. I realized then that although the words had registered in my mind—words that every bride was supposed to say and mean—they had not come out. I had not spoken them aloud. I tried again. But my mouth only opened and closed.

"Yesterday, when I saw your face, the look you had when Jason rescued your dog out of that frozen pond, I realized something. Do you know that you have never looked at me like that?"

"I don't know what you mean, Bryce."

He sighed. "I think you do."

Why was he doing this now? Everyone was out there waiting for us. The show must go on.

For the first time I think Bryce knew what I was thinking before I knew it myself. "There's no magic for you, is there, Chelsea? That's why you need all the trappings—the Princess gown, and the fairytale setting, and the white horse and gilded carriage."

"I don't know what you're talking about. Please, Bryce..." I glanced anxiously at the clock. "People are waiting...wondering...they'll be talking, speculating—"

"That's not a good reason to marry me."

A tear ran down my cheek.

"Would you rather have this conversation twenty-four hours after we're married? Tell me the truth, Chelsea. For once in your life, tell me the truth."

"I've always told you the truth. You just weren't listening."

He shrugged, and I realized now how handsome he was in his black tuxedo. He wanted me to say the words and I couldn't.

He looked down. "You're a good person. A kind, sweet person. But we don't have a lot in common, do we? You need the magic. I don't. I think that says it all."

What was he saying?

"The carriage is coming around to pick you up. One of Jason's handlers will be driving it. There won't be anyone to see you arrive if you still want to do it that way. If you still want to marry me come to the Orchard Room. The chapel is set up. If not, go outside to the croquet lawn."

Why?

He didn't say why. He got up and kissed me on the forehead. "It's been quite a ride."

I watched him leave.

I stared at the door. I turned and my eye landed on the bouquet of flowers on the coffee table. They were simple and elegant. The bouquet of white Oriental Lilies, red tulips, lush greens, arranged simply in a classic red glass vase. They bloomed as lushly as the day Jason had given them to me.

***

There was no one in the lobby when I went through the connecting tunnel to the main house and to the front doors. This wasn't the way it was supposed to be. I wasn't supposed to leave my room through this route. I *wasn't* supposed to be alone. Where *was* everyone? Even the reception desk was empty. I went to look out the windows. The horse and carriage stood waiting for the bride and groom.

I took a deep breath and went to the Orchard room, the

improvised chapel. There was a lovely white altar decorated with satin ribbon and blue and lavender flowers. The floor had a powder blue runner leading up to it. On either side were white fabric upholstered chairs trimmed with satin. No one was there. An unexpected wave of relief washed over me, then a crushing weight of disappointment and humiliation. I wasn't going to have to face everyone after all. Bryce had saved me that indignity.

I heard a sound from behind me, and Bryce came toward me carrying my white wool cape luxuriously trimmed with artificial silver fox fur. I gazed up at him and he smiled. I didn't know how to tell him.

He shook his head. "There's nothing to say, Chelsea."

He draped the coat over my shoulders.

"You know, all I've ever wanted was for you to be happy. But you can't marry me, can you?"

I shook my head, tears ready to spill.

"It's all right, honey. I don't want to marry you either."

I swallowed. I didn't understand. "I realized something, yesterday, when I saw you and Jason with the dog. I've never told you this but you've probably noticed. I'm allergic to them. Not severely, but enough to make me uncomfortable. I was willing to put up with that for your sake, but I can see that some time in the future...well, I might not."

I heard barking coming from outside and raised my head in the direction of the French doors. Honey was barking at the windows. She had sighted me. I smiled through my tears. She was dressed in a white shearling jacket with a green ribbon around her neck. Then I noticed that there was a lot of activity outside. The sun was shining through the trees making everything sparkle like Christmas diamonds.

Bryce straightened the fur around my throat. He opened the French doors. My brother was holding Honey's leash. The bridesmaids were gathered to the side in fur-trimmed capes similar to mine but with smaller collars. Beneath the flowered, sheer canopy Jason stood in a white tuxedo.

"Took some convincing," Bryce said and winked at me.

"But they managed to move the wedding outdoors."

"I do love you, Bryce," I said, eyes swimming. "Just not the way you deserve."

"Don't cry, darling," he said, handing me my bouquet of white roses. "Your fairytale is only beginning."

"You are an amazing person. I've always meant that."

"So are you. Merry Christmas, Chelsea."

My father came and offered me a tissue. I dabbed my eyes and whispered, "Do I look all right?"

"Gorgeous, sweetheart," he said.

From the corner of my eye I saw Melinda come and take Bryce's arm. They went to sit down and from somewhere to the side music began.

I passed Aunt Tessina as I walked down the white carpet in the wake of my bridesmaids to my groom. Her eyes smiled up at me. *To ease another's heart is to forget one's own.*

My sister and cousins led, with Honey and Holly in their holiday wedding finery on white leashes. For the first time they were perfect angels.

My father passed me over to my husband-to-be who looked down at me, a tender smile on his lips. Jason looked striking in his white tuxedo and black bowtie. "Was this the way you wanted it, Princess Bride?" he whispered.

Finally, I understood what it meant to be truly happy.

It was perfect.

A Very Catty Christmas

A Love Story for Pet Lovers

CHAPTER ONE

Uh-oh. Where is my cat? Giselle was always getting into mischief. And the last thing I need is for her to make me look bad in front of my boss. Not that Harry Snowden ever came to the Annex. But he might. One day he might. Ever since we moved to the new apartment upstairs from the Art Gallery of Hamilton's Design Annex, Giselle has been miffed at me. I know it takes time for a pet to adjust to a new home, but this was getting ridiculous. It wouldn't have mattered so much if it weren't for the fact that I wanted to impress the boss for more reasons than I care to express.

Why did he have to have a voice that made me melt? And those eyes. They pierced right through me. I always had a weakness for green eyes. Maybe that's why my preferred pets are cats. Only cats have green eyes. Although not my Giselle. She is a sapphire-eyed seal-point Siamese.

She had chosen the worst day, too, to disappear. I had to have my contest entry form—or should I say 'Lorelei's' contest entry form—on my boss's boss's desk in twenty-five minutes. That left me five minutes to get dressed and twenty minutes to get through James Street North's rush hour traffic to the main gallery's administrative offices downtown. Giselle was a smart cat and I knew she had the sense to stay away from traffic. She could take care of herself in the great outdoors. After all, the day I adopted her I had found her fishing in the slushy tarp of my neighbor's swimming pool. What she was fishing for I never discovered. She had hissed and spat at me, and when I tried to pry her out of the tarp she had jumped right back in. Unlike most cats she didn't mind water. In fact she seemed to be drawn to it. But that was six years ago. We had become friends—after a few more attempts to get her out of the pool—to which she finally conceded when I tempted her with an opened can of tuna. The neighbor did not know whose cat she was, and he certainly didn't want to be saddled with her. So I had taken her home with me, and posted her picture around the block. No queries came for her and she adopted me, so I named her Giselle and that was that. We moved since then—obviously.

By the time I turned up King Street I was out of breath from running. Worse—it was starting to rain. I had forgotten my umbrella and my face was cold and wet, beads of rain running from my temples to my chin. I ducked in through the glass doors and headed for the elevators.

Harry Snowden was coming out of the elevator just as I was entering. My boss! Well, my supervisor's boss. He really didn't have a lot to do with us volunteers. I felt self-conscience that he should see me as such a bedraggled mess. What if he chose today to stop and speak with me?

No such luck. He gave me a smile and nodded 'good morning.' It was the same every time I saw him. We never spoke because he was always rushing off to a meeting or something important while I, a lowly docent, volunteered two mornings and three nights a week leading tours through the art exhibits. I wished that he would notice me but except for this generic greeting he didn't. I sucked in my disappointment and stepped into the elevator, watching his handsome back. Harry was already halfway down the corridor. He was always dressed so stylishly. While I...I glanced down at my old wool coat, dappled and dark with raindrops…was just two steps up from Bag Lady.

At the top floor where the administrative offices were I hustled toward the door marked:

Marjorie Snowden, PhD, Director

No, it's not what you're thinking; it's worse. Madam Director whatever her proper title is was not Harry's wife, but his mother.

Just my luck, she shot out of the office just as I raised my hand to open the door. I had already removed the forms from the manila envelope, which was slightly damp.

"Lori Channing?" she said. "What are you doing up here. Aren't you supposed to be leading a school group this morning?" In her hand was the schedule that her secretary had left for her to check over. Madam Director, unlike most museum heads, liked to keep a tight ship, and that meant every now and then she randomly inspected her employee's work. Sylvia Simulivac was the volunteer coordinator and my supervisor, the person in charge of training and scheduling us docents. *She* was who I reported to and she in turn reported to Harry. I suppose at some level it was Marjorie Snowden—his mother—that Harry reported to. Sylvia was waiting in the docent's lounge for us volunteers; clearly it was her turn to be scrutinized today. And she was probably puzzling over what could have possibly happened to me.

In case you were wondering why the head of the Art Gallery knows who I am I may as well fess up. She caught me sketching in one of the galleries one day while I was supposed to be leading a tour. For some reason I thought it was an hour earlier than it was. She just happened to be with Sylvia when my supervisor was searching frantically for me. It happens a lot. I have a bad habit of getting distracted or just doing my own thing. That's what artists do. Oh, did I not mention that I was a closet artist?

I tucked the papers I was holding behind my back, and nearly lost the wet envelope. "Just have to drop something off with your secretary," I mumbled.

"What is it? Give it to me."

I started to shake. I literally began to tremble in my boots. Marjorie Snowden must not see what I had in my hand. If she did it would certainly bias her decision. Of course, I didn't even know if she had a vote. But I was almost certain that she did. She would at least have the deciding vote if there happened to be a tie.

Why was I so afraid?

Not only did her position, her appearance, and her manner intimidate me, but I also knew that Harry Snowden was her son. And I was determined to get Harry to notice me.

I have been in love with Harry for years. Ever since I started volunteering at the AGH. I know it's ridiculous and childish, and I shouldn't demean myself like that over a man. But he wasn't just *any* man. He was Harry Snowden. He was brilliant and kind, and so impossibly good-looking. At least to me. He was powerful and influential in the art world. He lived in a universe I could only imagine: one of famous artists and important people, elegant art shows and exclusive receptions. Yes, yes, I am not only a closet artist (i.e. in that no one knows I secretly weave intricate tapestries, and yeah sometimes I sell them) but I am also an ambitious artist who someday hopes to garner some sort of critical acclaim.

I'm pretty good, or so my teachers told me when I was in art school. In competitions, though, I scraped in third. Once I came in second. But mostly not at all. So I decided the best way to avoid humiliation is to never reveal my true aspirations. That 'pity look' gets old pretty quickly.

I've sold a piece or two as I've said, but not enough to get me any notice. What I need is a big art show, in a large venue—like the Art Gallery of Hamilton. My only real claim to fame is that some of my pieces are for sale in the Design Annex under the name of *Lorelei*.

Now you're wondering why Madam Director had called

me Lori. When I first started my volunteer position I was still in art school. I was registered as Lori Channing. My real name Lorelei was a bit of an embarrassment, so from the time I was in middle school I had everyone calling me Lori. Why my mother named me after a mermaid or mythical siren that lured men to their deaths was beyond me. Could it be it was subconscious revenge for my father skipping out on us when he learned that she was pregnant? Who knows? They were in university then, and maybe he wasn't ready to be a father. But as my ambition to become a professional artist took hold I realized that Lorelei was a perfect artist's pseudonym.

"Lori Channing," the stern voice cut into my thoughts. "You are such a scatterbrain. Please hand me whatever it is you were sent up to deliver and return to your post. Don't you have a group waiting?"

I knew the director was annoyed with me. I wished like I always did that I had never done something so stupid as to attract her attention. Now, she knew my name.

I pushed up the glasses I regularly wore when I was here in the capacity of a docent, and tucked a loose wisp of brown hair back into my bun. Suddenly, I was saved as the secretary flung open the door and said, "Oh, Marjorie. Thought I heard your voice. So glad you're still here. That call you've been waiting for finally came through."

The director immediately forgot about the papers and she forgot about me. Her arm dropped to her side and she hurried back to her office. The secretary, whose name was Sharon, shot me a sharp look of inquiry, and I smiled. "Am I too late to submit this?" I hesitated. "It's... for a...friend."

She extended a hand to take the forms from me. "Don't let Marjorie scare you so much, Lori. She's just tight as a wire because she's got her hooks into an important donor, and if she gets him it will be a massive amount of money. Something as you well know the gallery could use. That's him on the phone—"

"Hope it works out," I said as I handed her the papers.

She glanced down and smiled. "Oh, you're a friend of *Lo-relei*." She pronounced the first syllable of the name with emphasis. "I've heard of her. Isn't she that textile artist that does feline motifs? I hear she's quite unique."

My eyes shot wide open. "You've... heard of mm...her?"

"I think Harry Snowden has one of her pieces in his condo."

He does? I almost fell over backwards. I was so excited, so euphoric that the words wouldn't come out of my mouth. I wanted to tell her that I—yes *I*—was Lorelei.

But her phone rang and she nodded at me, "Gotta get that. I'll file this with the other entries."

I remained frozen in place as the door dropped shut in my face. Holy crap. Harry Snowden owned a piece of artwork that I—*I*—had created. I couldn't think of a finer thing to happen to me. I almost did the 'dance of joy' right there on the spot.

The door suddenly flew open again and I thought: *now's my chance to tell Sharon who I really am.* But it wasn't the dark, sophisticated secretary, it was the pale, catty Marjorie Snowden again and she was in a fierce mood. Crap, she didn't get the donation. So now was neither the time nor the place to tell her who I really was.

"What are you still doing here?" she snapped. "Do you want to be a volunteer or not?"

I was horrified at angering her, and was thoroughly cowed.

"I'm sorry," I muttered and scurried away. But once I was in the down elevator (thank goodness Madam Director wasn't headed the same way) the fear dissipated, and I began to feel euphoric again. Harry Snowden owned one of my art pieces!

CHAPTER TWO

The Art Gallery of Hamilton possesses one of the finest and oldest art collections in the country, featuring European, North American and contemporary art, and it was my job to present and inform the public of its offerings. The award-winning design of the building itself was one of the city's points of pride until leaks threatened the collection shortly after construction, and the structure was duly renovated. The renovations were recently completed but there were still some ongoing deficiencies that had to be addressed. Sticky elevators were one of them. Just my luck. As I was going down, the elevator stuck. Now I was in for it. If I failed to report to my supervisor she'd have to locate a substitute.

I must say I'm a mite bit claustrophobic when it comes to elevators. If I'm forced to remain inside one too long I start to panic.

I was panicking now.

I was alone in the elevator so no one was present to distract me. My only company was some generic Christmas music streaming over the PA system. I pressed the red emergency button until my finger ached. My silent screams were on the verge of becoming embarrassingly loud yells.

Next thing I knew, the elevator jogged and started descending again. It stopped and the door flew open, and Harry Snowden stood in my face.

"Hey, are you okay? We heard the emergency bell ringing. Did the elevator freeze again?"

I was so relieved to see him; all I could do was smile. My cheeks were still flushed with cold and excitement. I had totally forgotten how disheveled I must look. Harry saw that

I was all right and as some people were gathering behind us to enter the elevator, he said nothing more. I stood happily watching him walk away.

Oh dear. What was wrong with me? I was late!

I did the school tour with my head in the clouds. I barely heard myself speaking and when the students asked me questions I answered automatically. Half the time I was sure I wasn't answering their questions at all, but at least something coherent was emerging from my lips. I wondered which of my pieces Harry owned. After work I must stop in at the Design Annex before heading upstairs and ask the volunteer there if she had any information on the sale. Or maybe I could just snoop myself. After all, I was one of the Art Gallery's docents, although I did not volunteer at the Annex, but come to think of it, that might be a great place to work. It was just downstairs from my apartment. I could hardly wait until my tour group left. When they did, I barely said a word to Sylvia before I grabbed my coat and rushed out the door.

When I arrived at the Annex some sort of commotion was happening. Through the front window I saw Samantha— the girl who worked there—arguing, and my roommate Duncan berating her. So focused were they on one another that they missed spotting me. I had no idea what was occurring between them, but this was the perfect opportunity for me to sneak in through the back door and search the files to learn when Harry had purchased my precious wall hanging.

They were so engaged in their altercation that they didn't even notice when I glided through the back way and dropped down by the file cabinet in the office region. There was no partition between the studio display area and the office but I might as well have been alone. Fat chance. Just as I started sorting through the files I felt a presence behind me. You know how uncanny that is: the way you can tell when someone is watching you even when you have your back to them. It was like that now. Eyes piercing through my shoulder blades.

A shadow fell and I was suddenly aware of stark silence.

"What on earth do you think you're doing?" Samantha demanded, kicking shut the drawer and nearly taking my fingers off.

Now, I understood why Duncan disliked her.

"I...ah..." Stuttering wasn't helping. I had nothing.

"What were you looking for?"

"I just wanted to see which artists were showing in the Annex this month," I lied.

She grabbed a leaflet off the adjacent desk. "Here—This lists all of the artists and describes the work on display. The textile artist Lorelei's in it and so is *he*—" She stabbed a finger in Duncan's direction.

"Thanks," I said.

Her eyes ransacked the gallery before they returned to me. "Your pesky cat got into the gallery. She's wreaking havoc in here."

I had a wild search around. At first I saw nothing, then a slinky white body with classic blue-brown paws and ears slipped beneath a table. "Giselle," I called. "Come here, beautiful."

"Sorry," Duncan said to me from where he was standing in the center of the room. "She slipped out the door this morning when I went for a jog and couldn't get back in. She must have followed me to the Annex later on." Duncan Mackenzie was an artist too. A sculptor. He had a piece in the sculpture garden at the main building's outdoor terrace. "I just came in to check to see if *she* got my labels right." He scowled at Samantha who scowled back. Clearly these two did not get along.

"I am *not* stupid. That was just *one* mistake," Samantha spat.

"I just want to make sure that I get paid when you sell or rent out my work, and not someone else."

Giselle sat on the floor licking her paws nonchalantly. She blinked at us as though somehow we had disturbed her rather than the other way around, and slunk over toward me and started purring. I slid a hand under her torso and lifted her into my arms. "She didn't cause any damage, did she?" I looked around to be certain.

Samantha had been decorating the front windows with silver leaves and elegant white bells. "She just tore down my handiwork, that's all."

"Let me get her upstairs to the apartment, then I'll come down and help you decorate."

She nodded and crossed the hardwood floor to collect the delicate silver leaves that were scattered all over. It was a month before Christmas and the entire city block was already decked out in holiday cheer. The art gallery had a ways to catch up. Giselle struggled in my arms and I gave her a warning squeeze. Well, at least none of the art was touched.

"I'll just be a second." I motioned to Duncan with my eyes to accompany me.

***

"What's up with you?" he asked as we reached our apartment loft.

I unlocked the door, bracing Giselle on my hip, and turning the key with the other hand. I was breathless and flushed, and not just from the bit of excitement my cat had caused. "You have to watch her when you leave the house, Dunc," I said. "She's not used to the new place. I know it's been three weeks, but she wants to explore."

"Sorry, I forgot. So what's the news? I can see it in your face. And what *were* you looking for in the file cabinet? I don't believe for a second that you wanted to know who's showing at the Annex this month." He punched a fist at the coffee table where a stack of leaflets sat. They were identical to the one that Samantha had given me. I had been responsible for posting those around town—although I hadn't quite gotten around to it yet. But it was only the first of the month. "Did you get word on what's happening with the contest?"

I shook my head. I had just delivered my entry and it was late. Duncan had entered the contest as well. It was hard when you were competing with a friend, but all creative endeavors required stiff competition if one was to get noticed. Duncan and I had gone to art school together. We were both struggling artists. And every sale we made was another rung up the ladder.

"No. I haven't heard anything about the contest. But guess what?"

"What?" he asked.

"Harry Snowden owns one of my pieces."

"No kidding. How did you find out? Did he tell you?"

Duncan knew all about my crush on Harry Snowden. "No. It was Sharon who told me. You know, Marjorie Snowden's secretary."

"Ahh," he said. "Hey, that's fantastic." He gave me a quick hug. One thing I had to say for Duncan. He was generous. Even as a rival.

"That's what I was doing snooping in the file. I wanted to know which piece it was, and when it sold."

"And?"

I told him that I hadn't had time to find out before Samantha slammed the drawer on my fingers.

He shrugged. "I'm sure they'll contact you... So, did you make the contest deadline?" He abruptly reverted to our original conversation.

"The committee's meeting next week to do the final judging, and draw up the short list. I barely squeaked in."

"Hey, good luck."

"You too." I lowered my cat to the floor. "Stay here and be good," I ordered her. "I have to go clean up your mess. But first I gotta get changed."

I went into my bedroom and closed the door. In front of the mirror I stripped out of my conservative knee-length skirt and cardigan until I stood in only my white striped blouse. Oh, I did look so secretaryish, even dorky, when I put on my docent persona. But it was time to turn into Lorelei. If I was to get the goods on Harry's purchase of my wall hanging I had to appear as the artist. Only the artist had a right to ask for info on a sale. I understood why I hadn't been informed of this transaction yet. Statements weren't sent out until the end of each quarter. Sometimes—in fact most of the time—I didn't receive a statement because I had made no sale. And of course, Samantha had caught me in the act before I could find any reference to this particular transaction.

Glasses first. Those came off my nose and were plunked onto the dresser top. I had no vision problems except a very slight astigmatism. Most of the time I could see without glasses, but when I was tired my vision blurred.

I had nice legs and, as Lorelei, I often showed them off. I took off the classic blouse and searched my closet for something more artsy to wear. Skinny pants and a sexy tunic (in turquoise) on top. I yanked the pins out of my hair and let the waist-length locks fall out revealing copper and pink highlights that were usually buried inside my up-do. Lori Channing wore no makeup except for a touch of foundation and mascara. Lorelei went all out: smudgy eyes, liner, mascara and fuchsia lips.

"Hey Supergirl," Duncan said as I joined him in the living room. "I can't believe people are so cosmically stupid they can't see that you—Lori Channing—and the textile artist Lorelei are one and the same. What gives? Samantha is expecting Lori Channing to help her with the Christmas decorations."

"I—that is—Lorelei—wants some information on my sales. I'll just tell her that I sent Lorelei in my place. After all, she thinks the three of us are roommates."

"Aren't you worried one of these days someone is going to find out that you've been deceiving them? One day you might be famous."

"Ha!" I said, and shrugged. "One day. Well, it's too late now. I've been doing the masquerade too long. How could I possibly explain?"

Duncan knew my story. The humiliation of always

coming in third. Or never. My mom never wanted me to become an artist. Not because she didn't think I was talented enough (Oh no?) But because I couldn't pay the rent that way. Well, she was right for the most part. Without Duncan for my roommate—he had a job as an art instructor at the local college—that would be absolutely true. I told myself I was between jobs, and I was. I worked a whole year as a secretary at the university, now it was time to put all my energy into my art. The volunteer thing at the AGH was a way of giving me an identity. My real work took place at night when I textiled my heart out creating fabulous hangings—well fabulous to me. And now maybe to Harry Snowden, my dream man and a patron of my art!

"And what about lover boy?"

I scowled. I wished I'd never revealed to Duncan how I felt about the curator. But Dunc was one of those people who made you comfortable. Too comfortable. So it was easy to pour your heart out. Dunc had found me one day sitting on the back stoop, which was the entrance to the stairs leading up to our apartment, crying my eyes out because Harry Snowden never gave me a second glance. "You're a docent," Duncan had said. "A volunteer. He's not supposed to fraternize with the volunteers. It isn't kosher."

He had paused then, and asked me, "What do you know about him anyway?"

You feel what you feel, I thought. No matter how stupid.

Duncan had been patient and thoughtful. He never makes me feel stupid. Why does he put up with me? But he does. He's a wonderful roomy.

**

Back in the Annex Samantha was at the window applying magic tape to her silver leaves. I explained to her that Lori Channing was busy disciplining her cat. She didn't care. She, like most people, preferred Lorelei. Good to know.

"So nice to see you again," Samantha said.

"You too. Lori's really sorry about the cat."

"She should keep her indoors. There's a lot of traffic on James Street. She could get hit by a car or something." She was talking about the cat of course.

"I'll remind her."

I helped her finish decorating, and then I asked her if she was working the day Harry Snowden bought my wall hanging. "Oh, sure," she said. "That was some time ago. Really, no one has told you before now?"

I shrugged. "Which one was it?"

"Let me go look." She went to the desk with the file cabinet beside it. She squatted and searched through the bottom drawer for the record of sale. "Ah, here it is. *The Cat's Pyjamas*. I remember it. It was the one with ten cats dressed in nightclothes. Awesome. It should be on your next quarterly report. It sold for $2,000."

That was a grand fortune and enough for me to pay Duncan more than my share of the rent I owed him. I clapped my hands together in ecstasy. I wished I knew where Harry lived. I wished I could see my art hanging on his wall. I was beginning to sound like a stalker, and had to curb the direction of my thoughts.

"He said he'd like to meet the artist."

Whaat?

"I remember he was so impressed with the piece." She pointed to the wall over a stylish leather sofa and glass end table. The style of the furniture and the polish with which it had been arranged gave the viewer the sense that it, too, was art. Where my hanging use to be was replaced by an abstract painting of a waterfall. I looked around to see if any of my other pieces were in view. I saw one of Duncan's sculptures, a beautiful, almost erotic piece, composed of smoothly rounded sensuous forms that made one think of two people engaged in sex.

"I have another one of your hangings, an appliqué of cats within cats ready to hang." That was in fact the title of it: *Cats Within Cats*. I had had the idea of stitching the image of a fabric cat inside several more cats, the same concept as those Russian nesting dolls, where you had a doll inside a doll inside a doll. Except that my cats were two dimensional rather than three. The effect was wild, psychedelic. "I was thinking of putting it near the door so customers see it as soon as they come in."

"Wow, that would be fantastic, Samantha. Thanks." I could not see any reason why Duncan and Samantha did not get along. She loved artists, especially successful ones. She was an aspiring artist herself, though not quite as experienced as Duncan and me. I was going to say not quite as *'successful'* as Duncan and me, but that isn't exactly true. Duncan and I are not considered successful, although we sell a piece, now and then. We barely make ends meet with what we earn selling our art, and neither of us have had our work displayed in the big city galleries. The Annex was not the same. It was really just a display room for struggling artists. But to Samantha who was still in the learning stages anyone who sold their art was successful. So, yeah, she kind of had me on a pedestal. Or should I say she had *Lorelei* on a pedestal. What her problem was with Duncan, however, was a mystery. As far as I was concerned, she was great. But then I remembered how she treated me when she thought I was Lori Channing. I was beginning to feel a little schizophrenic.

"Yeah, so when Harry was in here last, he mentioned that he'd like to meet you. He had his eye on the appliqué as well."

"No kidding," I said. "I would love to meet him."

Samantha's eye went to the door. A stylish figure entered the gallery.

I was about to meet him sooner than I thought.

"Hello Dr. Snowden," Samantha said enthusiastically.

"Hi there, how's it going?"

"Great. Busy day. Sold five pieces."

"Wonderful," he said.

"Oh, Dr. Snowden. I'd like you to meet someone."

I tilted my head up toward him. He was tall, dressed in a nice suit with a cashmere overcoat and a blue and wine-colored scarf. "This is Lorelei. The textile artist."

His eyes brightened with interest. So, she had told me the truth. He really did want to meet the creator of *The Cat's Pyjamas*. I gave him a bold smile.

He didn't ask me if I had a last name. Good. Because what would I have said? But curators knew how eccentric artists were so he knew better than to ask. After all, nobody would ask if Cher had a last name.

"Lorelei... finally we meet. I'm so glad to have this opportunity. I'm a big fan."

I could have swooned. I was so overwhelmed I fell speechless. "In fact," he continued, "I bought one of your pieces...."

I wanted to say, *I know, I know and I am sooo thrilled.*

"I was looking for a birthday gift for my mother and when I saw *that* I thought it was perfect."

The world suddenly crashed. He gave it to his mother?

"She likes cats?" Samantha asked.

"Well, no. Not live cats. But artistically speaking, that wall hanging was perfect for her home library."

"But if she doesn't like cats...?" I ventured.

"She's a connoisseur of art. She appreciates a good piece when she sees it."

"And... she *liked* it?"

"Loved it," he said. "Anyway, I just had a thought. My mother is having a reception at her home for the visiting artist, Scotty Chang. I'm curating a special exhibit of his works. Some influential people will be there, people that would be good for you to meet. Are you free next Thursday evening, seven o'clock? There'll be finger foods and wine."

Was he asking me to be his date?

"Of course," I said, maybe a little too eagerly.

I wasn't on the guest list or I would have received an invite weeks ago. This was a spur of the moment thing. He *must* be asking me to be his date!

I had never been to the Snowden mansion before. I had driven past it many times, but I never imagined that I would be invited inside. How should I dress? I was terrified to ask because that would be exposing my ignorance. And I so wanted to impress Harry and his mother. I had gone to many art openings and the dress code was usually business attire. Business attire meant anything from a suit to casual chic or new age artsy—depending on whether you were the featured artist or a guest. I have to admit, no one had ever sponsored an art show of my works, and any shows I had participated in were group efforts.

But Marjorie Snowden was a stickler for convention. She lived in a mansion. This event could very well be Black Tie. And God knows nothing resembling an evening gown lived in my closet. Nor could I afford one.

But—and this was an important but—if Harry Snowden was asking me to be his date then I would cut off my right arm and sell it, if that would buy me an appropriate evening gown.

"Bring a guest if you like," he said. "Do you have the address?" He quickly wrote it down on the back of one of his business cards. "Hope to see you there."

For the second time in twenty-five minutes my world crashed around me.

I was *not* going to be his date.

Before I could ask him about the dress code, he returned his attention to Samantha and asked to see some files.

Should I disturb him over something so stupid as what to wear to his mother's artist reception?

CHAPTER THREE

Scotty Chang was a Chinese artist who had immigrated to San Francisco. He was a rising star, and the AGH was lucky to get him as part of a travelling exhibition. His style was influenced by German expressionism and his subject matter derived from his experiences growing up in China. The result was striking. I hoped one day that Marjorie Snowden would host a reception for me. But first I had to make an impression.

Duncan agreed to be my date. Who else could I bring? Chang's opening wasn't for another two weeks and this reception was a special gathering for VIPs. This weekend, I promised myself, I'd go shopping and find a dress. Thank goodness I had sold that hanging to Harry. Even though I hadn't seen a cent of it yet, the fact that the payment was forthcoming was reassuring, and gave me the confidence to splurge.

What did people wear to these things? I called Sharon, the director's receptionist for the dress code. She wasn't answering her phone and I could hardly leave a message for something so trivial. Besides, I had pretty much decided to take a chance and invest in an evening gown. That is before I consulted Duncan. "Don't buy a ball gown," he said. "It's not like you're Cinderella or anything, and besides you'll never wear it again. Go with the LBD."

LBD was Little Black Dress. I had a couple of those but they were old.

"That never goes out of style. And you look fab in LBD. I'm telling you right now, I ain't buying anything to impress Madam Director. She can take me or leave me the way I am.

Still want me to come?"

I hesitated for a second. He just better not embarrass me. Duncan Mackenzie had a way of putting people off. But the one thing I liked about him was that he was always himself. No surprises that way. What you saw was what you got. And I always felt comfortable with him. In fact, I felt so comfortable I had forgotten that my upper lip was covered with Jolen creme bleach and neither of us had noticed.

"What *are* you going to wear?" I demanded, grabbing a tissue from my pocket and wiping the white stuff from under my nose.

"Clothes," he said.

"What clothes?" My voice had a tone of exasperation as I turned to look at him.

He grabbed the tissue from me and wiped the rest of the cream from my face. "Why do you feel you have to bleach your moustache? You don't really have one." He tossed the tissue into a decorative trash basket under the side table by the entrance, and answered my original question. "Black jeans, white shirt. Okay by you?"

"What if it's formal?"

"I don't care if it is."

He was right. Evening gown was not my style. Lorelei wouldn't be caught dead in a ball gown. LBD it was.

I went shopping with that in mind and found the most adorable little black dress. I was five feet five inches tall. I won't mention my weight. Let's just say the LBD makes almost everyone look good. This one was a couple of inches above the knee with a cinched in waist, a fit and flare skirt and polka dot mesh neck and shoulders, cap sleeves. I bought a pair of black stilettos to go with it and a red wool coat. My bling consisted of a wide sliver bracelet and silver choker. I wore nighttime glamour makeup with hot red lips.

"Like I said. You look fab," Duncan remarked on the night of the reception. "Glad you took my advice. Who wants to look like an old fuddy-duddy in a Cinderella gown anyway? That's not you. *This* is you. *This*—is Lorelei, the cat girl."

"I just hope you're right," I said nervously.

Duncan was wrong.

When we got to the Snowden Mansion I could see through the living room's opened drapes that it was a formal affair. Crap and double crap. I should have listened to my instincts; they were never wrong.

I wanted to swing around and go home but I had nothing to change into there, and I didn't want to miss this opportunity to see Harry again. The mansion was a heritage manor on Ravenscliffe Avenue. It was huge and from the street looked like it had close to one hundred windows. The grounds were massive and neatly manicured. Winter had changed the colorful foliage of the numerous trees to grey bare branches and the white peeling bark of a stand of lovely birches. The only spots of color were some dark green yews and blue spruces. I looked at the inkiness of the sky beyond the peaks of the grand mansion. The only thing I had going for me this evening was the weather. It was relatively mild and dry. No sign of snow or rain.

The door was opened by a butler. Yes a butler. I had no idea 'butler' was still a job. I thought that went out with the Victorian era. But what else could he be? He was dressed in formal black and white and was taking everyone's coats and scarves. Yeah, 'butling' is a profession Duncan's eyes said. There were more millionaires and billionaires than ever and they needed staff to run these humungous properties. I know the Snowdens did not make their money from the art business. Theirs was old money. I believe Marjorie's grandfather was a wealthy industrialist who moved here from upstate New York. She also married money, so Harry had wealth from both sides.

The butler was a middle-aged man who glanced briefly at my dress as he took my coat. Was that a look of disdain—disapproval? He indicated we cross the black and white tiles of the massive foyer to the party room, which was bustling with guests dressed in—you guessed it—ball gowns and tuxedoes.

Needless to say I felt underdressed and out of place. I saw Harry across the room, looking dapper in his black tie, white shirt, and black tails—but he didn't see me. Duncan clad in black jeans, a white shirt and a casual sport jacket didn't care that he was underdressed. There was only one person I noticed who was not dressed to the nines, and *that* was a slim, good-looking Chinese fellow garbed in a taupe t-shirt and blue jeans with a black jacket on top. I had no doubt he was the artist.

Most of the women had their hair fashionably done in up-dos, while mine was unfashionably down like a girl's, waist-length and sleek.

She had noticed me; I felt Marjorie Snowden's pinprick eyes jab me, but she didn't approach. Then I realized she probably didn't know who I was. Duncan was gabbing with some of the guests. In fact he was acquainted with one or three of them. He never had any trouble mixing because he didn't care how he was perceived in social situations. I had a sudden urge to powder my nose—or something. Maybe it was a panic attack. All I knew was: I had to get out of there. *Fast.*

I found myself in the lobby. Then wandering down a hallway lined with numerous entries into spacious rooms. Here was one with double glass doors and when I looked inside I saw it was the library. On the wall was my textile hanging, *The Cat's Pyjamas.* I don't know what compelled me to do this, but I opened the door and walked in.

The walls were lined with fine wooden shelves filled with books. There was dark leather furniture and a marble coffee table on hardwood floors. The area rugs were plush and modern. Everything looked brand new in here. Suddenly, I heard a sound behind me. I turned and looked into the angry face of Madam Director.

"Who *are* you?" she demanded. "I don't recall having placed you on the guest list."

I extended a nervous hand. "Lorelei... the... a textile

artist," I muttered.

"Well, speak up girl, I can't hear a word you're saying."

"I'm Lorelei," I repeated. "Harry.... Your son invited me." I pointed to the hanging on the wall. "I'm *her*."

"You're the cat?"

I shrunk from her iron voice.

"Well, if you're afraid to make yourself known how do you expect anyone to learn about your art?"

I swallowed. What did she want from me?

Marjorie Snowden moved her graceful pearl-beaded torso over to the wall hanging. "It's a lovely piece," she said. "But could be better. You have potential."

Potential? Was she dissing me or complimenting me? Invisibly, I tossed my hands up in despair. She, of course, had no idea what I was thinking.

"You have imagination. And your technique is good. It's very effective. But has a rawness about it."

Was that good or bad?

"So, Lorelei, pleased to meet you. But the way to get ahead in the world of art is to talk to the folks who matter. Get to know people. They want to know what you look like. Don't hide. If you hide you will guarantee yourself oblivion."

Ironic, I thought as I stared at her. *You're looking at me but you can't see me. You haven't a clue who I really am.*

"I have to get back to my guests. Stay here and admire your talent by yourself if you must, but your ego is best used in the public eye."

Was she calling me egotistical? I had no response. She was already gone.

I stood stunned by her cattiness and her arrogance. How could this woman be the mother of the man I loved? I paused as I studied my artwork. But she *did* say the piece was lovely, didn't she? Even if it *wasn't* perfect? So maybe she didn't totally hate me. If only I wasn't so claustrophobic around people, maybe I could hobnob with my betters the way Duncan did. He was on his way up. And he didn't give a hoot what the critics said.

"Lorelei?"

It was Harry's voice and I almost collapsed from pleasure at the sound. I swung about, the color rising to my cheeks. How mortifying to be caught in the act of admiring one's own work! Not only was I admiring it, I was reveling in the fact that *he* had bought it, and that it was hanging in the home of the AGH's director!

I had no excuse. It was obvious why I was here, in his mother's library, with my neck bent at an awkward angle studying the perfection of my stitches when he caught me.

"Your first major sale?" he asked me empathetically.

I nodded, still fighting the heat from my face. Most of my works sold for under five hundred dollars—no—that was being generous. Most of my works sold for around a hundred dollars. Sales were few and far between. Like maybe two or three a year. Harry had paid two thousand dollars for *The Cats Pyjamas*. It was my best effort. I had used expensive materials and had invested months and months in its creation.

"I understand. I've known quite a few young artists over the years. It's quite a triumph. But let me reassure you this was not a sympathy sale. I was truly struck by the piece."

"Thank you," I said.

"I'm glad you could come, Lorelei."

"I'm so sorry, Dr. Snowden. I can't tell you how embarrassed I am—"

He smiled. "All forgotten. Mother told me you were in here. And since you are my guest I thought I should join you. You don't mind, do you? Or would you rather be alone?"

I could see he was teasing me. I shook my head.

"And please, call me Harry. 'Dr. Snowden' makes me feel old. And I like to think that I'm not *all* that much older than you."

Was he asking me how old I was?

I'm twenty-eight. The words did not emerge aloud. Harry, I knew, was in his mid thirties. I had done my homework.

He came to me and held out his hands and I placed mine

in his. "You don't have to be so worried. No one here bites."

Except your mother.

His eyes glimmered as though he had read my mind. "Mother is always skeptical of the women I take an interest in."

You're interested in me? I almost swooned.

His hands felt warm and firm in mine. He was a man in control of his life. Was he inviting me to be part of that life? I could not take my eyes away from his. "Harry," I said. "Am I dressed all right for this party?"

He glanced down at my little black dress and at the simple silver jewelry. "You are stunning," he said. "Why haven't I ever seen you around the gallery before?"

Oh, you have, I wanted to say.

"Well, we're going to change all that. You are a very talented artist, Lorelei. No more hiding in back rooms and libraries. Okay? I want to see you succeed. Now come, we have a lot of people to meet. Have you been introduced to Scotty Chang yet? He's an impressive man. You must meet him—"

CHAPTER FOUR

The party at the Snowden mansion was a hit and made all the papers. There was a photograph of me and Harry, his arm around my shoulders. I clipped it out of the *Hamilton Spectator* and taped it to my mirror. When Duncan saw it, he snorted. I didn't care. Harry had asked me to be his date at the official opening of Scotty Chang's show next week. Before I left the party with Duncan, Harry had kissed my cheek. I was flying.

My only problem was getting Harry's mother to accept me. She thought it a bit odd that her son was interested in me, but I suppose as long as it appeared casual she wasn't going to cause trouble. I was high as a kite when I went to my volunteer job the next morning. I suited up in my dowdy Lori Channing clothes. Black rimmed glasses, cardigan sweater, knee-length skirt and boots. Now that things were looking up I was considering eliminating Lori Channing from my alter egos and coming out exclusively as Lorelei. But to be honest I loved my volunteer work at the art gallery. It gave me the opportunity to inspire young people and engage older folks. I had also made some special friends among the staff. Speaking of which, here came one of my favorites now—Mr. Rudy Donner.

He had to be seventy-five if he was a day. Since they had abolished mandatory retirement many of the gift-shop and cleaning staff were seniors. He had a short white beard and bushy eyebrows. In winter, he always wore a red sweater under his janitor's uniform. Steel-rimmed glasses. He never failed to show up every Friday morning to watch my tour from the sidelines. Even though he had heard it a hundred times he said he loved hearing me talk about art.

When the tour was over, that's when he usually took his break and stayed to chat with me. Today, I suggested we head to the cafeteria in the lobby of the art gallery for coffee. He agreed, went to tuck his janitor's uniform inside his locker downstairs and met me in the cafeteria. It was called the Horse and Train Bistro and served soups, casseroles, and made-to-order sandwiches as well as offering a fabulous selection in the coffee bar.

"Have you heard the results of the contest yet?" he asked me.

I set my Mochaccino down on the table, and hesitated. "Umm, what did you say?"

Why would he think I had entered the contest?

"Big opportunity for someone like you."

"Mr. Donner," I said. "How did you know I had entered the contest?"

He smiled and did not answer me.

"I've been watching you a long time, Lori. No one that takes such a deep interest in art isn't an artist herself. That contest has been publicized for *months*."

"*You* take a deep interest in art, Mr. Donner. Are *you* an artist?"

"Me?" he laughed heartily. "Not a chance. Couldn't draw to save my life. But I can sweep the heck out of a floor. You though. I've seen you sketching in the exhibits on quiet afternoons when no one was around."

No one, but *you.* That disconcerted me somewhat. Nonetheless when I looked at him I simply saw a sweet old man who reminded me of Santa Claus.

"Oh, Mr. Donner," I moaned. "Sometimes I think I'm just barking up the wrong tree. Maybe I'm not as talented as I think I am. I suspect there are more than a few people— especially around here—who would agree."

The old janitor shook his head. "No one has any power over you unless you give it to them. Don't let those who choose to criticize what they cannot do themselves make you quit."

How did he know I was thinking about what Marjorie Snowden had said to me in her library the other night? Her remarks about my art had sounded complimentary, and yet oddly had not come across that way.

"One day you're going to be famous, Lori Channing."

I blushed. "Thanks, Mr. Donner. But I don't think so. I'll be pleased just to sell a few pieces and make people happy."

His eyes lit up. "You already do that, lass."

I noticed that he had a pamphlet in his hand, the one that listed the featured artists exhibiting in the Design Annex. "Oh, have you been down there?" I asked. "They support local artists. They have some nice work on display."

"As a matter of fact, I have," Mr. Donner said. "And Lori, I've known you so long, don't you think you could call me Rudy?"

I laughed. "I'll try."

"I like *this* artist's work." He pointed to a name. It was *my* name. My alter ego Lorelei. "If I had the money I would buy a piece of her art."

I was so flattered I almost hugged him; I was also conflicted. I wanted to tell him that *I* was Lorelei. But I couldn't do that. "You like cats?" I asked.

"Love them. Before my wife died we always had a trio of cats."

"And now?"

"Now, I'm too old to take care of them."

"You're never too old to take care of a cat. They practically take care of themselves."

"Easy for you to say, lass. You're young."

I smiled. He sipped his coffee and glanced down at the pamphlet. "Says here, the results of the contest are to be released today. Have you checked your email, Lori?"

I had not. He urged me to check it. It's true I hadn't exactly denied participating in the contest. When he saw me hesitate, he knew he was right and that I had entered it. What he didn't know was that I had registered as Lorelei, not as

Lori Channing.

"I saw you once in the Annex," he confessed.

I paused. "You did? Why didn't you come over to say Hello?"

"You were busy." He didn't say anything more, and, although at first I thought nothing of it his silence started to make me suspicious. Was it possible? Was he the *only* one who could see through my disguise?

"When?" I asked.

"The other day, when the curator Harry Snowden paid a visit. I was outside, looking in through the window. I saw you with the shop girl. Harry Snowden had just walked in."

My nerves began to shake. Harry was unaware I had two identities.

"Mr. Donner…." I began.

"Rudy," he said.

"How…?"

"I've been watching you a very long time. You deserve better. You deserve to win."

"Sooo…" My eyes returned to the pamphlet that he had spread out on the table between our coffee cups. "…You *know*."

"I know," he said. "But if you want to keep your identity a secret I won't tell. Why you want to keep it a secret, however, well that is the real question. You deserve better. Much better."

"I've sort of trapped myself, I guess," I admitted weakly.

He shrugged. "Check your email. Maybe you have nothing to worry about."

I pulled out my smartphone and touched the envelope icon. A string of emails appeared. I glanced up at Mr. Donner…at…Rudy.

He smiled. "Well?"

I glanced down and tapped the message labeled **'Emerging Star' Art Contest**.

My heart stopped.

It literally stopped.

I had to breathe, clutch my chest—not that that did anything. But then my pulse began to race. Oh, my gosh—I had *won*. Of all the contestants—*I* had won. I had even beaten out Duncan!

There was going to be an award ceremony to announce the winner. I was going to have one of my pieces exhibited in a prestigious art show. I would be the star of an opening, have my own reception... Now I was getting carried away with myself. The date of the opening was set for Christmas Eve.

I felt a breath of wind rush at me as the cafeteria flew open and closed, and suddenly my roommate Duncan was standing at our table. He took one look at my face, and knew I already had the news. "Hey, I came to hunt for you as soon as I found out."

"But nothing's been officially released yet."

"No, but I was upstairs talking to Sharon. She didn't mean to, but she let it slip. Hey, congrats, Lor, I'm really happy for you." He leaned over to hug me, and suddenly noticed I had company and grinned. "Hey, Rudy. How are you? Nice to see you again."

"Good to see you, Duncan. Well, it looks like our girl is going to be famous after all."

My phone chimed. All of my messages for Lorelei went directly to voicemail. I switched it on. An unfamiliar voice requested my presence in the Director's office at my earliest convenience. It was Friday. Could I wait until Monday to learn officially that I had won the contest? Not on your life! I had to go home I told the guys. They both understood, and I wondered if they realized that the other knew my true identity.

No time to waste finding out. Must get home to transform into Lorelei. If only it were as easy as Kara Danvers (or was it Linda Danvers?) mild mannered assistant, changing into Supergirl. In that case, I would only have to rip my shirt off.

I left a message that I could be there within two hours. I

did not receive a confirmation but decided to take the chance that someone would be there to see me on my return as Lorelei.

***

When I arrived at the director's office, everyone was out dealing with a minor art gallery emergency. Sharon told me to wait and that she'd be right back. I waited but got impatient after ten minutes. Her desk was a mess of papers. My eye roved over them, bringing to my attention that these were the judges' checklists. There were several piles and as my curiosity won out, I found myself on the other side of the desk scanning the names of the contestants. The judges seemed to have narrowed the shortlist down to two. The finalists were me—Lorelei—and an artist named Lara-lee. Well that was confusing, I thought.

I had *no* idea *how* confusing. There were scores at the top of each contestant's file. I was pleased to see that mine had come out with top marks—receiving 25 points for all twenty-five criteria. Lara-lee was a close second with 24 points out of the twenty-five critical marks.

Then I gasped in horror. They had miscalculated.

I have an abnormal ability with numbers; I can see an error a mile away. There was an error.

At that moment I heard voices in the hallway. I quickly glided around the desk and flew to the waiting area and sat on the plush white sofa with its artistic row of black, yellow and red pillows.

Marjorie Snowden entered the office accompanied by Sharon, her administrative assistant. Marjorie nodded at me and went into her office. Sharon grinned and sat down at her desk. I raised an inquisitive eyebrow.

"Nothing serious," Sharon said. "A minor complication with the installation of Scotty Chang's exhibit. All fixed now." She beamed across her desk at me. "Sorry for keeping you waiting, Lorelei. You *are* Lorelei, aren't you? What a momentous day for you. And might I add that it's a great pleasure to meet you, finally! Marjorie will just be a moment. You must be so excited."

I was. In more ways than I cared to express. There's a reason why people should not snoop. What was it? You might learn something you don't want to know. Now, what was I supposed to do? If I came forward with the information it would be clear that I had peeked at things I wasn't supposed to see. And yet I knew the truth about the results of the contest. There was no other way I could possess the information.

But was it even my business to call them on a mistake? It wasn't *my* mistake; it was theirs. I racked my conscience for an answer. What would Duncan do? What would anyone in my position do?

I decided to let the situation play out. It was none of my business. If I hadn't snooped I wouldn't have seen what I saw, and I wouldn't now be cognizant of the mistake. They didn't know there *was* a mistake. It wasn't my job to verify the judges' math—or to match the correct names with the correct scores. It wasn't my fault!

"Lorelei? You can go in now." Sharon studied me with concern. "Are you all right? You look ghastly pale."

"I'm fine," I said, hoping my voice sounded warm. I know it sounded hoarse and very unlike Lori Channing's alto soprano. Which was good. I could read upside down (another gift *or* curse depending on the situation) and I had just recalculated the figures.

I was not mistaken.

I raised my eyes. Sharon had not noticed that my focus was on the judges' scores. Subconsciously, I wanted her to look. I wanted her to catch the error, so I wouldn't have to say anything. At that instant she *did* look down. Her eyes roamed over my score sheet and then Lara Lee's. Perhaps I was wrong. But I was never wrong when it came to simple addition.

"Hey," she said. "You sure you're not coming down with something?"

I looked into her eyes. "I'm fine. Just in shock." Wasn't *that* the truth. "I didn't expect to win."

"Well, it's all down here in black and white. Congrats! This is the opportunity of a lifetime. A game changer."

I have to say it was all I could do to squash the guilt, and react appropriately to Sharon's exuberant show of support, and then a few minutes later to Marjorie Snowden's congratulations and her plans for the exhibition where my art piece *Catterwall* was to be featured. My winning entry depicted a number of felines metaphorically and literally climbing walls. For those who don't know, 'catterwall' is a play on the word 'caterwaul', which means a shrill harsh sound like that made by fighting cats, or a female cat in heat. I think the rest speaks for itself—and if it doesn't, then think about it. That's what art is supposed to do. Make one think.

And boy did I have a lot to think about.

CHAPTER FIVE

The announcement of the winner was to take place next week. My featured piece *Catterwall* was to be delivered to the gallery two days before so that it could be mounted for display. The announcement was to formally take place at the Scotty Chang reception. So if I hadn't been invited to that before, I was invited now. Of course I was already attending as Harry Snowden's guest. This news made it doubly special.

But my conscience was troubling me. The truth was the judges had added up the scores incorrectly. Or they had misread the numeral. Could a **3** look like a **5**? Yes, absolutely. Because when I mentally calculated the numbers my scores had added up to 23, not 25.

Duncan noticed my brooding but I refused to tell him the truth. It wasn't my fault they'd made a mistake.

"Wow, you seem awfully down for someone whose dreams are finally coming true. And Harry Snowden is your date? Come *on*."

I smiled at Duncan. He was right. All of my dreams were materializing.

"Well, baby cakes, I think this calls for a celebration. How about if I take you out for dinner? We'll order champagne *and* dessert. The whole shebang."

"That sounds marvelous, Dunc." It really did. I should be celebrating. After all it could be *me* that had made the mistake. I had no business checking their math. I know I said that I never fail at simple addition, but hey, there's always a first time.

"Go doll yourself up. Maybe I'll even shave." He guffawed and started for the bathroom, whistling.

Duncan always could make me smile.

I returned to my bedroom, Giselle slinking up to greet me. She was bored and wanted me to hold her and pet her. I sat her on my lap and she immediately began to purr. "Two minutes," I murmured into her silky white fur. "Then I have to get dressed."

I was in the middle of changing my ensemble when the phone rang. My smartphone was in the living room somewhere between the sofa and the armchair. "Want me to answer that?" Duncan shouted through my closed door.

"Yes please." I was in the midst of trying to get my hair untangled from my zipper. I finally managed to free myself and wiggled into my tight Banana Republic Sloan dress with the cream-colored bodice and deep purple skirt.

"You look sharp," Duncan said as I padded out of my bedroom in bare feet. He handed me my phone. "It's Harry Snowden."

My heart leaped. "Hello?" I gasped, almost choking from excitement.

"Lorelei," he said. He hesitated a second. I guess he was wondering who the man was that had answered my phone. "Are you free right now? I just heard the news. Unofficially, of course. I'd like to take you out to celebrate."

Oh my gosh! My eyes must have lit up like lightbulbs. "I'd love to have dinner with you."

Whatever noises Duncan had been making in the background suddenly ceased. I glanced over and saw him removing his shoes. Oh crap. In my excitement at Harry's dinner invitation I'd forgotten about my date with Duncan. I noticed that he had also put on a tie. Duncan never wore ties. He was in the process of unlooping it, too.

"Just a moment, please," I said.

I hedged and Duncan grinned at me. "It's okay, baby cakes. Not the first time you've ditched me for someone richer." He laughed.

"Love you," I mouthed.

He blew me a mock kiss.

"What time?" I asked into the phone.

He said he was in his car on his way home when he'd had the idea. "How about in ten minutes?" he suggested.

Holy crow. That was hardly any time at all.

***

The next day was Saturday. I had spent the night with Harry and it was the best night of my life. It was unexpected. I had not thought Harry to be such a fast mover. But at the time I did not regret it. I only wished that I had not drunk quite so much wine and that the evening had not been such a blur. Don't get me wrong, I don't usually jump into bed with a guy on the first date, but this was Harry. I have been in love with Harry Snowden for years.

In the morning I got out of bed before he did. I couldn't let him see me before I'd had a chance to make up my face. Though he probably wouldn't have recognized me as Lori Channing anyways. He barely gave her a nod, though he was always pleasant enough. Still, better safe than having to give an awkward and probably incriminating explanation. He told me he had to be at the gallery. So many special events were scheduled just before Christmas and he was working overtime. He apologized for having to leave me like that. I asked if there was anything I could do to help. "There is *one* thing," he said after a moment's perusal. "There's an art catalogue I need, but it's at my mother's house. I'm already late for a meeting so I won't have time to go and fetch it. Would you be an angel and pick it up for me, and bring it to the gallery? I'll call Pickford to let you in." Pickford was the butler. "It's his day off, but I'll ask him to wait for you before he leaves."

No problem, I assured him. He kissed me, a long, deep absorbing kiss, and then stared lingeringly into my eyes. Oh, perhaps it was me staring longingly into his. "I'm late," he said, abruptly tearing away.

He was gone and I was left to shower and find my own way home. Unfortunately, I had no car. I called Duncan.

"Giselle's been puking her guts out," he said. "I was just on my way to take her to the vet."

"You sure it's not just a hairball?"

"Pretty sure, but I'm no expert. I'm in the car and I've got her in the carrier." I told him I was still at Harry's condo. "Should I come pick you up?" he asked.

"Please."

When they arrived I was waiting at the front entrance. I jumped into Duncan's ancient jeep. It was a millennial car and could conk out at any second. I twisted around so that I could check out Giselle in the pet carrier. Her eyes were bright and she was licking her paws. "Doesn't look like an emergency," I said. "Can we make a quick stop on the way?"

"Sure," he said.

Then it happened. As luck would have it the old jeep chose today of all days to conk out. The engine died as we sat at a stop sign, and Duncan couldn't get it to start up again. A lit icon continued to flash red from the dashboard. "Battery's dead."

"Great," I said. "I promised Harry I'd pick up something from his mother's house, and now, how am I going to get to the vet?"

"I have to stay with the car until the CAA comes to give me a tow or replaces the battery. Look, there's a bus. It heads up near Ravenscliffe. You can catch it if you run."

I leaped out of the car, detached Giselle's carrier from the backseat and ran pell-mell after the bus. It saw me and stopped. I stumbled onto the bus, and five minutes later I was at the corner of the exclusive neighborhood where Madam Director lived, and clumsily debarked. I lugged Giselle with me up Ravenscliffe Avenue to Harry's mother's house. Thank God, Marjorie was at the gallery today. I stood at the front door feeling foolish, wearing evening clothes and bearing a pet carrier with a very annoyed cat inside it. Pickford gave me an onceover with emotionless eyes and directed me to the library. I think he noticed the pet carrier, but resisted asking me why I had brought it or what was inside it.

"I'm afraid I have to leave, miss," he said. "Mr. Snowden informed me that you came to pick something up for the gallery. I'd appreciate it if you would hurry so that I can lock up."

"Just be a second," I said. I went to the library where Harry said the catalogues would be in a bookcase. He had written out the title and volume number. I set down Giselle's carrier. I noticed that French doors opened out from the library onto an exquisite garden where there was a large swimming pool covered with a tarp. It was mild outside and what little snow had been left from a former snowfall had turned to slush. I looked behind me. Pickford had left me alone. I went to the French doors and opened them to smell the fresh air. The bright green yew trees at the far side swayed gently in the cool breeze. The library was a bit warm and stuffy. I was sweating from all the rushing around. Then I returned to the bookcases to search for the catalogue.

Found it. Out of curiosity I flipped the pages of the thick tome, squatting at the bottom of a tall bookcase. The AGH had a much larger collection than I realized.

A sudden hiss drew my attention outdoors. Through the opened French doors I saw Pickford the butler with a broom hovering over the tarp of the swimming pool. What on earth was he doing? Was there a snake in the pool? Then I gasped. My eyes darted swiftly to my pet carrier. The cage door was open!

That Giselle! She was not only smart, but she was clever. Cleverness in a cat spelled trouble. I placed the catalogue on the marble coffee table and approached the door. Hells bells, I was in big trouble. This wouldn't go over well with Madam Director.

"Scat!" Pickford shouted at the pool, the broom swishing over his head.

"Don't hit her!" I screamed. "That's my cat."

"What the deuce is she doing in Dr. Snowden's pool?" Pickford's normally pasty face was red with rage. I had messed up his illusion of domestic perfection by letting my cat into the picture.

"Please, Mr. Pickford. She won't hurt anything. But you have to stop waving that broom around."

Giselle was trapped in the tarp, splashing around in the slush where the canvas dipped into a wide depression. "Giselle," I called. "Come here, beautiful. There are no fish in that swimming pool."

She wanted to ignore me, but she was miffed by Pickford's threatening broom. She gave him what sounded more like a growl, then hissed and spat, while he kept the broom at face level to protect himself in case she attacked.

What was wrong with this man? Didn't he have any pets? And then I realized what a stupid question that was. Of course he didn't. He lived in the Snowden mansion, and Madam Director had no pets, none that I detected anyway. I forced myself to be considerate. After all, he might be afraid of cats. Well, clearly he was or he wouldn't think he needed that broom to protect himself against a defenseless animal. Then horror of horrors, Giselle decided to show just what she thought of him. She coughed up the biggest hairball I had ever seen. I could have laughed, but when I saw the horror in the butler's face, I swallowed what would have been a burst of uncontrollable guffaws.

"I'm so sorry, Mr. Pickford. I'll clean that up."

"Just retrieve that hairy beast, and get out of here."

No need for name-calling.

I crawled on my hands and knees to the edge of the pool. "Come here, kitty." I stood up, frustrated and a little afraid now. What was he going to tell his employer? She would hate me; think I was a bumbling fool. What would Harry think. I knew the story would reach him. There was nothing I could do to prevent it. Pickford disliked me from the moment we met.

Standing up, I shouted out of desperation. "Giselle!"

She leaped from the slushy puddle in the center of the tarp to the edge nearest to me, dug her claws in for traction, and crawled inelegantly out. Oh, Lord, if she left holes in the tarp I was a goner. I lifted her with one hand and tucked her against my now filthy coat. She was wet and dirty from her escapade in the swimming pool tarp.

Pickford remained on the far side glaring at me. I hurried back inside the library, shoved my cat inside the carrier and latched it. How she had unfastened the latch was beyond me. But like I said, she was clever. A real feline Houdini.

I grabbed the catalogue. By now Pickford had followed me into the library. He left the broom outside and locked the French doors. I opened my mouth to apologize again, to beg him not to mention the mishap, but ultimately I knew it would do no good. He never wanted to see me in this house again, and he would make certain of it by making Marjorie Snowden aware of every last detail of my visit.

I left with the catalogue under one arm and the cat carrier in the other, and ran down the hill as fast as I could go without falling flat on my face, until I reached the bus stop where Ravenscliffe Avenue intersected the main thoroughfare of Aberdeen.

CHAPTER SIX

One thing was clear. Giselle was not seriously ill. Now that she had coughed up that hairball she was fine. I decided a visit to the vet was unnecessary after all, and made a beeline for the art gallery. Only problem was I still had the pet carrier, inclusive of cat. Would they mind if I brought her in just long enough to leave the catalogue with Harry's secretary? Of course, they minded. I was told at the door that pets were prohibited inside, and that only service animals were allowed. I could hardly convince the security guard that Giselle was a service animal.

"I need to get this to Harry Snowden," I said, setting the cat-filled cage on the floor and waving the catalogue in the security guard's face.

"You will have to leave the pet carrier outside."

I couldn't leave Giselle outside. Someone might steal her—or worse, she might decide to break out of her jail cell and explore. I wouldn't put it past her. The security guard turned his nose up at the soiled cuffs and hem of my coat. I must look like a hooker to him in my stilettoes and short purple skirt, and my hair in disarray. I was at my wits end when my friend the janitor, Rudy Donner, came along on his way to fix some light fixtures. "What's the problem?" he asked.

I pointed to the pet carrier.

He grinned. "Is it bring-your-pet-to-work day?"

"No," I said, abashed. "Harry Snowden asked me to deliver this catalogue to him, and I was on my way to the vet—" I raised my hands, palms up, as though that explained everything.

"And animals are not permitted inside the gallery," he finished for me. No problem. I'll drop the catalogue off at his office. I'm headed that way now."

He could see the disappointment in my expression. An amused look came into his eyes. "Would you rather I waited outside with the carrier and *you* delivered the catalogue personally?"

Oh crap, now he knew. This was infuriating and mortifying, and—what else did he know about me? You would think that he was Santa Claus or something. And that he had decided I was very naughty, but in a good way.

I handed him the catalogue. "Thanks Rudy, I appreciate it."

He glanced at my dress coat, now soiled from my foray into the Snowden swimming pool to wrestle out my cat, the long, highlighted hair around my shoulders and my dramatically made-up face, sans eyeglasses. "No problem, Lorelei. And if he happens to be in his office I'll let him know you had a cat emergency."

Oh, please don't, I pleaded with my eyes.

He smiled at me. *Don't worry, I won't.*

As I escaped outside with Giselle it dawned on me that this was the first time I had greeted Rudy Donner as the artist Lorelei. He had spoken to me the way he always did when I was dressed as docent Lori Channing. Why was it he was the only one who could see through my disguise? I pushed my long hair out of my face as a puff of wind caught it. No point in having an argument with myself on the street. I wasn't about to win no matter what persona I employed at the moment.

I headed home humming Christmas tunes to myself. All was not lost. On the whole this was the end to a pretty great week. I had spent the night with Harry Snowden, my dream man. I loved him. I knew I did. Everything was so perfect. It felt so good to be with him. He had promised to call before the Scotty Chang exhibition. The announcement of my win would be made the same night. By Christmas Eve I would be the star of a provincial-wide exhibition. Thousands of entries had come from all across Ontario. I had beat out the emerging artists from Toronto, of which Lara Lee was one.

Then my heart sank. Crap. It wasn't my fault. Why did I have to keep thinking about that miscalculation—which could very well not be an error? After all, I was the only one that had seen it. Or thought I'd seen it.

As I approached James Street North on foot, my right boot sank into a puddle. I barely noticed. What had caught my attention was movement inside the Design Annex, the renovated glass and stone building to which I now stood in front. I recognized the artist who was talking to Samantha. Speak of the devil. Lara Lee was right there. I assume she must also have work in the Annex, and if I were a little less self-obsessed and a little more observant I would probably have noticed that her name, too, was on the list of artists showing here this month.

She left the gallery without noticing me. We had never met in person but I knew of her work, and recognized her from a photo Duncan had once shown me. She was an emerging star. Her looks were nothing to brag about. She looked like she hadn't combed her hair or showered in a week. Her clothes were loose and even more out of fashion than struggling artists normally flouted, in their never-ending attempts to defy convention. Was it an affectation?

I guess I wasn't as famous as I would like to be. In artist's circles I was just slightly above a 'nobody.'

I shrugged and decided to forego a visit to the Annex, and went directly to my apartment. Giselle fidgeted in the carrier, and I was pretty sure Samantha would frown on my bringing her inside with me, even in the persona of Lorelei whom she liked rather than Lori Channing, my other persona—the one she disdained.

Duncan was home.

"How's Giselle?" he asked.

I let her out of her jail cell, and she snapped at my fingers when I tried to pet her. "Guess she's a little ticked off because she spent the entire day inside the carrier. Thanks for worrying about her and offering to take her to the vet. She seems back to normal. Let's see if she'll eat." I opened a can of Iams wet food and dumped it out into her dish. She sniffed at it then immediately started to lick it up. "I believe whatever upset her stomach earlier today has past."

"Good. She really was puking her guts out this morning. I was a bit concerned."

"Thanks, Dunc. You're a gem."

"So… I take it the date went well?"

I grinned. "Oh, I am so happy, Duncan."

"I can see that. I'm happy *for* you. You deserve it." He glanced away.

Was he just a wee bit jealous? It was selfish of me, I know. But why did I have that inner sensation, that inside prickle that told me something was off between us?

"Did you hear about Lara Lee?"

I frowned, guilt irrationally creeping up my neck. "No. What happened?"

Please don't tell me that you knew Lara Lee had come in second. He was pretty chummy with Sharon, Madam Director's administrative assistant. She might have told him.

"She got kicked out of her apartment in Toronto for reneging on the last three months rent. It's impossible for an artist to live in the big city. Everything is too expensive. She's moved to Hamilton where the rent is cheaper, but she doesn't know if she can make it even here. She was really counting on winning that award and the chance to exhibit a piece of her art in a major exhibition." He paused. "She could use a break."

More guilt.

"Can't she bunk with somebody like we do? It cuts the expenses in half."

"Yeah, and in your case it cuts the cost down to a third. You still owe me your share of the groceries, or did you conveniently forget?" he teased.

"Soon as I get paid, you're the first payee on my list."

He laughed. "I'm just riding you. You eat like a bird."

"No, seriously, Dunc. I saw her leaving the Annex downstairs as I was coming home. She looked pretty done in."

"Well, if we had a spare room I'd offer her a place here. But it's a tight squeeze as it is. And we're using the living room as a studio."

No, that would be impossible. Couldn't fit another person in this loft.

"I just hope she doesn't end up on the street."

"Don't say that. She's not that hard up, is she? Surely she has friends. Family?"

"I don't think she does. Or if she does she doesn't want anything to do with them."

"So sad," I said, softly.

"Makes you appreciate what you've got, huh?" He came over and gave my arm a pat. "Hey, since I didn't get to take you out last night, how about tonight? What time do you finish at the gallery? Or, are you too hung-over?"

I scowled at him in jest, glanced at the time. Then grinned. "Actually, I *am* a little tired."

"I *bet* you are," he said, reprovingly, but with humor in his eye.

"Quit being so crass."

"Well, you did it, didn't you?"

I stuck my tongue out at him. "A lady never tells."

"Hope you didn't do *that* to him."

"Shut up, Duncan."

"So, rain check?"

"Rain check."

I went to my bedroom to scrape off my heels and peel out of my dress. I hadn't had a change of clothing in eighteen hours. I was looking forward to putting on my Lori Channing persona. Her fashion sense was a bit cheesy and unadventurous, but it made her almost invisible. And there was nothing I wanted more than to be invisible tonight.

I flopped down sideways across the mattress in my lacy

underwear. I had a few hours before I had to be back at the gallery. I was troubled. I had to know for sure. The AGH was open late tonight. I was giving a tour. If I waited until the doors closed, I could get inside Sharon's office and find out once and for all whether or not the judges had made a mistake.

And if they had?

What are you going to do about it, Lorelei?

My conscience had an annoyingly loud voice at the most inopportune moments.

I wriggled out of my lace underthings and dragged on my more practical stretchy sports stuff. I should dress in dark clothes just in case I had to make a disappearing act fast. And they had to be comfortable because who knew how long I would have to wait inside some broom closet before all the staff, security and custodians went home.

Giselle had followed me into my room and was slinking around the windowsill. I would have to learn to move like her, silent and stealthy. Where was I going to hide until the doors of the AGH closed? And how was I going to break into Sharon's office? I grabbed my black-rimmed eyeglasses. Time to suit up.

CHAPTER SEVEN

There were ten people waiting for me at the Visitors Services desk when I arrived that evening. I greeted them with the usual spiel, and handed out pamphlets. It was hard for me to concentrate on my talk and then afterwards on their questions. We visited all of the galleries ending up at the last exhibition, a collection of historical Canadian women artists and their self-portraits. Emily Carr was the cherry on top. She was the most famous of all these female artists.

I was anxious for everyone to leave, and forty-five minutes later, the last visitor thanked me and left me alone in the gallery. I fetched out my smartphone and checked the time. Almost closing. The offices upstairs were long vacated. In fact, I could probably sneak up there now without being seen. I was hoping that the cleaning staff had left the office doors open as they usually did when they were doing the offices at night. The foyer was deserted when I went to the elevators. There was very little sound. I decided I had better clock out first then backtrack to the administrative floor.

"Lori," Sylvia said as I went to say goodnight to her. "The director wants to see you before you leave."

My heart leaped to my throat. *You mean she's still here?* Then—*Why? What did I do?* I nodded, grabbed my coat from the coatrack and my purse from the plastic storage cubes, and went to the elevators. That really threw a wrench into my plans. I stared at the blank elevator door. What could she possibly want to see me about?

By the time I reached the top floor I had worried myself into a tizzy. Stop it, I warned myself. I really had to get a grip or I would blow it.

I smoothed down my pencil skirt, and patted my tightly twisted hair, that showed only brown on the top of my head. I tapped on the door marked **Marjorie Snowden, PhD, Director.**

Sharon her secretary had already left. Her desk was clean and any papers were stacked into neat piles. The computer was off.

"Come in," the iron voice said.

I nervously pushed open the frosted glass door.

"Don't just stand there like a mouse."

I didn't know what she expected me to do.

"Sit down."

I sat.

She shuffled some papers in front of her and then shoved them aside. She sighed.

Okay, that wasn't good.

"Lori Channing."

Yes, that was my name. Well—one of them.

I couldn't meet her eyes. I was so terrified that she might see Lorelei staring back at her through the black-rimmed glasses.

She shook her head. "Why do you want to be a volunteer here at the AGH?" she asked. Her voice had noticeably softened. Was she planning to fire me? You can't fire a volunteer, can you?

"I love art, Dr. Snowden," I said miserably.

"Do you." It wasn't a question. It was more like a statement.

"If you love art so much, why are you always late?"

Was I late? I didn't think that I was.

"And this business with your cat."

Oh shit. I cupped my mouth and hoped I hadn't said that out loud. I never swear, honestly I never swear. Except when I'm in trouble.

"It's come to my attention that your cat has escaped into the Design Annex, not just once, but a couple of times."

I was silent.

"And earlier today, Security reported that you brought your cat here. *Here,* to the main gallery."

Oh no, I could feel it coming. She knew about Giselle's misadventure in her swimming pool. But wait a minute. She wouldn't have known that the perpetrator was me. I had been in the guise of Lorelei. But if she put two and two together… Would she figure it out? Oh, Lord, if she figures out that Lori and Lorelei are one and the same I'll be dust under her feet. I think I was beginning to shake but she hardly noticed. I barely heard the next five minutes of her reproach. I was busy trying to look innocent.

"Keep that cat out of the Annex, Lori. And no pets are allowed in the downtown gallery—at *any* time—is that clear?

I nodded. She sighed and I could detect the exasperation in her face.

She rose from her desk and went to the oak rack holding her coat and Hermes scarf. When I didn't move—I was literally frozen in the seat from fear—she turned and said, "You may leave now. I have to get home. My son and I are going Christmas tree shopping tonight."

Honestly, can you imagine Marjorie Snowden decorating a Christmas tree?

I nodded and dragged my inert body to a standing position. I refused to take the elevator downstairs with her. I had to invent an excuse, and said, "I think I need to use the ladies room."

She nodded as we left her office and entered the corridor. "It's around the corner."

I scurried off as she sought the elevator.

I waited a full ten minutes before I left the women's washroom. I could hear whistling down the hall. It was probably the cleaning staff. The whistling disappeared into one of the offices. Lucky for me, the office doors were all opened so that the janitors could do their work. I slipped inside Marjorie Snowden's outer office to the reception area and scoured Sharon's desk. The judge's forms must have been filed away. I moved to a likely filing cabinet. Where would they be filed and under what label? I started at the top: **ART CONTEST**. And there they were. Fortunately, the file cabinet where I was prying was behind the opened door. No one could see me from the corridor. I dared not close the door, otherwise someone might wonder why it was shut when it had been left open. So, I had to be very quiet, with an ear to what was going on outside.

It took a very short time to find what I was looking for. My stomach sank as I added up the figures. It was true. I was right the first time. They had made a mistake in the addition. My score was a 23 and not a 25, despite the fact that the hand-written number looked like a 25. No one had thought to double-check the calculations.

I heard a sound outside in the hallway. I fumbled the forms back into the file and eased the drawer shut. I straightened, grabbed my coat and purse from where I had flung them onto a red-pillowed chair and turned around. Rudy Donner was standing there with a mop in his hand and a frown on his usually pleasant face.

"Find what you were looking for?" he asked.

I blanched from my heels to the roots of my hair.

"Rudy," I gasped.

"The same." He studied me as the color returned to my face. "You didn't answer my question."

"Are you going to report me?"

"Why, lassie? What have you done?"

"I was snooping in the file cabinet."

"Why?"

I collapsed on a nearby chair. "Oh, Rudy," I said. "Something awful has happened."

He propped his mop against a bookcase and looked compassionately down at me. "What did you do?"

"The truth is, I haven't actually done anything. Except check my contest scores because I thought I detected a mistake when I was here before." I was babbling semi incoherently. I don't know why, but I trusted Rudy not to judge me until I had finished explaining, and even then I knew he wouldn't judge me. He wasn't that kind of person.

I told him what I saw. I told him that Lara Lee's score was higher. I offered to go back to the cabinet and show him myself. But he said no, he didn't want to see it.

I was practically in tears. He watched me and said nothing until I had finished babbling.

He exhaled and leaned toward me, tipped my chin up so that I was looking through glassy eyes into his warm brown gaze. "Lassie," he said. "What have you done wrong? Except maybe snoop inside a file cabinet that doesn't belong to you."

I nodded and dried my cheeks with my sleeve. I fished inside my purse for a tissue and found one slightly used. I blew my nose.

"I wish I had never glanced down at Sharon's desk when I came for my interview with Marjorie Snowden that day."

"And now, through no fault of your own, you have knowledge you can't un-know."

Exactly.

"Tell me," he said. "Why did you come back? Why not just leave it alone? You could have been the one to make the mistake. Since when is it your responsibility to find someone else's mistake?"

I don't know, I wanted to wail. But I did know. Lara Lee, the artist who actually won, was homeless.

"She's broke," I told Rudy. "Kicked out of her home. I saw her as I was headed to work tonight having dinner inside a soup kitchen."

"You're a good person Lorelei Channing," Rudy said.

"What should I do?"

Rudy extended a hand and I took it and stood up. "You should go home. Get a good night's sleep. Everything will be less cloudy in the morning."

"You're not going to advise that I should tell Dr. Snowden?"

"I have no knowledge of what you are talking about."

I frowned. He picked up his mop and ushered me to the

door. I kissed him on the cheek. "Go home, lass."

I left the AGH. I don't know why, but Rudy Donner always made me feel better, even though he hadn't solved my problem. He was right though. Things always seemed bleaker at night. I walked down King Street to James North. Duncan was always warning me not to walk downtown at night on my own. It was relatively early. Just after nine-thirty. I'd be home in about fifteen minutes.

There were some seedy characters on the streets. Most of them were harmless. Most in fact were just poor. They couldn't help the way they looked.

The lampposts sent harsh light onto the wet street. Steam furled from the ground and a foul smell came from the sewer grate. Cars beaded with rain parked bumper to bumper, cloaked in shadows. It all seemed so incongruous with the Christmas decorations and twinkle lights. A couple of gruff-looking men in dirty blue jeans and baseball caps eyed me as they walked by; I kept moving. A woman was ahead of me. She had long, scraggly, greasy hair and layers of loose clothing. I picked up the pace, I wanted to get past her and home. I was starting to feel jumpy.

I slipped beside her and speed-walked along the curb to get past. In my haste I accidentally jabbed her with my elbow. "Sorry," I muttered.

"Spare change?" she asked, extending a grubby palm.

I fished in my pockets for loose coins and came up with a couple of dollars worth. "Sorry, it's not much."

"Thanks. Every bit helps."

I had a quick glimpse of her haggard face behind the unruly hair before the wind swept it over her eyes in unpleasant strings. My heart stopped. I felt something click inside my chest like my heart valve had stuck. She moved on and turned the corner toward the homeless shelter.

I had seen that face before.

It was Lara Lee. The artist.

CHAPTER EIGHT

The weekend passed without my receiving an irate call from the Snowden Mansion concerning an errant or itinerant cat. So either Pickford had let me off the hook or Marjorie Snowden was unimpressed with my antics. Either way I was relieved. However, that didn't mean that she liked either Lorelei *or* me. When I saw Harry at the Annex Monday morning, however, he never mentioned the incident so perhaps I was in the clear.

He had come to pick me up to take me to lunch. He had booked a table at Il Fiasco in Dundas, a trendy sort of place with an intimate atmosphere and fine food, but affordable. We were just getting ready to leave when the forlorn form of Lara Lee came straggling into the Annex. I instinctively felt Harry flinch as she walked in the door, the smell that wafted in with her was offensive and he made an effort to hold his breath. So she hadn't showered in a few days.

Samantha had told me that nothing of hers had sold recently so she was still penniless. I was almost tempted to purchase a piece of her art to assuage my guilt. But when I saw how expensive her art was I knew I couldn't afford it. I guess like the rest of us she just didn't sell enough pieces.

Harry pinched his nose as we stepped toward the door. Suddenly Lara Lee swung around, and said, "Excuse me. You're Harry Snowden, aren't you? Curator from the AGH?"

Harry gulped uncomfortably before turning. "Hello, yes I am."

"I'm one of your artists. I show here at the Annex— occasionally."

He nodded without extending his hand. "Nice to meet

you."

I noticed he didn't ask her name and oddly she had not offered it right away. I could see she was about to when she realized that Harry was clueless to her identity. But he quickly brushed her off, and pretended not to notice when she shot out a hand. "I'm sorry, but I'm late for an engagement. Perhaps we could discuss your work another day?"

"Yes. Of course," she said dejectedly, arm swinging to her side. And then she answered more severely. "A busy man like you has no time for someone like *me*."

I was a little surprised at her bluntness, but she was honest. I had to say that for her.

She pivoted to me, scrunched up her eyes. "Don't I know you? I swear I've seen your face before."

I hoped to high heaven that she didn't recognize me from last night, that I was the one to drop those few measly coins into her hand.

"I'm Lorelei," I said.

She nodded. "That's right. The textile artist. I've heard all about you."

Harry was a little startled at her outspokenness. I was stunned that she knew who I was. Talk was fast and cheap on the artist grapevine but I never thought I would be a subject to go viral.

Harry nodded that we were leaving, and I smiled, trying to make things right between us fellow artists. He ushered me out the door ahead of him before I could say anything else to her. Then he gasped as he exhaled before drawing in a deep intake of air. He laughed. Honestly, he could be a bit more discreet. I didn't see anything funny about a person having nowhere to bathe.

"I don't imagine she's gone in there to purchase anything. Hope she doesn't plan to stay in there for long or we'll have to have the whole place fumigated."

"Harry!" I said, shocked.

"You have to admit. That smell is still lingering. Thank

heavens she didn't force me to shake her hand."

"That was the artist Lara Lee."

"No. Seriously?"

"She hasn't been able to make ends meet."

He frowned. "I've seen her work. Had no idea she was that hard up. She's very talented. But the world of art is a rat race. She may not be cut out for it." He shot a studious look through the window. "Not getting any younger either. Looks like she might be in her forties. And that attitude—" He shook his head.

For the first time I saw past my rose-tinted glasses. And caught a glimpse of a very different Harry. Was this who he really was? I was taken aback.

"It's a tough business. Retaliating against circumstance and bad luck with a nasty attitude is not the best strategy. Maybe she should get a day job."

He had a point. Most of us had to work at something other than our art. Duncan was an art instructor, and a sometime administrator for the local college. I have had all sorts of totally unrelated jobs. At the moment I wasn't gainfully employed because to be truthful there was no gainful employment to be had. Well, there was always waitressing, I suppose. Or I could become a barista at the local Starbucks.

The only reason I wasn't in the same position as Lara Lee was because of Duncan. His day job paid our rent. And his friendship meant my salvation.

Speak of the devil. Here came Duncan now. He raced around the corner shouting at the top of his lungs: "Giselle, you felonious feline. Get back here."

I stooped and scooped Giselle up into my arms as she scurried toward me.

"Sorry, Lori...elei." He had almost made a gaff that could have signaled disaster. He ground to a halt in front of me and apologized for nearly crashing into us. "Darned cat slipped out as I was leaving."

Harry had a puzzled look on his face. Duncan smiled.

"Hello Harry. Nice to see you again."

Harry continued to frown but followed with polite protocol, and gripped Duncan's outstretched hand.

"Duncan Mackenzie, sculptor. We met at your mother's home. At the reception for Scotty Chang."

"Oh, of course," Harry said. "Apologies. I recognize your face, but the name slipped my mind."

"Here, I'll take her upstairs," Duncan said, reaching toward me for Giselle. "Come on, gorgeous. Your mommy's going out. You have to stay home."

I handed the reluctant Siamese over to Duncan like a zombie. What was Harry thinking? Was he wondering why Duncan had referred to me as 'Mommy?'

Duncan glanced from me to Harry. Then back again. As he said his adieus Giselle hissed from under his arm in Harry's direction. Harry jumped back.

I patted his wrist. "It's all right, she's just nervous with strangers."

"No kidding. Am I mistaken in thinking that that's *your* cat?"

Now I've done it.

"Actually, she's *mine*," Duncan cut in. "I just call Lorelei mommy as a joke. The cat really likes her."

"Hmmm," Harry said.

"We'd better go," I urged Harry, "if we don't want to lose our reservation."

"Yeah, don't want to lose that reservation," Duncan echoed.

I scowled at him then mouthed 'thank you.' He shrugged. Harry tucked my hand under his arm, and led me to where he had parked his car on the street.

Once we were seat-belted inside his Lexus sedan, he turned to me. "Do you live with him?"

I froze. What was I supposed to say?

"From the sounds of it, I'd say you do."

Okay. No point in lying. "Yes. Duncan's my roommate."

He went still for a few seconds. "Roommate... How so?"

Was this really any of his business? I glanced his way and by the expression on his face I saw that it was. It *was* his business if we were going to continue seeing each other. Why did this annoy me?

"Duncan and I are old friends from art school. Nothing more."

"Never?"

I shook my head. "We've never dated, if that's what you mean."

"But you live in the same apartment? You said you lived in the loft above the Annex. That's where I assume Mr. Mackenzie was going, as there are no other apartments on this block."

"What are you asking me, Harry?"

Why was he such a prude?

"You *know* what I'm asking you."

"We have separate bedrooms."

"That doesn't say much."

"We don't sleep together. Ever. And never have."

He glanced backwards at my apartment overtop the Design Annex. "I'm surprised. Attractive woman like you." He smiled. "You know I think you're very pretty."

Truth was, Harry had never actually seen me without makeup. I hadn't washed my face before we'd hit the bed the other night, and I had redone my face before he had risen the next morning. He didn't know if I was pretty or not. Duncan on the other hand had. He'd seen it all. The good, the bad— *and* the ugly.

"Roommate," I said adamantly. "We are roommates. That's all."

He pressed the ignition. "If you say so."

***

The Scotty Chang opening was in a couple of days and I was in a tizzy as to what to wear to it. The contest winner was going to be announced during the speeches and I wanted to look my best when I was introduced. It was my bad luck that the restaurant we chose for lunch was the same restaurant that Harry's mother and Scotty Chang were at that day. Il Fiasco was a charming recently renovated eatery that served upscale international cuisine. The prices were reasonable so I was surprised to find Harry's mother there. Unfortunately, she insisted that we sit with them. So much for a romantic luncheon with the man of my dreams.

I smiled and sat down, Harry holding my chair solicitously. He was a gentleman through and through, and this was the woman who had raised him to be that way. I had to curtail my terror of her. After all it was Lori Channing who annoyed her—not Lorelei.

She seemed guarded when it came to my dating her son, but not offended. She was coldly polite. She did not show any overt dislike for me the way she did when I was Lori Channing.

"So, Lorelei," she said. "Scotty was just telling me where he gets his inspiration. He has returned to China several times and is very inspired by the Chinese inner cities as well as the plight of the peasants."

Clearly I was not inspired by the inner habitats of cats or their plight. I was more conscious of the feline as a metaphor i.e. the evocative characteristics that reminded us of our own humanity.

"You know, Lorelei actually *owns* a cat," Harry said, winking good-naturedly at me.

Now the cat was out of the bag. I guess he had figured it out. Giselle was mine, not Duncan's.

"Isn't that so?" Harry asked, turning to me.

It was difficult to keep the color from rising to my cheeks. "Always helps to have real life inspiration."

Marjorie Snowden observed me suspiciously. "It wouldn't happen to be a Siamese cat, would it?"

I nodded, nervously. How could I deny it? Harry had seen it and could attest to it being a Siamese cat.

"Pickford mentioned that you were over at my house the other day."

"That's right, Mother, I sent her over to fetch something for me."

They were making me sound like a dog.

"Lorelei," Marjorie said, her voice sounding louder than it probably was. "Do you have a last name?"

"But of course, she does." Everyone laughed. "She just chooses not to use it. Isn't that right, Lorelei. You have to admit, Mother, it adds to the mystique."

Why did I find his enunciation of the word 'Mother' when he addressed her so annoying? And why did he sound like a peevish boy trying to please her.

"It certainly does."

"Well, then, we probably shouldn't insist on the artist revealing her family name," Scotty Chang said. "It *is* part of the mystery and the persona."

Thanks, Mr. Chang, I wanted to say. And sincerely meant it.

"You know," Marjorie interrupted. "You remind me of someone."

Oh, no. Here we go.

"Do you have a sister or a cousin who works at the AGH?"

Harry's face suddenly brightened. "Hey, you're bang on, Mother. I know who you mean. It's one of the docents. Hmmm," he frowned. "She's a mousy little creature, but the features are similar. Not as vivacious as you, pretty lady. Ahh, my memory fails."

"Yes, mine too. The name draws a blank at the moment."

Scotty Chang shot a puzzled glance in my direction slightly perplexed at the turn the conversation had taken, and the peculiar discourse between mother and son. He was used to being the center of attention and couldn't believe how this non-conversation was circling around some nondescript and, no doubt, inconsequential docent. I decided to return him to his pedestal. "Congratulations on your wonderful exhibit, Mr. Chang. I read the rave reviews from all across the country.

You must be so pleased."

But Marjorie Snowden wasn't finished baiting me yet. Her eyes landed on where Harry's hand covered my own on the tabletop. "Actually, I was thinking it would be nice to invite some of the docents to your opening, Scotty. They are such hard workers and they *are* our connection to the outside world of potential art lovers. Yes, we must do that. She took out her smartphone and made a note to herself. "We must be sure to invite the docents."

CHAPTER NINE

Marjorie Snowden was nothing if not true to her word. An invitation came for me addressed to Lori Channing. A separate invite was addressed to Lorelei. And since Madam Director did not have my artist address she had sent it to the Annex where she was certain I would get it, since the shop girl Samantha knew exactly where I lived. The AGH must have gotten my address when I filled out the forms for the volunteer job as docent. On my contest entry form I had used the Design Annex address, begging Samantha to collect all of Lorelei's mail, which she had done. I had told her *and* them that I was between apartments, and if they were to ask now, I would say that I (Lorelei) was bunking temporarily with Lori Channing and her roommate Duncan Mackenzie.

"What's the matter?" Duncan asked me. "You look like someone who just lost her cat."

I managed a weak smile as Giselle greeted me at the door and did the figure eight dance around my legs, purring in unison with the rubbing of her cheeks. I quickly elbowed the door shut before she got any ideas of escaping, and tapped the invitation on the side table by the door where we stashed the mail and keys and other junk when we came home. "I think Marjorie Snowden may be on to me. What am I going to do, Dunc? I've woven a web so deceitful I've got myself all tangled up inside it."

I opened the envelope with a finger to verify my suspicions. The invitation was identical to the one delivered to Lorelei.

"You mean she suspects you're both Lorelei *and* Lori Channing? So what?"

"She'll wonder why I did that."

"*I*—wonder why you did that. Why *did* you do that?"

I slumped onto a chair and groaned. "I don't know. When I first started volunteering at the art gallery years ago, I was a student. I loved being a docent so much I didn't want to quit. But when I became an artist I wanted people to respect me. It's not cool to be a volunteer when you're supposed to be one of the artists."

He laughed out loud, I mean *really* loud. "You are an idiot."

I scowled. "I hate you."

"A cute idiot," he amended.

He squatted at my feet so that we were eye to eye with me slouched in the armchair. "Nobody cares if you're a volunteer. Everyone cares that you're an artist. I love what you do. And who you are."

"Oh, Duncan. I am so confused. I've really messed things up."

"Well, it's nothing that can't be fixed. You're not the first person to have two identities. Besides, who have you harmed? I'm just surprised that nobody knows you have an alter ego."

"One body knows."

"Oh? What body is that?"

I hesitated for a second. Oh, what the heck. "Rudy. Rudy Donner."

"That nice old guy? You worried he's gonna fink on you? Don't worry. I've seen you two together. He adores you. Like you were his own granddaughter."

"I think he's disappointed in me."

"Why? For pretending to be two people? You weren't really pretending. You really *are* both those people. It's just that most people don't make such an enormous effort to disguise themselves, and hide it from other folks. You really are more like Supergirl than you think."

By now Duncan was holding both of my hands in his and it felt good. His fingers were strong and calloused from manipulating clay and stone, and metal, and using sculptor's tools. His skin felt masculine, not soft and unused—like Harry's hands. Harry had never done any sort of labor in his life.

"You're drifting," Duncan said. "Okay now?"

He moved to withdraw his hands and stand up. I gripped him with my nails gently.

I said, "I didn't mean it. I'm sorry. I *don't* hate you."

He grinned. "If you gave me ten bucks every time you said that, I'd be a rich man."

I tugged at his hands. "Please. I was just embarrassed for getting myself in such a fix. You're right, I *am* an idiot."

Duncan frowned. "What else is going on, Lor? There's more to this cloudy mood than you're saying."

I debated whether to tell him the truth or not. My two personas had become Lori Channing art gallery volunteer, the Angel; and award-winning textile artist Lorelei, the Devil. *Tell him. No, don't tell him. Fix it. No, don't fix it.* Then I realized why it was so hard for me to tell him. It wasn't just that I was embarrassed about my alter egos. I didn't want him to know what a bad person I could be. I was going to take something that rightfully belonged to someone else, something that *that* someone needed more than I did. If the AGH gave me the cash award and placed a piece of my art in the upcoming international travelling exhibition, it could mean great things for me. This kind of opportunity was life changing. At the same time I was condemning Lara Lee to poverty and perhaps a life of artistic obscurity.

"Lori, you're white as a sheet. What's the matter?"

I leaned over and threw myself into Duncan's chest, wrapping my arms around his neck.

"What the...?" he said softly.

I hugged him and could not let go.

He allowed me to wrap myself around him for a few more seconds, and then he slowly disengaged my arms from his neck.

"What else is going on, Lori," he said.

He forced me to look into his beautiful brown eyes and I realized this was the first time I ever noticed what color they were. They were chestnut with tiny flecks of gold in the center of one iris.

"Don't do that," he said, getting to his feet.

I noticed now, too, how tall and strong he was. "Don't do what?"

"Don't hug me like that."

"I always hug you," I said, defensively.

"Not like that."

I didn't know what he was talking about but he looked disturbed. Duncan was never disturbed. Not by me.

Saved by the bell. My cellphone rang, and Harry was at the other end to advise me to send in my RSVP ASAP. He did not know that Lorelei had already done that.

Even Harry noticed that I wasn't quite myself. Of course he really wouldn't know what myself sounded like. He had only ever heard Lorelei's voice. Lori Channing was just a plain, quiet, unobtrusive girl who he occasionally gave a nod and a 'hi there' to.

I wanted to tell him that I wasn't in a temper conducive for talking, but this was Harry and I just couldn't do it. He was in a chatty mood and after a while he stopped noticing my lack of humor and continued to talk about the upcoming event. It was only when I was totally silent after he had ceased his speech that he said, "Lorelei, is there something wrong? You're awfully quiet."

I wanted to ask his honest opinion. What would he do in my place? And yet I couldn't tell him the truth without him thinking badly of me. But *would* he think badly of me? That was the thing. The art world was as cutthroat as the business world. He was the first to admit it—because in the end it *was* an extension of the business world. Weren't people supposed to grab opportunities? Wasn't that the recipe for success?

I tucked my smartphone up against my ear. Duncan was watching me, but when I flicked my eyelashes in his direction he turned away and started for the kitchen. I bent down and tucked Giselle under my arm and went into my bedroom. I closed the door.

I couldn't stand it any more. I had to tell someone. Rudy had been no help at all. He had not told me what to do. He had suggested I go home and sleep on it. I had slept on it and still had no answer. If the universe wanted me to be successful—even through a mistake—shouldn't I allow the course of events to play themselves out?

Only one idea came to mind. I couldn't make this decision by myself. And Harry was my boyfriend. That thought felt weird. I ignored it. I said forcefully into the phone, "Harry, I have a problem. I'd like to discuss it with you."

"Sure," he said.

"It has to do with Lara Lee."

"I still can't get the smell of her out of my memory. Makes me feel like taking multiple showers."

"She's a brilliant artist. You said so yourself."

"That was *before* I met her."

CHAPTER TEN

I told him the truth, not quite certain how he would react to it. But on retrospect, maybe somewhere in the back of my mind I already knew what his response would be. That was why I had told *him*—and not Duncan.

Deep in my gut I knew that Harry Snowden understood the business. And that he would be on my side. But I also knew that if he kept my secret he would have to keep the secret from his mother. I was laying it all down on the line. All my cards exposed. I suppose what I was doing was the same thing I had tried to do when I told Rudy Donner the truth. I had wanted my dear friend to make the decision for me. He hadn't. He had refused to allow me to shift the responsibility onto his shoulders. Not so with Harry. Harry was a go-getter. He was self-motivated and resourceful and a power player. It wasn't only because he was Marjorie Snowden's son that he had his job. And I wondered, after he did not condemn me for keeping my secret, what sly and illicit deeds *he* had committed to attain and keep his position.

"It's a rat race," he repeated.

I had heard him say this several times since we had started dating. "You do what you need to do to win."

Even cheat? No sound came from my lips but he knew what I was thinking.

"You are such a neophyte, Lorelei," he said. "You aren't cheating. I would never sanction cheating. This is undisclosed information, information that no one has. And you certainly *wouldn't* and *shouldn't* have it under normal circumstances. But chance sent you on a different path. You didn't look on purpose. You weren't snooping. And I am not on the panel of judges. I am not involved in the running or administration of this competition—in *any* capacity. I have not seen the score sheets or the score totals of any of the contestants. You are not culpable. You have done nothing wrong by not reporting something you are not suppose to be aware of in the first place. If you hadn't happened to glance down at Sharon's desk, we wouldn't be having this conversation." He paused. "Do you understand what I'm saying? You do nothing. I don't want Lara Lee to receive this prize. It's yours. Regardless of the mistake, it's yours. In fact the idea that they even made a mistake means they have to honor the decision. They are the ones at fault, not you."

By 'they,' I wasn't sure whom he meant. I guess whoever it was that had added up the scores incorrectly.

"This conversation never took place," he said.

Funny, this was virtually the same dialogue that I had experienced with Rudy, only with different words. But the gist of it was the same. Somehow the advice had sounded different coming from him. Somehow, Rudy Donner had not seemed complicit even after receiving the knowledge of what I had learned that fateful day. So, why did Harry come across as guilty as I felt?

And yet what it came down to was that it was okay. Harry was saying that it was okay for me to receive the prize because of a mistake in the final calculations. To be honest, neither Harry nor I knew who was responsible for the final calculations. He said it was best we didn't know, and that we didn't try to find out. It wasn't our problem.

Did I feel better? Yes, yes I did. It was like a burden had been lifted from my shoulders. Harry, my beloved Harry was on my side! I could go to the art show opening with my head held high!

But I still had one problem. Scotty Chang's opening was in one week. Marjorie Snowden was going to make the announcement of my win in a speech sometime during the presentation. She expected to see both Lorelei and Lori Channing there. I had not yet decided what to do. I had returned Lorelei's RSVP of Yes to the AGH as soon as I received it. I still held on to Lori Channing's invite, undecided how I could appear at the same place, at the same time, as two different people. If I were to attend the event as docent Lori Channing as well as Lorelei the artist I would have to hand-deliver my answer today. I sighed. It was probably too late. The only reason I wanted to show up as both artist and docent was to get back at Marjorie Snowden for trying to trap me. Well, maybe that was a hopeless case, and I was already trapped. Rats. If it wasn't one thing, it was another. Why was life so complicated?

***

"What a tangled web we weave…when first we practice to deceive."

I scowled at my roommate who stood in my bedroom door. "Haven't you ever heard of knocking?" I asked.

"Send your regrets, Lori," Duncan advised. He indicated with a gesture at the familiar envelope in my hand. "What can she do to you if all the docents she invited don't turn up. She'll be so busy she probably won't even notice."

"Then she'll win."

"Win what? You don't even know that she suspects you and Lorelei are one and the same."

"Oh, yes she does. You weren't there at that lunch. She knows, or at least suspects, and she's baiting me."

"Then I guess you'll *both* have to go."

I collapsed onto my bed.

"Want me to run your RSVP over to the gallery? I'm headed that way anyway."

"You'll do that for me?"

"Of course." He shot out a hand to take it from me.

I hesitated for a split second then released my grip on the envelope.

"So what's the plan," he said. "How are you going to be Lorelei and Lori Channing at the same time?"

I paused to peruse the idea over in my mind. My hand

was on Giselle's head that was now propped up on the bunched purple and lavender wool blankets on my mattress. Her eyes were half-slits, showing sapphire irises that seemed to glow in the pale light of my bedroom. She too seemed to be questioning my wisdom.

"I'll go as Lori. Meet everyone, and then get changed in the bathroom as Lorelei. After the transformation Lori will have to have gone home with a headache or something. Lorelei has to be there for the contest winner announcement—"

It dawned on me what that meant. I guess Duncan noticed my face fall.

"Lori," he said. "This isn't like you. You look really ill. What is wrong?"

I sat up on my bed, disturbing Giselle who scowled at me. "You're right, Dunc. I have a problem."

Interesting thing I learned about myself that day. Even though Harry's support had lifted my spirits, Duncan's opinion really mattered to me. I knew what Duncan would say if I told him the truth. I did not want to know the truth. And I did not want to hear him say it. And yet I knew if I refused to discuss some aspect of this issue with him he would never leave me alone.

"Hypothetically speaking," I said.

"This happened to a friend?"

I nodded. "Yes, this concerns a friend."

It really did. I liked to think that I could be friendly with all of my artist colleagues.

"Okay—so what terrible thing did this friend do?"

"She didn't do a terrible thing. It's what she *didn't* do."

"Huh." He frowned. "So, you gonna tell me about it?"

I exhaled. "Yes," I said.

"I'm listening."

I went back to the beginning, to the day when I was called into Marjorie Snowden's office to be told unofficially that I had won the 'Emerging Star' Art Contest. I had stood in front of Sharon's desk waiting for everyone to return from an art installation emergency. And there it was, right in front of my face. The judges' scores. I shouldn't have looked, I told Duncan. Only my wording was a little different the way I explained it to him. The pronoun 'I' was substituted with 'she'. *She* should have dragged her eyes away, in fact *she* should have torn her whole body away from that desk and sat on the white sofa with its red, yellow, and black pillows, legs patiently crossed and waited. But she hadn't. She had looked.

Duncan's kind expression darkened. His silence was thunderous. When he finally spoke I already regretted revealing my secret.

"Who really won?" he demanded.

I had forgotten that he, too, had entered the contest. Did he want to know how he had ranked among the others? I had not looked that far. All I was interested in were the top two scores—mine and Lara Lee's.

"Who?" he repeated.

"Lara Lee."

It was as though he had been holding his breath. He inhaled now after a rush of expelled air.

"This didn't happen to a friend, did it?" he said. He snorted. "Of course it didn't. I knew that even before you started to talk. This happened to *you.*"

I neither confirmed nor denied the accusation.

"And no one knows?"

As I glanced at his fiery eyes I realized he was angry. Angry at me? It wasn't my fault. Just because people couldn't add and subtract, that didn't make me a criminal.

"Why aren't you answering me? Does anyone else know?"

The heat was rising up my neck to my face. Just who did he think he was, judging me like that? "I don't like your tone. I thought we were friends. I thought I could trust you."

"Trust me? Trust me to do what? Keep another one of your secrets?"

He really was mad. I didn't understand. Duncan was usually so compassionate and understanding. Harry had said that I hadn't done anything wrong.

"Forget it," I snapped. "I should never have told you. This is why I hesitated to tell you in the first place."

His eyes blazed at me, then they softened. He sat down on the edge of the mattress beside me, laid down the envelope. He took my hand but I withdrew it like his touch burned. And it did.

He sighed. "Look, Lori. I know it's been tough. Being an artist *is* tough. It's tough for everyone. But you have it better than most." He paused. "So, do I."

"Don't preach to me, I'm not a child."

"I am not trying to tell you what to do. But if this weren't weighing on your conscience you wouldn't have told me. You would have kept it to yourself."

"I haven't kept it to myself. I just didn't tell *you* first."

He looked hurt but then quickly got over it and said, "Who *did* you tell?"

"None of your business."

"What did they say?"

"They said it wasn't my fault. I didn't have to do anything."

"Lara Lee is staying at the homeless shelter down the street."

"I know that!"

"Why are you mad at me?"

"Why are *you* mad at *me*?" I spoke with strong emphasis on both pronouns. Just in case he didn't get it.

"I am not mad at you." He fell silent for a while before he added, "Okay, you're right. I *was* mad at you. At first. I'm not now. I understand how you are choosing to look at it."

"I am *not* choosing anything. I'm innocent here. Whoever tallied up the scores made a mistake. Not me."

"So why are you talking to *me* about it?"

I scowled. Trust Duncan to bring out the Angel Lori, while the Devil Lorelei seethed.

"Hey, you aren't evil. I never said that."

Why did Duncan know me so well? He was the one who

had labeled my two personas Angel and Devil.

"It's *my* turn," I said. "I deserve this."

"And what does Lara Lee deserve?"

Now I was fuming mad. How dare he make me feel guilty when it wasn't my fault! It wasn't! It wasn't fair to be put in this position. "You know what? I don't want to talk about this any more."

"Fine," he said. I could see he was exasperated too. He got to his feet and made to depart. He turned around and gazed at me. I glared back. "Do the right thing, Lori."

He had forgotten the envelope and it was lying on the bed beside me. No way was I going to ask him for any favors. I would deliver the RSVP myself. To add to my sense of utter betrayal, Giselle leaped out of her nest of colorful blankets and tiptoed out the door after Duncan.

I refused to go to the gallery as the mousy Lori Channing. I needed to feel confident and powerful. Only Lorelei could help me feel that way.

I dolled up in skinny jeans and a skintight white sweater. I wrapped a red scarf around my neck and painted my lips to match. I added extra mascara for extra confidence. I would tell Sharon I was dropping it off for Lori. She knew that Lorelei and Lori Channing were friends.

CHAPTER ELEVEN

I dropped the envelope off at Sharon's desk without incident. Sharon was too busy to chat with me, so I left shortly after I arrived. Just as well, since the last thing I needed was to run into Marjorie.

I went outside to the outdoor sculpture garden. This was one of my favorite places to visit when I was troubled. I wished Duncan and I had not quarreled. I needed him on my side.

I stood in front of the *Centerpiece*, a welded steel sculpture, distinctly modern and resembling a human figure standing in a position both majestic and relaxed. My next stop was *Two Seated figures*, a bronze diptych. I finally stopped at the temporary display area, where local artist's works were rotated. A piece of carved stone called *Bodies in Love* caught my attention. It was one of Duncan's works.

Voices suddenly came from behind me—a woman's voice and two men. It was Marjorie and I was glad that she had company. That meant I could slip away without being rude. She nodded at me but didn't introduce me to the men. I saw now why she hadn't. They were tradesmen come to fix some sort of crack in the tiling of the floor. I planned to slip away, but just as I ducked toward the door she called out my name. The two workmen had gone to the far end of the garden to where the repairs were needed. She summoned me over to talk behind a bronze statue where we were certain to be out of earshot. She cradled a large artists tube in her arms.

"Dr. Snowden," I said. "So nice to see you again."

Marjorie Snowden glared at me.

Now what had I done?

Then I caught a glimpse of my reflection in the window behind her. I was dressed as the stylish textile artist Lorelei, with long, flowing, highlighted hair, thick-mascaraed lashes and no eyeglasses. My thin willowy form was like one of these sculptures, with no hint of the mousy, cardigan-toting, Birkenstock-wearing geek that was Lori Channing. She couldn't possibly recognize me.

And she didn't. Her reason for detaining me was not to accuse me of moonlighting. "It has come to my attention," she said, "That you were about to pull a fast one over on us."

Words froze on my tongue. I was stumped for a suitable response. After all Harry had counseled, had he ratted me out? "You are not the true winner of the 'Emerging Star' Art Contest."

My guilt must have colored my face.

"So it's true. You knew who the real winner was, but you chose to stay silent."

Shattered though I was, it never occurred to me to lie. It did occur to me to wonder if someone finally double-checked the results. Or was it really Harry or Rudy who had spilled the beans? No not Harry. Harry had adamantly advised against it.

I swallowed a gasp. The sinking sensation of cold betrayal descended. Was it Duncan? All it would have taken was a quick telephone call or text.

"Who told you?" I asked.

"That's none of your concern. The fact remains that you intended to steal this prize knowing full well that there had been a mistake in the calculation of the judges scores."

In some ways I was relieved. It was no longer my problem. I could relax and slink back into my loft/studio and create art in peaceful obscurity.

"Do you know who the real winner is?" the director demanded.

I nodded meekly. I hoped Lori Channing's personality wasn't showing through Lorelei's disguise. I had taken acting classes when in school and I knew how to modulate my mannerisms and my voice. But at the moment I had no control. I had better not speak or I would sound exactly like squeaky Lori and then, not only would the cat be out of the bag, but furthermore—Madam Director would have more ammunition to use against me.

She stood immobile and quiet for a few seconds. Then she accosted me with her iron voice. "How much did you want this opportunity, Lorelei?"

I gulped. *More than you could imagine.*

When I didn't speak she nodded as though she knew my mind. "I can't have people knowing about this error. It would create a vicious scandal and disaffect our most important donors." By important she meant rich. "I've also met the real winner. She may be talented, but times have changed and talent is not enough. I can't have her image as the face of the AGH. It's…it's just not right. In fact—" she cut herself off, and then concluded. "I find her appearance downright disgusting."

More than a little shocked, I could not find my voice.

"So I ask you again, Lorelei. How much do you want to win?"

I felt like I was a runner up for the Miss Universe Pageant. *You mean I still have a chance?* She seemed to have finished berating me, and now awaited my response.

"I think you know, Dr. Snowden. It's why I didn't say anything before now. I didn't think it was my place to say." I was beginning to find my voice again—and with it my confidence. She was gearing up for something, and I wasn't about to let her abuse me.

The men on the other side of the sculpture garden had activated some machinery, a drill or something, and it was generating enough noise to mask our discussion. Marjorie Snowden removed the lid from the tube she was carrying and unrolled a tapestry, letting the tube fall to the ground. The tapestry hung from her chest to the floor. I recognized it. It was the hanging Harry had bought for her birthday. *My* textile: *The Cat's Pyjamas.*

"I hate this thing," she said. "I loathe cats. But I hung this in my library because of Harry. I'll make a bargain with you. If you keep the bargain, no one will ever know how deceitful you are and perhaps you will even have a chance at making something of yourself. I don't know how talented or untalented you are, Lorelei, but if I were to decide from this piece I would say you are just a tad more talented than that sculptor over there." She pointed to Duncan's statue in the local artists' temporary display, to which I said nothing. "But then my job is not to judge talent. My job is to run the institution that showcases it. It is someone else's job to decide who is worthy and who is not. The bargain I want to make with you is this. I will award you the prize money and the opportunity to showcase your work in the upcoming international travelling exhibition. But—I want you to break up with my son."

I have to admit I was not surprised. She had never warmed up to me but at the same time she had not seemed adverse to our relationship. Why now?

All of my righteous indignation was steaming to the surface. She was blackmailing me, using the gallery's mistake and my misjudgment to steamroll me into giving up her son. At the moment I felt more weary than anything else. My anger had mutated to resentment, and then into a strange and totally inexplicable sense of relief. I still wanted to know why she objected to our relationship. I decided to ask her. After all, if she expected me to dump Harry I would have to give him a reason. It was easier if she articulated the reason for me.

"I don't like you. You aren't good enough for my Harry. But worse, you're a gold-digger."

"Excuse me?"

"Don't pretend that you're not dating my boy because he's powerful and wealthy, and heir to an enormous estate. He has the power to make or break your career. As do I. Don't ever forget that."

She was threatening me. And I had absolutely nothing to

fight her with.

"Harry doesn't love you, Lorelei."

It was like she had shoved cotton into my mouth. I wanted to retaliate with, 'Yes, he does.' But he had never spoken the words. And why would he? It was too soon.

"He'll break it off with you sooner or later. That's guaranteed. This will save you the heartache."

If she thought he would break it off with me, why not wait until he did? How was my dating him temporarily threatening her? Then it came to me.

Her confidence was phony. She had no way to know if he would fall in love with me or not. He *might* fall in love with me—against her will.

"All you have to do is decide how much you want the prize and the spot in the exhibition.

A true manipulator. How dare she bargain with my affection for Harry? She was not getting away with this. She was not. But I had no obvious plan to thwart her. I said, "I'm going to Scotty Chang's opening as Harry's date. How will I explain?"

"You'll think of something."

Was that all? Was I missing something? Just dissolve my relationship with Harry and I would be announced the legitimate winner?

"Furthermore, you will never breathe a word of this mess-up to anyone. Not even to the staff. Am I understood?"

Yes, I was beginning to understand.

"Lara Lee must never find out that she was the actual winner. Are we agreed?"

She dropped one edge of my hanging and let it drag on the floor while thrusting her right hand into my face.

She wanted me to shake on it.

Before I knew what I was doing I felt the cold grip of her fingers almost breaking mine.

"Now take this back to my house." She clumsily rolled up my beautiful wall hanging. "Pickford will let you in. I've decided it suits my library after all."

I submitted to her request. I knew why she wanted it returned to its place in her home. She did not want to have to explain to Harry why it was gone. She did not want him to suspect that she had any part in it when I dumped him.

Pickford was not pleased to see me, but at least this time I had come without the cat. He took the hanging from me and returned it to the library, closing the door in my face.

CHAPTER TWELVE

I bought a very special gown for Scotty Chang's opening. It was floor-length and a startling shade of royal blue. Thin spaghetti straps were all that held it up. On my feet I wore black satin, open-toed stilettoes and carried a matching clutch. Duncan stared at me when I came out of my bedroom, with a look that demanded: 'how can you afford that getup?' I left his accusation unanswered. He was attending the event also, but not as my date. I had not broken up with Harry yet. I had told Marjorie that it was too soon. Did she really want me to hurt him? She had delivered an ultimatum. If we were not broken up by the evening of the announcement, my prize would be revoked. She suggested I do it right there at the reception. I wasn't sure that I could.

There was Christmas music playing in the background when we entered the gallery, and a beautiful silver Christmas tree that rose from floor to ceiling. It was tastefully decorated with tiny white lights and white pinecones and white sateen ribbons.

My original plan was to arrive as Lori Channing and then ditch her trappings and appear as Lorelei for the rest of the evening. I had forgotten that Harry was going to come and pick me up. It almost would have been better had I broken it off with him before tonight. But I could not bring myself to do so. I had wanted this for so long.

More than your chance to be a famous artist? I asked myself.

That was the million-dollar question.

I still felt I had the right to the prize as well as to Harry. And I don't know why I cared if Madam Director knew I was

Lori Channing, except that, then she would have been right about me all along—that I was a liar.

Duncan was still peeved. He told me he would not assist in the charade. He wanted no part of the deception. "You're better than that, Lori," he insisted.

So I recruited Rudy Donner's aid. God knows why he agreed to my plan. It was full of holes.

When I arrived on the arm of Harry Snowden, everyone gasped at my gown—except Marjorie Snowden. She stared at me suspiciously, knowing full well that I had not yet kept my end of the deal. She drew me aside. "You have one hour before I announce the winner of the 'Emerging Star' Art Contest," she warned. "Think very carefully about your next move. Your future is in my hands."

When I failed to tremble in terror, her mouth twitched cynically. "You can come out of this a star or a fool. Make the right choice."

She turned to go, and then she said, "By the way, where is your friend the docent, Lori Channing? My secretary, Sharon, tells me you two are as tight as kittens."

My glare made no impression on her. Apparently, I had delivered exactly what she expected for an answer. She arched a well-manicured eyebrow, and left me to speak a few words to her son, before she sent her attention in the direction of some of the VIPs. I was fuming mad. I had almost given up my plan to appear as Lori Channing because I figured being exposed with double identities was peanuts compared to winning a life-changing opportunity that included a big cash prize.

Harry was busy with some of the guests. Duncan was nowhere in sight. Servers in classic black and white blouses, skirts and slacks were passing around champagne and canapés. I made a B-line for the elevator and once the doors had slid open and closed with me safely inside, I pressed the DOWN button. I would have to go to the basement to the custodians' lockers where Rudy had stashed my Lori Channing clothes. He had promised that no one would be there.

Lori's dress was a simple black affair. Another LBD but much plainer than the one I'd bought as Lorelei. This one had no lace or sheer parts. It had a high scoop neck. I replaced my stilettoes with black flats, rolled up my glossy highlighted hair into a tight bun until only the underside, which was brown, showed. I wiped off my makeup and applied a clear gloss on my lips. I unclipped the dangling crystal and silver earrings and replaced them with simple gold studs. Last, I popped on my black-rimmed eyeglasses. I adjusted my posture, mentally changed my persona from Lorelei to Lori Channing, stashed my fancy clothes inside Rudy's locker, and stepped out of the empty locker room with no one the wiser.

The elevator stuck once, mid floor, and I almost panicked when I realized I might miss the whole show. I had this image of myself turning the place upside down when the alarms went off to bring everyone rushing to the elevators to rescue me. I almost, *almost* jabbed the emergency button. There was music streaming through the PA system, Bing Crosby singing Christmas songs to keep me company. I wanted to scream. No amount of jolly *Santa Claus is coming to town* was going to break me out of this panic.

But something about the lyrics caught me off-guard:

> *He knows when you are naughty*
> *He knows when you are nice*
> *He knows if you've been good or bad*
> *So, be good for goodness sake!*

Next thing I knew, the doors slid open and I raced out of there like a rat on fire. I stopped at the entrance to the reception hall to catch my breath and compose myself. Duncan had arrived, and he was with a woman in an oddly familiar little black dress. He glanced my way and nodded. I nodded back. The other docents were at the far corner huddled together, many feeling out of place. Some, though, were brave and were mingling with the crowd.

"Lori, Lori," my fellow volunteers greeted me. I was well liked among my peers. "Did you see what Marjorie Snowden, the director was wearing? Isn't her dress gorgeous?"

I caught my breath, gazed dazedly around as though I had just arrived. I had to admit I had not noticed the director's outfit when she was admonishing me. But now I took the time to send a curious gaze toward the front of the gallery where a piece of mounted art was draped in white cloth. Marjorie Snowden stood just aside of it. Was that my hanging? It had to be. I evaluated the director's appearance. She looked stately as usual, this time in a black and white evening gown that had a bright splash of green. It was artsy and yet at the same time sophisticated.

"And did you see the textile artist Lorelei? She is so beautiful. Her gown is exquisite."

I smiled sheepishly, and agreed. I nervously smoothed out the creases from the front of my black cocktail dress. "I love her dress," I said, which I did. I had paid a bundle for it.

"Oh look, here comes Dr. Snowden now."

The 'Dr. Snowden' the docent was referring to was not Harry—whom I was hoping it would be—but Marjorie. I tucked a loose strand of hair behind my ear. It was show time. Was I going to pass muster or was Madam Director going to trip me up somehow, and expose my charade.

"Hello Lori." She nodded to the other docents and called them by their first names. I was impressed. I was pretty certain that Sharon or Sylvia, our volunteer coordinator, must have pointed out to her who everyone was—so that she would appear to care about them. "Nice to see you all here," she said politely. "So glad you could come." She turned to me. "I'm surprised to see *you* here, Lori."

"I wouldn't have missed it for the world," I said, in my best breathless and deferential voice. I wished she would stop repeating my name. Was she taunting me?

"Where is your lovely artist friend, Lorelei?"

"She's around her, somewhere," I replied.

"I saw her with your son," someone said.

"Did you?"

Marjorie scowled slightly, but so briefly that I was probably the only one to detect it. She immediately readjusted her expression to reflect her usual phony, pleasant face. "I must get a Christmas photo of all the artists present with our precious volunteers."

"Fabulous idea," someone piped in.

Now it was my turn to scowl—though ever so swiftly.

"Well, I hope she's here in the reception hall and not in the Ladies room powdering her nose. I'm about to give the presentation." She looked meaningfully at me.

Crap. I had to race back downstairs, make up my face and change my dress and shoes. Oh, how I wished I hadn't started this masquerade in the first place.

And then I saw the woman Duncan was with. He had brought a date, but not a date I would have expected. The little black dress she was wearing was familiar—because it was one of my discards. I had been packing away some of my old dresses to give to charities, now that I was planning to have some real money, and able to purchase new things. The dress was not awful. It was just a teensy bit faded. It was a classic...well, maybe a little dated, but with a flared skirt and sleeveless, unlike the tulip-shaped skirt on the dress I was wearing now.

The woman in my little black hand-me-down was Lara Lee.

I felt the rage burn my cheeks. How dare he? How dare he guilt me like that? But then I realized it wasn't rage that was flushing my face so horribly. It was shame. I was caught in my own web of lies.

"Hello, Lori," Harry said, coming up to me. "It is Lori, isn't it? You're one of the docents?"

I smiled at him. I could feel Madam Director's eyes burning a hole in my back.

How was it that Harry didn't know that I was Lorelei,

his girlfriend?

I stared hard at him. He seemed a little taken aback. "Something wrong?" he asked.

Yes, there was something wrong. *Something terribly wrong, if you can't see who I am.*

My eyes strayed to the doorway and I saw Rudy standing there in his janitor's uniform, but instead of a broom in his hand he was carrying what looked like a pet carrier. What was he doing here?

A silver spoon ringing on a glass drew everyone's attention. Oh, hell. Now what was I going to do? How was I going to slip away, transform into Lorelei and be back in time to receive my prize? I excused myself from Harry. Harry had already forgotten about me. He was moving up to the front of the gallery where his mother was standing at a podium. His eyes flitted around. Was he searching for Lorelei?

I made a beeline for the exit where Rudy stood holding the pet carrier. "Can't talk now," I gasped at him.

It wasn't a pet carrier that Rudy was holding. It was some sort of sports bag that looked like a pet carrier. "Your things are in there. Go to the Ladies Room. It will be faster. No one's there right now as they are all waiting on Dr. Snowden's presentation."

I can't explain how relieved I felt. Bag in hand, I made a mad dash for the bathrooms, already plucking off my eyeglasses and shoving them into my clutch. When I got inside, I saw that Rudy was right. It was empty. Just to be safe, I changed inside one of the stalls. Once I got my gown and stilettoes on, it was just a matter of making up my face. I dumped out the make up on the counter and drew two elegant black lines overtop my upper lashes, and beneath my lower ones. I added mascara and eye shadow, highlighter and blush. The last thing to paint were my lips—a deep fuchsia pink. I yanked the pins out of my hair and let it tumble into a side wave, and clipped on my silver and crystal earrings.

I shoved all of Lori Channing's clothes into the sports

bag, just in the nick of time. Sharon had been sent to look for me.

"What are you doing here?" she demanded, swinging the door wide. "Marjorie's almost ready to announce your name."

I left the sports bag tucked under the sinks and rushed out in the wake of Marjorie's secretary. I passed Rudy in the entranceway, and paused for a split second. His white shirt and red sweater peeked out from beneath his janitor's coveralls, and for a crazy instant I swear I heard the lyrics of *Santa Clause is Coming to Town*.

Duncan was there too, and beside him stood Lara Lee.

Marjorie was standing at the podium. Harry was up near the front of the crowd. I made my way toward him and stopped by his right. All of the formalities welcoming Scotty Chang and congratulating him on his avant-guarde art— which was displayed all around the gallery—had been completed. There was a loud show of hands and the tinkle of glasses. She was studying me now, trying to decide if I had done as promised and broken it off with Harry. I had not. My phone hummed against my hand inside my clutch, and I discreetly opened it. Why was I not surprised to see a text from Marjorie Snowden? She must have pre-timed it to send at exactly eight o'clock. She had warned me that 8:00 pm was the time when she would announce the winner of the 'Emerging Star' Art Contest.

Did you break up with Harry?

There was no point in my texting her back. She could hardly leave the podium to read my text.

I shook my head.

Her eyes blazed at me. People were starting to get restless at the silence and some were even looking our way.

Her eyes left mine and turned toward Lara Lee. The painter was not a great beauty but she did clean up better than one would expect after having witnessed her at her lowest point. For one thing, she no longer cleared out a room when she entered. However, she didn't seem to be able to shake the 'homeless' look, even in my hand-me-downs. I had no idea what Marjorie planned to do. I don't think I had extrapolated this far. I think all along I had intended to break up with Harry because the prize money and the opportunity to have work displayed internationally was too big a temptation to resist. But now it was crunch time and I hadn't done it. I could do it now. Harry was standing right beside me. All I had to do was say, "Harry, it's over. I am so sorry, but I'm breaking up with you."

But the room was so quiet except for a few restless feet, and the rustle of gowns, and one or two people clearing their throats nervously. If I spoke now, everyone would hear me.

Marjorie finally broke the tension by smiling. Sharon had come up to whisper something in her ear. Marjorie brightened at whatever news it was that her secretary had imparted. "I was drawing out the suspense," she said, laughingly. "This is a very special opportunity for an emerging artist. And I was waiting for the news. I've just been informed that the Emily Carr University of Art and Design has added a bonus to our grand prize. The winner of the 'Emerging Star' Art Contest will also serve one year as paid writer-in-residence at the prestigious Vancouver school!"

There was an enormous thunder of applause.

Marjorie was holding a silver envelope with a red seal in her hand.

Oh Lord I thought, Oh Lordy, Lordy, Lordy. I wanted that prize. Thirty thousand dollars, plus a one-year paid residency, plus a piece in an international art exhibit? I could not turn this down.

"Harry," I whispered.

Marjorie was watching me. The audience was still clapping so they couldn't hear me.

"Yeah." He turned and looked at me gently. Then his face changed as Duncan brought Lara Lee up to the front of the crowd and stood her beside me. I glanced at her, annoyed. Harry gave her a polite nod but I could feel the change in his manner and the tenseness in his muscles. I realized something at this moment.

True she did not smell like summer flowers but so what? At least she no longer smelled like she slept inside a dumpster.

Harry took my hand and pulled me closer to him at the same instant as he moved a safe distance from her. I don't know if she noticed. She was staring so hard and with such longing at the envelope in Marjorie's hand.

Marjorie's eyes were on the dowdy Lara Lee. "And who is this lucky artist?"

Marjorie's eyes returned to me. She was staring at the hand that held mine. When she raised her eyes they were telling me to drop his hand as a sign that I would break up with him as soon as it was convenient. I almost did. I felt my grip slacken.

I turned slightly to hide my face from Harry. I couldn't do this and look him straight in the eyes. What my sight landed on was Duncan watching me intently over Lara Lee's head. The look was without malice or judgment. He was telling me he understood—no matter what decision I made. But it wasn't he who had me so mesmerized. Beyond him, in the doorway stood Rudy Donner. Like my guardian angel he hadn't left since I first noticed him standing there earlier this evening. If Marjorie were aware of Rudy's presence she would have sent security guards to hustle him away. Oddly, he went unnoticed.

He returned my look with an encouraging smile.

No one has any power over you unless you give it to them.

No one had spoken these words out loud, especially not Rudy since he was so far away. And yet I heard them as though they had been whispered in my ear.

"Well, the moment of truth," Marjorie said from the podium. Her voice was teasing, and she was purposefully drawing out the suspense. All of the artists who had made the short list were present. Even Samantha from the Annex stood amongst the crowd. Beside her stood a man whose face I recognized. He was the director of the MET, the New York Metropolitan Museum of Art. I had never met him before but had seen his picture many times. What was such an important person doing here at the AGH? I knew Scotty Chang was a famous artist, but was he so famous that a VIP from New York City would fly all the way to Hamilton Ontario to see his exhibit? I shivered. I guess so. And that made me even more nervous because if I chose to, he would witness my winning of the prize. I held my breath. I could hear Lara Lee nervously tapping her foot on the hardwood floor beneath us.

No one has any power over you unless you give it to them.

The moment of truth.

I clutched Harry's hand with both of mine, and drew his curled fingers to my chest. He glanced down at me at once surprised and delighted. He kissed the top of my head. That was enough for Marjorie to know what I had decided. She glared, with a spite that only I felt. I was certain no one else detected her rage and malice. Maybe only Harry—who glanced swiftly at me—had a troubled expression on his face that soon disappeared as his mother began to speak.

I could almost taste the vindictiveness as I braced myself for the backlash.

But the words that came out of her mouth were the last thing I expected to hear.

"Our winner," she said, "Is the lovely and talented textile artist, Lorelei!"

CHAPTER THIRTEEN

Applause boomed and I felt Lara Lee visibly shrink.

I was stunned beyond belief. Here I was ready to reveal all, and Marjorie Snowden had given me not only a reprieve *but*—the grand prize.

"Congratulations, beautiful," Harry said. "This is stupendous. I am so happy!" He kissed me on the cheek, then uttered under his breath: "This was the best scenario, believe me. Anything else would have been unacceptable."

Sharon and Sylvia had simultaneously released the cord that held the drop-sheet overtop my tapestry. It hung fully exposed, mounted by invisible wires from the ceiling, overtop a plinth with a description of the work of art. It was a massive piece and it looked magnificent. And I could barely breathe.

Everyone was urging me to rise to the podium to give a speech. As I moved forward to comply, Duncan reached out and squeezed my hand. "Hey, Supergirl," he said. "Good luck."

I walked to the podium, my royal blue gown trailing like summer waves.

I stood for a few awkward seconds, wordless.

"I am so grateful… and so honored," I stuttered. I was so filled with emotion the words choked in my throat. "I can hardly believe my good fortune."

I was about to continue with my acceptance speech when I saw in the doorway someone I hadn't seen in years. You heard me mention my mom, earlier. She was never much of a supporter of the arts. She was disappointed when I went to art school and told me she couldn't help me. It was all she could do to make ends meet as a secretary working for a small insurance firm. But I was her daughter and she wished me well.

You know that resentment you resist but can't help feeling when your parents won't or can't help you achieve your dreams? Well... I had it big time, which was why I seldom spoke about my parents. Forget my dad; he isn't even in the picture. And it wasn't my mom's fault; hey, she was there for me as much as she could be, but for her to fly out all the way from Vancouver to come to this art show? That was a surprise. After all, it was by invitation only. Who could possibly have invited her? Harry?

Harry was oblivious to the fact that my mother was standing in the doorway dressed in her tacky best. Rudy was encouraging her to enter the gallery as she hesitated.

Marjorie had stepped aside when I took the podium, and now I could see her eyes reach far across the other side of the room where they landed on my mother. It was Marjorie? Marjorie had invited my mother to the art show? Had told her that I had won an art contest? With all the guilt tripping I had been doing, it never occurred to me to tell her myself.

The audience was waiting for me to conclude my speech. I was speechless. What was Marjorie up to?

The director signaled to Samantha who was nearest, to lead my mother up to the front of the crowd.

Marjorie was using my mother to ensure my silence. She knew I would never demean myself in front of my mother by admitting what a liar and cheat I was. Well, she was wrong! *Dead* wrong!

"Everyone," I said. "That beautiful lady in red is my mother."

My mom turned proudly to receive the audience's oohs and aahs before she turned back to face me with tears in her eyes and an enormous smile on her lips. Maybe for the first time in my life I was going to do something to make her truly proud.

I turned in the direction of Duncan and Lara Lee. Dunc

was watching me, a puzzled look on his face, but then he realized what I was about to do. He smiled, and blew me a kiss. I looked at Harry who hadn't a clue what was in my mind. He was beaming, thinking that this event had turned out fantastically.

Will you still love me after this?

I took a deep breath and glanced down to compose my thoughts. Then I said, "I'm afraid there has been a mistake." Then I told them the whole sordid story. I apologized for not speaking out before now. I did not implicate Marjorie or Harry Snowden. I made no mention that they both knew and were complicit in my decision to withhold my knowledge. I looked at Lara Lee with true remorse and sorrow. "I am so sorry Ms. Lee, you are the real winner. Not me."

To say that she was stunned would be an understatement. The whole room was silent. Harry's mouth was hanging open in disbelief and for the first time he looked more unattractive to me than Lara Lee had ever done. Marjorie had to save face and quick. She rose to the occasion, rejoined me at the podium and gave a speech to show her shock and outrage, and then her compassion for me for being brave enough to admit the error of my ways.

I was not surprised that she chose this route. I expected it. In fact I half-expected her to send the security guards after me to throw me bodily off the premises. She did not do that. Such an act would have been even more disgraceful, would have shown a deeper lack of sophistication than anything I had done.

I left the podium with my head held high. In my heart I knew I had done the right thing. Before I left the podium to Lara Lee, I whispered to her, "You are a true artist, a brave woman and the best of all of us. You deserve this, and I am so sorry I caused you so much grief."

She grabbed my hand, her eyes wet, ready to spill. I shook my head. "You don't have to thank me. I've done nothing deserving thanks."

I couldn't stay to listen to what else they had to say. I

needed, wanted to speak to my mom. We hugged and I urged her through the crowd and out into the corridor with me.

I hoped I had not embarrassed her. And by the look on her face I knew I had made her proud. "I raised you right, sweetheart," she said.

"Yeah, you did." I laughed through my tears because I knew I had just destroyed my career as an artist and probably my relationship with Harry. My phone hummed indicating a text. Out of habit I pulled out my phone from my clutch and read it.

Goodbye, Lorelei, it said. That was all.

"More bad news, honey?" my mom asked, taking my hand.

"No," I said. "Good news."

It was from Harry. I mopped my eyes and blew my nose, looked around. Where was Rudy? He had been hovering in the doorway the whole evening, and now he was gone. I had wanted to thank him for being such a good friend. Had I lost him too?

That was more than I could take.

"Lorelei," my mom said. "What's wrong?"

I shook off the bad feelings. I hoped I had not lost Duncan as well. I moved to the entrance of the gallery and peeked in. The speeches were all concluded. Samantha was talking to Duncan. They both had enormous smiles and were laughing at each other's remarks. Oddly, it looked like they had become friends. Wouldn't you know it? On the day that my life fell apart, whatever animosity was between them would be repaired. Good. I was glad. I liked them both and was happy that they were now friends. A twinge of jealousy stabbed at my heart. I had to get out of here. I didn't have the courage to go back inside after admitting what I had done. Besides, Harry had just broken up with me. By text. I could not face him.

"Let's go, Mom." I didn't want to stay in a place where I was unwelcome.

"Wait, there's something going on in there. Isn't that

your artwork all the fuss is about?"

A large group of people had clustered around my hanging. What could possibly be happening? Did they want to burn it because they were so disgusted with me?

Samantha suddenly left Duncan's side and came rushing toward me. "There you are," she said, her voice trilling with excitement. "I've been searching everywhere for you."

"Whatever for?" my mom asked.

I quickly introduced Samantha to my mother before she replied. "You see that big imposing man in the dark suit?"

Most of the men were wearing dark suits.

"The VIP. The distinguished white-haired dude from New York. He's the—"

Yes, I knew who she was talking about. The director of the Metropolitan Museum of Art. "What about him?"

"He just bought *Catterwall*. Your wall hanging!"

"What?"

"For twenty-five thousand dollars!"

This time I really was speechless. I nearly crumpled to the floor.

My mother squeezed my arm. She too failed to find words.

"Lorelei, do you understand what I am saying? Your art is going to be hanging in the Metropolitan Museum of Art! In New York!"

Samantha dragged me by the arm into the gallery. When Sharon saw me, she also ran over, and so did Sylvia. Everyone was congratulating me. Lara Lee approached me with a huge smile on her face. "*You* are the brave one," she said to me. "And very talented. Congratulations!"

There was not an ounce of resentment in her voice. She was truly happy for me and I wasn't sure I deserved it.

Harry came up to me a sheepish grin on his face. What, was he going to congratulate me, too? "Lorelei," he said. "Please don't read your text from me. I didn't mean it. I was just embarrassed for the gallery. But everything has worked out. We can start again—fresh."

Seriously? He thought I wanted him back?

"Sorry, Harry, I already read it. You were right the first time. This is goodbye as far as anything romantic between us." Anyone who could not tell that Lori Channing and Lorelei were the same person did not know me at all. And someone who did not know me could not possibly ever love me. The good news was: I *didn't* love him. I loved somebody else. Was it too late? Oh, I hoped not.

Where was he?

Marjorie Snowden came up to me, fake as ever to congratulate me on the sale. The director of the MET had been impressed with my honesty she sneered. Which was what had made him take a second look at my work. He had found it riveting. "*His* words," she said. Then she introduced me to him. It would have been the best Christmas present ever, but there was one thing I wanted more.

I tore myself away from them as soon as I politely could. I saw that my mom was happily engaged talking to Sharon and Sylvia and Samantha. If he wasn't with Samantha, where was he?

I searched the entire room. Surely, he had not left without speaking to me?

Then I saw him. Through the glass doors that led to the sculpture garden on the patio outside. No one else was out there because the weather had turned cold. I opened the door and slipped out.

He was standing in front of his own statue, gazing thoughtfully at it. I wondered if he had heard the news. Maybe he hadn't.

"Dunc," I said. "Everything okay?"

"Yeah." He smiled. "Hey, congrats. I heard about your big sale. You're on your way, Lorelei."

For the first time when something great happened for me he didn't call me Supergirl. "I thought you'd be happier," I said. "I mean... not about the sale. I mean... that... I finally did the right thing."

"I *am* happy. And proud. I never doubted you for a

second."

"No?"

"Well, maybe for a nanosecond. It didn't last."

"Then why do you look like you just lost your cat?"

He was quiet for a long while before he answered. "Because I think maybe I just did."

I frowned. "I don't understand."

"Hey, you'll never guess what happened after you left the gallery…after you spilled your guts out."

"You make it sound so pathetic."

"It wasn't. You were eloquent and divine."

"So, what happened?"

He looked away from me for a long while, his eyes penetrating the glass panes of the door into the gallery where figures hobnobbed, and champagne was drunk and talk was of art and artists.

"Nothing will happen right away, but there's talk now that Marjorie will be replaced. All the bigwigs at this event did not like the way she handled things tonight. They've suspected her of corruption for a long time. Oh, don't worry. Harry's innocent in all of this. He's just her son and something of a minion…" His eyes flickered away before he apologized again for demeaning Harry.

"I don't care what you say about Harry. He and I are kaput."

His eyes brightened. "Really? What happened?"

"He didn't like my honesty."

His lips tightened in a grim line. He was fighting emotion and a smile.

I placed a hand on his arm, forced him to look at me. I should be the one having trouble looking into his eyes, not the other way around. "There's something else, Dunc. I can see it in your face. What aren't you telling me?"

He cleared his throat, wet his lips. Why had I never noticed what yummy lips he had? I shot my gaze to the floor. What was I doing?

"You have to keep mum about this. Nothing is official

and I don't know if I'm even going to take the position. But I've been asked if I would consider succeeding Marjorie Snowden as the next director of the AGH."

I felt an explosion of warmth and happiness for Duncan. I threw myself at him but he held me at arms length. "You'll take it, of course," I insisted. "You can do wonders with this place."

"That depends," he said.

"On what?"

"On where *you're* planning to live."

"What do you mean?" I frowned.

"They want you to move to New York."

I did not hesitate. "I can do my art here."

"But in New York you'll get greater exposure."

Then it dawned on me what he was saying. "You mean... you would come *with* me? Give up all this?" I spread out my arms.

"Hey, I'm not half bad as a sculptor." He grinned.

"You are a *fantastic* sculptor."

His eyes were glowing in the semi illumination coming from the inside of the art gallery and the streetlamps on the periphery. "I love you, Lorelei. I always have."

"I think I've always loved you, too. I was just too stupid to see it."

He bent over and kissed me on the lips. I felt a thrill traverse my body as I gazed up into his starlit eyes. I was right. His lips *were* yummy.

I suddenly felt something move at my feet. I looked down and a sleek seal point Siamese cat started doing the figure eight thing around my legs. "Giselle?" We reacted simultaneously. "Where did she come from?"

A soft whistling was vibrating the night air. *He sees you when you're sleeping. He knows when you're awake... He knows when you've been good or not. So be good for goodness sake!*

Christmas lights hung high over an elderly man's head but he was in shadow. Rudy Donner was sweeping the patio with a broom. On the ground beside him was the pet carrier I had thought I'd seen earlier, and which had magically turned into a sports bag filled with my clothes. The whistling grew a little louder. I recognized the tune and laughed. Duncan turned to me, a perplexed expression crowding his brow. I threw back my head and let the snowflakes drift down onto my tongue in joy. It was the season for miracles. I wasn't about to question this one.

I bent down and lifted Giselle into my arms. The three of us cuddled together for warmth. We should go inside now before the snow really started to fall. But I wasn't cold. I had Duncan and Giselle for warmth.

Rocky Mountain Christmas

A Love Story For Pet Lovers

CHAPTER ONE

"I mean it, Joy. We're on deadline. We're number one because we stay on schedule. Don't disappoint me."

I sighed. This job meant a lot to me but I was tired. My heart was broken. I needed a vacation badly. And my creative juices were blocked. I needed inspiration.

"That's not my problem," Susan said after I had made my feelings vocal.

I know, I know. Feeble excuses. It's not like I was the first woman in the universe to get dumped. But she could have been more sympathetic. She wasn't really mean. It was just her manner and the fact that she was my boss. In fact, we were great friends, but she never let that get in the way of the magazine.

"Are you there, Joy?"

I roused myself out of my stupor and nodded, although it was only to myself. "I'm here. Don't worry. You can count on me."

I ended the call to my editor with a deft touch of my

right forefinger on my smartphone. I'd been working on this story for months, and the deadline was creeping up. If I wanted to be free to join my family in the Rocky Mountains for Christmas I'd better get this story submitted. Susan made that quite clear.

But first I must write it.

You're wondering what the story's about. Okay. That's fair. My editor Susan Lopez is the head honcho at *Cats and Dogs Magazine*. This magazine started out as a little rag ten years ago, but soon ballooned into one of the biggest print and online monthlys in the world. It has an audience of millions. Why, you're asking? Because it's about pets, of course. Everything you ever wanted to know about dogs and cats. And who doesn't love their 'fuzzy snugglies'?

I write a social column. It's called 'My Best Friend is my Fur Baby.' My current assignment is to compose a heartfelt article that explains why women today are skipping marriage, and why they prefer dogs as companions to men.

You may not be one of those women who feel that way, because you haven't been cheated on, neglected or betrayed. Or simply dumped for no better reason than because something younger, fresher, maybe prettier came along. But most of my thirty-something friends are firmly in that category. As is my fortyish sister, who is twice divorced and swears she will never marry again. Since her last divorce ten years ago she moved out to Emerald Lake to run the family lodge with my father and my mother (the latter now passed away), and has had one dog after another. No more men, she swears. And after I told her about this article I was researching, she jumped on the bandwagon to be interviewed. She is part of the growing unofficial club choosing dogs for roommates over men. And being unexpectedly dumped by my ex, now so am I. That is—I *was* in the club until I met Jack.

Jack Tinsle changed my mind. He bowled me over like I had never been bowled over before. He was gorgeous and nice and made me laugh from day one. So why am I alone? I wanted to be with him so much. Am I just stubborn, do I have too much pride? Do I want him to say the 'L' word first? Do I feel guilty?

It was all of the above. Especially the last. So what happened?

I guess we should go back to the day I met him.

It was a mild, but windy autumn afternoon and I was researching my article for the pet mag. Pets had been part of my life since I was a girl, but as a career woman I had no time. That didn't mean I no longer loved dogs and cats. It just meant I'd lost touch and had forgotten how fickle they could be when they were suspicious of you.

I needed to know what it felt like to be in love with a pet again so I did a dumb thing, I went to the Humane Society, completely ill equipped and ignorant, and told them I wanted to foster a dog. Fostering implied the living situation was temporary. It required me to care for the animal until a permanent home was found. This was perfect. For me and my research that is. For Rocky, the Australian shepherd dog I took home, it was otherwise. Apparently, he knew from the start that I was just using him to get a magazine story. My idea was to compare my experiences between canine love and human love. Who I was going to use for my human guinea pig was up for grabs. My original idea was to compare Rocky's love with Lonny's (my ex-boyfriend). But neither of them particularly loved me at the moment.

I was just lucky that Jack happened to come along.

Rocky and I were outside my apartment, which is inside a converted house on a quiet side street in Calgary, Alberta.

I had taken the dog outside to do his business and had forgotten his leash. The Humane Society had told me that he was a very gentle, docile animal, and I should have no trouble with him. Boy, were they ever wrong!

Not that Rocky was vicious or a biter or anything like that. It's just that I was a stranger. And he was wondering where the people who loved him and fed him at the shelter were. I think maybe he thought he could find his way back to them, so after lifting his leg and leaving a dark patch on the trunk of a tree, he trotted nimbly down the street. "Rocky!" I shouted. "Come boy!"

Either Rocky disliked the way I pronounced his name or he didn't like me giving him orders. As soon as I got anywhere near him, he raced off down the sidewalk leaving me in a panic.

"Please, Rocky," I wheedled. "Come to Mama." I was worried he might decide to really take off, and I would never be able to catch him. A few blocks down, and this street intersected with a main thoroughfare.

He stopped at the next block, and I rushed up to him gasping, totally out of breath. I tried to grab his collar, but he dodged me.

He was heading for the intersection and I screamed, "Rocky!"

A man at the crosswalk turned, and tackled my dog by the collar.

"Oh, thank you so much," I said as I rushed up to them.

"You should have this dog on a leash," the man said, rather gruffly.

"I know. I'm sorry. I wasn't thinking."

He frowned. Then his faced turned gentle when he saw how distraught I was. He undid his belt and looped it through Rocky's collar to use as a makeshift leash. "Where do you live? I'll walk him—you—home."

"I just got him," I said, trying to explain my reckless behavior.

"All the more reason to keep him on a leash." He smiled.

I returned the smile and kept pace with his long stride. I have a tendency to wiggle when I walk quickly and struggled to keep that characteristically feminine gait in check. I have been teased one time too many on my so-called swivel hips. Why does that matter to me? Because I'm a modern career girl, and much as we love to flaunt our sexiness with skinny jeans and high heels (and yeah this tight little leather jacket in chocolate brown that I was currently wearing), it's frowned upon by our professional colleagues. I can think of more than once when Susan reminded me to dress appropriately. But when you're trying to attract a guy, and it's part of the research...?

"He is walking really well with you," I said. "He never does that with me."

"You have to let him know who's boss."

"It's been a long time since I've had a dog."

We were almost in front of my house. I liked the way this man looked and the way he spoke. He had a nice deep voice and muscles that flexed when he lifted his arm to guide Rocky at an even keel beside him.

"You would think he was *your* dog," I joked.

He grinned. "Actually, I have an advantage. I train dogs for a living."

"Really?"

Hot, commanding, *and* a dog trainer? This guy I would like to see more of. "My name is Joy Zamboni," I said quickly. "What a coincidence that we should meet."

"Coincidence?" he asked.

I hesitated to tell him what my plans were for him. The little cogs in my brain were turning. He could be my guinea pig! I needed a man's point of view for my article.

"I'm Jack, Jack Tinsle."

"Like in the Christmas decorations?"

He laughed. "Yeah like that, but spelled T-i-n-s-l-e. And you," he said after a pause. "Are you related to the Zamboni that invented the ice resurfacing machine?"

"Probably somewhere down the line, we're related. Why? Do you like ice skating?"

"Some," he said.

Cool, I thought.

"But I run a business. In fact, I've just opened a dog-training center in your neighborhood. It's called K-Nine."

Was this fate or what? Clearly I needed help. "Sign me up."

"You'll have to come down to the center. And remember

to bring a leash."

He unlooped his belt from Rocky's collar and clicked his tongue twice. For some reason that got the dog's undivided attention. "This your house?" Jack asked indicating a pale yellow, vinyl-sided bungalow with a wooden porch painted white, and birch branches in ceramic planters on either side of the steps. Obviously it was, since I had stopped in front of this house.

"Yup," I said nonetheless.

"Up boy," Jack commanded. And to my complete and utter surprise Rocky skipped up the stairs to the front door.

"How did you do that? Rocky never pays attention to me when I ask him to do something."

"You have to say it like you mean it."

"But I *do* mean it."

"Hmm." He smiled at me. "You come across as a softie to me."

I rolled my eyes at him, but secretly I was delighted.

"See you tomorrow?" he asked. He dipped his hand into his shirt pocket and drew out a business card. It read:

K-NINE
Expert Dog training
Kensington Village, Calgary AB

"Awesome," I said. "See you tomorrow."

CHAPTER TWO

Tomorrow could not come quick enough for me. I spent the whole evening tearing my wardrobe inside out. What did one wear to train their dog? Why did I care what I looked like? I caught up my dark auburn hair and swept it back in a loose twist with a few tendrils about the ears and nape. For a top I chose a sweater with a cowl neck overtop super skinny jeans. And on my feet high-heeled boots, though I probably should be wearing running shoes. However, Jack did not specify what type of footgear I should wear. Or did it even matter? It contradicted the 'Susan Code.' So why was I fussing about these things?

Uh huh, that's right.

Mr. Jack Tinsle.

In the morning I imitated what I had done last night in the mirror. I looked fab. More than acceptable. Would Jack be Rocky's instructor? Or was he just the boss and did he have a bunch of trainers doing the grunt work?

Lucky for me Jack's dog school was only a few blocks from where I lived in the trendy neighborhood of Kensington Village. I had Rocky in tow and this time I had him on a short leash. He resisted when I told him we were going to school, and I had to coax him all the way. Halfway there the treats came out, and I lured him like a horse with a carrot on a stick. It was embarrassing. People stopped to look and laugh at me. I was one lousy dog mom.

By the time we arrived I was frazzled. We walked in the door and Rocky refused to move another step once inside. A young woman came up to me. "Hi, can I help you?" she asked.

"I'd like to register Rocky for classes." I looked around. "Um, is Jack Tinsle here by any chance? He's the one who suggested we come."

"Oh, sure. He's in his office. I'll go see if he's available." She left and I gently tugged Rocky's leash to get him to move away from the door. "It's not like this is the vet's. Nobody's going to hurt you. Come on, big boy. We're going to learn our ABCs."

Rocky sat down and turned his sad-sack stare at the window.

"Look, Rocky," I said. "There are lot's of dogs here. You can make friends."

There were indeed a number of people with pets waiting for a class to start. Many of the pets were puppies and were bouncing around, excited to see so many of their compatriots.

"Rocky, come!" I was beginning to get frustrated. Why did this dog hate me?

"Hey, Joy," a familiar voice said. "So glad you made it."

Jack Tinsle came over and crouched down in front of Rocky. "Hi big fella. Long time no see." He scratched the dog's ears and ran his hands over his neck and back. Rocky shivered with pleasure and rewarded Jack with a lick on his face.

"Do you want to adopt him?" I asked. "He seems to love *you*."

"How long have you had Rocky?" Jack asked me.

"Not long. Just a few days."

"You need time to bond. Give him at least a week. He misses his previous owners."

"His previous owners neglected him. He ended up at the shelter which is where I got him."

"Well, that was very nice of you to do that. All dogs need a permanent home."

So true, I thought, but I was only Rocky's foster pet mom. After my assignment he would go to someone else.

"Pat," he said to the girl who had greeted me at the door. "Joy needs to fill out some paperwork and then I'll give her the tour."

Jack took Rocky from me as I filled in the form that Pat handed to me. When I finally joined him it looked like he and the dog were fast friends.

"Rocky has a gentle disposition," Jack said giving me his preliminary evaluation. "No real behavioral problems."

"Oh, he's an angel. It's just that he defies *my* commands."

Jack laughed.

"What? What's so funny?"

"The fact that you think a dog is *supposed* to obey commands."

"Well, isn't that the whole idea behind doggie school. Don't you teach them to obey their owners?"

"I think we've identified the problem, Joy. It's not just Rocky who needs to be schooled. You do too. And that's what we do here."

What? My objection stayed inside my head. Was he insulting me? Was he insinuating that I was doing everything wrong?

The look of amusement remained, while I was certain my face was as red as a beet.

I shook it off. Yeah, like a dog. "Okay. So what's the solution?"

"Go to that wall over there. Then call him to join you."

I did as I was told and when I had my back to the wall, I squatted and yelled, "Rocky, come!"

I knew what he was going to do. We had done this many times before. The dog just sat there and stared at me.

"Okay," Jack said. "Lesson one. Picture this scenario. You're late for work. You call Rocky from the backyard but he won't come. You run outside and try to grab his collar. He dashes away with a 'catch me if you can' glint in his eyes. What do you do?"

"I run after him and try to coax him in."

"And if he refuses?"

"I try to drag him inside," I said, my face burning with

embarrassment.

"Do you shout at him?"

"If I'm really late. Then yes, I suppose I raise my voice a little."

"A little? Or a lot?"

"It's frustration. I don't hurt him or scream at him." Now *I* was getting frustrated.

"It's okay, Joy. I know you wouldn't hurt him. Not on purpose."

He dug into his pocket and pulled out a dog treat. Immediately Rocky perked up.

"I've tried that," I said. "Sometimes it works, sometimes it doesn't."

"But do you do this?" Instead of moving forward toward the dog, Jack started running backward. Rocky followed. When they reached the far wall. Jack stopped and handed Rocky the treat, which he scarfed down instantly.

"Now you try it. Call him. Then move away and have him come to you."

Jack passed me several treats. Then I did as I was told. I was nervous. At first Rocky ignored me. I shot Jack a helpless look. He gave me an encouraging nod and urged me to try again. I did.

This time Rocky came. Suspiciously at first. But then he realized I only wanted to give him something delicious to eat.

"Now, back-step in my direction. Keep your hand out with the next treat."

I backed away from Rocky. He followed slowly. I started to move faster with Jack's praise, shuffling backwards in my high heels—as fast as I could go. Rocky was coming. He was enjoying the game.

Suddenly I tripped and fell butt first into Jack's lap. I landed smack into his chest with my head. I felt his strong hands clasp me firmly and we both slid down the back wall to the floor, me wedged between his knees. He laughed. "You okay?"

I was more than okay. I'd forgotten how nice it felt to be

hugged by a big, strong man. The accident sent Rocky into a frenzy of excitement. He started to bark. I raised my fist that had managed to hang onto the dog treat and offered it to him. He stopped barking and picked it out from between my fingers with his teeth, and dropped it down his throat.

"Good boy."

We were inspired to join a special class for adult dogs, and for a newbie, Jack assured me Rocky would perform well. "He'll be getting his PhD in no time," Jack joked.

First I had to get him to 'stay.'

Jack stood on the sidelines and sent me and Rocky in to join the class that was already in session. I was finding it difficult to concentrate because Jack might leave. The lesson lasted for about two hours and I learned a lot. For one thing I discovered that for many dogs the command 'Come' is an invitation for a game of canine keep-away. "This happens with a lot of dogs," the trainer instructing the class explained. I recognized her as Pat, the woman who had greeted me when we first came in the door.

"How did your dog's skills go from perfect-puppy 'recall' (that was the trainer's professional term for 'come') to 'catch-me-if-you-can' as an adult dog?" She paused before elaborating. "Think about this: exactly what does 'come' now mean to your dog? Are you about to clip his nails, shove a pill down his throat, give him a bath or lock him inside the house so that you can go to work? Don't make the 'come' command negative. Just go fetch the dog without a command if what you're about to do to him is something he'll find distasteful. There is no point in warning him that he won't like what's coming.

"So what to do to get him to obey the 'come' command? Call him several times for no reason at all except to do something pleasant, like giving him a treat or a nice scratch behind the ears. Then send him off to play again. After a while he'll learn that obeying the command is more likely to be a fun rather than an unpleasant experience."

I have to admit that was the most enjoyment I had ever

had going to school. When the class was over and I turned around; Jack was still there leaning against the wall watching us.

"An excellent first class," he said to me.

"I'm so grateful to you, Jack. Can I buy you a cup of coffee?"

He grinned. "You realize you *do* have to pay for the lessons?"

It was a joke and I almost thumped him playfully, but caught myself in the nick of time. Much as I liked him, it was too soon for casual touching. He was practically a stranger.

He checked his calendar, and decided he could take a half hour break. We went to a sidewalk café for coffee. The place next door had not packed away their patio furniture (although the chairs were stacked and the umbrellas absent), when we asked if we could sit outside. The barista obliged. I explained that it was only because of the dog. It was November after all. But it was unusually warm.

"Thanks so much, Jack," I said. "That was a real eye-opener."

"Glad I could help. You have a great dog there. He just needs a few classes to help you two to bond."

"He really is a good companion. He likes the same TV shows as I do."

Jack laughed.

***

Two days later I was in the village doing some Christmas shopping. I planned to have this magazine article wrapped up by mid December so that I could drive Rocky and myself to my dad's guest lodge at Emerald Lake in the Canadian Rockies. It looked like there would be no snow in the city for the holidays so it would be nice to spend it in the mountains, but maybe I was being premature. After all it was almost three weeks before Christmas.

I was inside a gift shop with Rocky tied up outside, when I heard that distinctive voice. I recognized it instantly and when I looked up I saw Jack talking on his cellphone while rummaging through some sale boxes of last years Christmas cards. Talk about a coincidence, I only bought Christmas cards on sale. And the ones that were on sale were usually last year's. He noticed me and ended his call. I wanted to ask who he was talking to. The conversation seemed rather intimate, and by that I mean he had lowered his voice as soon as he saw me, turning away slightly.

"Hey, Joy, nice to see you again."

Likewise I thought, but for answer I smiled.

"Good choice," he said, eyes dropping to the box in my left hand.

The cards were oversized with cute, realistic-looking chickadees perched on snow-tipped rushes, trimmed with holly and bright red berries. I was hesitating over buying them because large cards always cost more to mail. But these were seventy percent off. A steal.

"I never pegged you for a Christmas card sender," I remarked.

"And why not?" he asked. "Just 'cause I'm a guy?"

For exactly that reason, I thought. My ex, Lonny, would never purchase cards on his own. That was *my* job. I glanced down at Jack's hand and saw that he was clutching the exact same design as the cards I had selected. Coincidence or what? Or perhaps it was…fate?

I know it was aggressive on my part, but I really wanted to ask him out. I saw no ring on his finger so I assumed he was unmarried. Question was: did he have a girlfriend?

His phone rang again. He sent me an apologetic look. "Answer it," I said. "It might be important."

I think it *was* important because the next minute he was in a heated discussion with someone. He quickly apologized to me and slipped away. I went to the cashier and paid for my Christmas cards, then looked to see if Jack remained engaged. He was, whispering fiercely into the phone. I wondered if he had a girlfriend, a wife? I noticed earlier that he wore no wedding band, but men often didn't. Who else did one speak to that way? Dejected I went outside, unfastened Rocky's leash from the lamppost where I had left him and headed for home. On the return trip Rocky was pleasantly obedient. He walked without pulling or putting on the brakes. He walked where I walked, and stopped when I stopped. Jack Tinsle was a miracle worker, and I wanted desperately to see him again. At the very least I wanted to interview him for my article. Then it dawned on me. Maybe he had been arguing with one of his employees. Of course. That was it.

I was lying to myself if I thought this man didn't matter to me. He did. And the more I thought about it, the more I disagreed with the premise to my story. Given a choice between sleeping with my dog or with Jack, I think I would choose Jack. I felt torn and frustrated. What kind of career woman was I if I just wanted to hop into bed with the first good-looking guy that paid me any attention? I grinned to myself. It had been a long time since I had thought about sleeping with anyone.

On the way I stopped off at a Starbucks and bought myself a latte with extra cream and a touch of caramel drizzle. I'd go on a diet tomorrow. Today I wanted to indulge. Rocky started barking while I was inside the coffee shop, so I quickly paid for my purchase and steered him home.

CHAPTER THREE

Should I call him? Or not? I took a sip of my lusciously sweet coffee and placed the heat-proof paper cup on the kitchen table, slung my leather bag onto the back of a chair and disengaged myself from my short white puffer jacket. Not exactly my most dog friendly coat, but remember I had only been doing this dog thing for less than two weeks. But honestly I was loving it. If it weren't for my darling Rocky I would never have met Jack. I gave him a hug. Wonder of wonders, he did not reject me. A couple of quick licks came from his tongue. And I kissed him back. Not with my tongue. With my lips on the top of his soft, warm head.

I should call him. But not yet. He probably wasn't home. I had left him at the boutique, what, forty minutes ago? I had no idea where he lived. At Rocky's next class I must ask him where he lived.

My cellphone rang. My heart skipped a beat and then started racing. Maybe it was him? But why would he call me? How would he have my number? Of course he had my number. I had had to write it onto the form when I registered the dog for training.

"Hello?" I said, trying to sound nonchalant.

"Joy? It's me Ellie."

My cousin Ellie! We had grown up together in Calgary until she had moved to Edmonton with her parents and *my* parents had moved to run the lodge in a lakeside town called Field in the Yoho National Park in the gorgeous Rocky Mountains. Mom and Ellie's mom, my Aunt Liza were sisters. They were close—up until the time my mom died—just like Ellie and I. We were the same age so I had more in common with her than I did with my own sister.

Only I hadn't heard from Ellie in months. And the last time we saw each other was over a year.

"I heard you got a dog," she said.

"You heard right. And I heard you have a boyfriend. A hockey player?"

"That's right. He plays for the Edmonton Oilers."

"Really? That's awesome. Which one is he? Not that I know anything about hockey."

"They call him Rocket T. But his friends all call him Rocco. He's been playing for fifteen years and wants to retire. He's got plans, but I'm hoping that's down the road. He's still young. Got a lot of play in him still... Well, let's not get into that right now."

"You sound a little upset, Ellie. What's wrong?"

"Oh, it's just that we seem to be *so* perfect for each other in most things. And I love the fact that he's a professional hockey player. He has no idea how lucky and how talented he is. So many guys would give an arm and a leg to have had the opportunity to play professional hockey. But he *is* headstrong. When he gets an idea in his head it's glued like cement. Let's put it this way. He's not the best at compromising."

"Who is?" I paused. "That's why I like dogs. As long as you feed them, give them a warm bed and lots of fun time, they're yours forever." This was something I was beginning to learn about Rocky. All he wanted was to be treated kindly. That was all anyone wanted. So why was it so hard for men and women to treat each other with kindness?

"But surely that's not why you got a dog? Honestly, Joy. What compelled you to foster a dog? Surely, you haven't given up on men entirely—"

I laughed. No, not entirely. "The pooch's name is Rocky."

"No—really? Well, this can all get a bit confusing."

"No kidding. Rocket, Rocco, Rocky—but you're steering me off course. You've been together such a short time, and you're having problems already? Is it because he has to be out of town all the time?"

"That, and the fact that he refuses to discuss his plans with me. He says it's because he knows I'll disagree with them."

"Do you?"

"What, disagree with them? Only when it's important and it affects me too."

"Do you love him, Ellie?"

The phone went silent for a few seconds. "Yes. Yes I do. And if he'd ask me, I'd marry him."

"Wow. That is serious. So, what has he done that's upset you so much?"

"Well, like I said. He wants to retire from professional hockey. I don't want him to do that. He's only thirty-five and he makes great money. He wants to move. He wants to—oh, let's not talk about this anymore. It's getting me down."

"So, when do I get to meet him?"

"Who? Rocco? Soon," she said. Her mind was clearly distracted. "Your dad has invited us up to the lodge for Christmas."

"That's fantastic. That means I better get this stupid article written and submitted so that I can get up there early. I want to go skiing. *So* bad." I hesitated for a second. "Hey, Ellie. I want to ask you something."

"Sure, what is it?"

"I met this guy."

"Oh, fabulous, Joy, I'm so happy for you."

"Hold your horses. We haven't even gone on a real date yet. Just coffee."

"Well, what's stopping you?"

"Nothing. It's just that I don't know all that much about him. But the thing is: this article I'm writing for the magazine is about dogs replacing men in the loves of modern women."

She giggled. "Really? That's a story? So, what's the problem?"

"I want to write him into the article. Do you think I

should tell him? Do you think he would mind? I mean—I just have no idea how he would take it."

"He'd be flattered, I'm sure. Just tell him that's what you want to do. And then invite him up to Emerald Lake for Christmas."

"That would seem really weird. I hardly know him."

"Then get to know him. *Fast.*" Ellie was silent as she searched her digital calendar. I could hear the clicks. "You have less than two weeks. Bring him up there, I want to meet him."

"Ellie, he's probably got people that he spends Christmas with. Family, parents, you know—like us."

"Well, at least go on a date with him."

I couldn't get up the nerve to ask him for a date. Our next class at the training center wasn't until Monday. It was Saturday afternoon and I had just brought Rocky home from his walk. I was restless. I had written part of my article but it rang false. My belief in it was wavering—that a dog could replace the love of a man in a woman's life? I picked up the phone. I should probably be calling my sister Carrie. She would soon straighten me out. Instead of phoning Carrie, I dug out Jack's business card. It also had his cell number on it and I tapped in the figures.

"Hey," he said. "Jack Tinsle here."

"Hi Jack, it's me. Joy Zamboni."

Hey, Zamboni," he said. "Nice to hear from you. What's up?"

He sounded like he was out of breath, so he was either out on the street somewhere or he was working out. I was about to ask him where he was, but my hesitation must have suggested the question for me.

"I'm at the ice rink," he said. "What are you doing right now, want to join me?"

Did I ever. "Be there in a jiff," I said, hugging the phone to my ear.

"You *do* skate?"

Not really, but I wasn't about to let him know that. I

could ski—so wasn't skating similar? I could fake it.

I ended the call and kissed Rocky on the head after giving him a Milkbone.

When I got to the ice rink, I could see Jack speed skating, clockwise, around the outer periphery of the rink. I wondered if something was wrong. He seemed to be trying to work off some energy or anxiety or anger. It was hard to decide which. He didn't see me until I had donned my skates and was tentatively testing the ice. I could ski so I could skate, I told myself. It's just that I hadn't skated since I was a kid. Was skating one of those things you never forgot—like riding a bike?

Not exactly. I fell flat on my butt, just as Jack came skating up to greet me. "What happened?" he asked.

My face was red but I don't think I had injured myself. Jack held his hands towards me to help me up. I gripped his outstretched arms, rose, and fell into his chest. This time it was my face and not the back of my head that met his collar. He smelled good, clean, like freshly laundered cotton that had been hung outside in the sunshine, and whatever brand he used for shampoo.

I giggled into his sweatshirt. That was the second time I had collapsed into his body since we met. It felt good to have his arms around me, so good that I held onto him slightly longer than I had intended.

It seemed to me that the feeling was mutual. I felt his lips brush the top of my hair. Was I imagining things? I looked up into his eyes. They smiled back at me like limpid pools of clear pond water filled with green and yellow lilies. The moment lasted but an instant, and the smile was gone.

When I moved away, he had a puzzled look on his face.

Oh no, maybe I had read him all wrong.

But then when he saw the troubled look on *my* face, he smiled. Honestly, I wasn't throwing myself at him on purpose.

"Hey, are you just a klutz? Or are you trying to tell me something?"

If that wasn't up front and blunt I don't know what is. He was giving me an opening. I paused, but not too long. "Jack, I want to go on a date with you."

The look on his face was a mixture of stunned and pleased. I guess in writer lingo we might call the expression 'bemused.' I had mere seconds to muddle over it. He was waiting for an explanation.

Ellie was right: he *was* flattered. I'd better deliver the rest of the proposition before I lost my nerve. "I'm writing an article," I said, and prepared to explain the details of my research plan. Oh, and also the fact that I was a professional writer.

"Oh, so you haven't just fallen hopelessly in love with me." This last came with a chuckle.

"Don't flatter yourself," I retorted, hoping my true feelings were adequately buried. "How could I be in love with you, I don't even know you."

"I think you know plenty."

I twisted my lips, uncertain how to respond to that.

"I've been interviewing women for this article, but I need the perspective of a man. Are you game?"

"So—you want to date me?" He mock-scratched his head, and cocked it like a spaniel. "Then compare the experience with that of your dog?"

I laughed. He made it sound so ridiculous. And yet I had spent many a pleasant evening watching *Big Bang Theory* with my dog.

"I just want to go out with you, once. And then we don't have to ever see each other again."

"Oh, you mean because it might not go well."

"Well, I don't know. We haven't done it yet."

"By 'done it'… you don't mean—?"

"Jack! I'm not that kind of girl." I was laughing, and so was he. If the truth be known, I *would* have done it with him—right here—right now—if he had wanted to. My mind went off on an erotic fantasy that involved heli-skiing and me in a sexy ski suit getting lost in an avalanche rescued by a hunky rescuer that looked exactly like Jack Tinsle. But he wasn't allowed to know that. "I meant—"

"I know what you meant. All right. I see no harm in it. But if you decide you hate me, will you still finish training your dog at my center?"

"Of course, you big lug!"

He was roaring now. We were both laughing so hard I had tears in my eyes. This assignment, I decided, was going to be fun.

CHAPTER FOUR

It's funny but all throughout the date I had a feeling there was something that Jack was keeping from me. Well, fair was fair. I had kept mum about Lonny. Why would I talk about my ex? Why would he want to know about him? We knew what each other did for a living, but our personal lives were a mystery.

What was I trying to prove by going on a date with him? That dogs make better companions than men? So far, Jack was proving me wrong.

We decided that for our date we would stay in the area so that we could drink without driving. I met him at my favorite cellar restaurant—the Kensington Winebar. This place serves tapas style food, and cheese and charcuterie platters, and offers wonderful wines by the glass.

We started with a plate of very thinly sliced artisan salami accompanied by homemade potato chips dolloped with aioli and homemade pickles. Next came a mushroom flatbread with a white sauce, fresh baby arugula, and shaved Parmesan cheese. Last we shared a charcuterie board, which had cured, sliced meats and four semi-soft and hard cheeses, all served with different breads, crackers, pickled vegetables, mustards and chutneys. Every cheese was labeled.

With this last order we enjoyed a glass of Mourvedre and a glass of Malbec. As we raised our glasses in a toast to the success of my controversial article, I noted our hands clasped around the sparkling stemware, the shadows flickering in the background. We clinked glasses, and the skin of our fingers inadvertently brushed each other's. Maybe it was the ambiance, maybe it was the heady food and wine, but I swear in that moment a thrill went up both our spines. We let our hands linger longer than was normal for a toast, especially a casual toast, and neither of us wanted to pull away first. But then *he* did.

Still the spell remained unbroken. The hearth blazed with a roaring fire, and it was decked out in Christmas cheer. There was a candle floral arrangement lit on the garlanded mantle. I felt all warm and fuzzy, and whether that was the result of the alcohol and the fine cuisine or the excellent company, it was irrelevant. I was on cloud nine and having a wonderful time. The music was soft rock, and some jazz, and both Jack and I admitted to being grateful that Christmas tunes weren't in the mix yet.

"Don't you like Christmas?" he asked me.

I shrugged. I had loved Christmas when I was a kid, especially after my parents had bought the lodge on the lake. But after some unsuccessful relationships I started to resent the holidays. It seemed like everyone had somebody for the holidays except me. Lonny and I had not lasted more than two years. He had only just met my family and then he was gone. I couldn't seem to keep a relationship afloat. My dad was worried that I'd never get married. He'd given up on my sister. But my brother, you see, was the perfect son. He was married, had a house, a great government job and a wife who also had a great government job. Throw in two perfect kids and a cat—and little sister Joy looks like a loser.

That might have been one of the reasons I decided to foster Rocky. At least I would have a dog to cuddle with when everyone was all huggy by the fireplace.

But what was I doing thinking about all of that when I had Jack sitting across from me in the firelight, appearing pleased, albeit slightly bemused. He looked especially handsome, rugged, with a fashionably stubbled jaw and kind eyes. He was dressed in a nice shirt and tailored pants, so he had taken me seriously when I had called our get-together for dinner a date. I too had taken extra care with my ablutions and choice of clothing. For the first time I wore a dress, a warm wool thing with a cinched-in waist and a tulip skirt. Around my neck I wore turquoise beads and a matching bracelet and earrings. Black stockings and stiletto boots, and a fake fur jacket finished the ensemble, since I was walking.

"So, Joy Zamboni, tell me what your Christmas plans are."

"Headed to the Rockies to spend it with my family. My dad owns a lodge on a lake, in the mountains. And he lives there all year round with my sister."

"Sounds amazing."

"Do you ski?" I asked.

"Downhill? No," he said. "Never had time to learn."

"Oh? Why's that? I thought everyone who lived near the mountains learned how to ski."

"I didn't grow up near the mountains. I grew up in a small town where we had lots of frozen ponds in the wintertime."

"Oh, I see." He mentioned that he enjoyed cross-country skiing, but he was reluctant to elaborate so I didn't press him. "What about you?" I asked, changing the subject. "What are *your* Christmas plans?" I heard Ellie's voice in my head urging me to ask him to join me for the holidays. But that was absurd. We had known each other all of six days.

"Not sure yet," he said, his voice sounding a little troubled. "Had plans, but they might be falling through."

This was my chance. *Just ask him!*

If only.

***

The day after my date with Jack, when I told Susan my editor what I had planned for the article and that I was experimenting by coming out of my shell and actually dating again, she decided to give me an extension. "But I expect to have that article emailed to me by Christmas Eve," she insisted.

Not a problem, I told her.

"There's one more thing."

Oh-oh. "What?"

"I want you to take my photographer up with you to get some candid shots. You say your cousin Ellie is going to be there with her beau. Like all couples, from what you've told me, they have issues. Maybe they can be the headline couple for traditional relationships and your sister and her dogs can illustrate the benefits of canine companionship."

Great. Would Dad mind me bringing a stranger to Christmas dinner, and would my big sister give him a hard time?

I phoned my dad to inform him that I was driving up to the lodge in a couple of days, and to expect an extra guest. Susan's photographer, Graham Harlan, had insisted on taking his own car in case, for any reason, he had to leave. It was agreed that we would meet at the lodge in a few days. So as it turned out, the beginning of my holiday was going to be a working vacation. But at least I would get to see my family.

I had to get my car serviced and then pack for myself and Rocky before we were off for a well deserved vacation. I was feeling lighter already.

Finally my Rav4 was ready. I loved my SUV because of its high visibility, spacious cargo room, fuel economy and four-wheel drive. I was expecting snow on my way up the mountain passes and it was nice to know that the car had passed muster.

***

Rocky sat in the backseat belted behind me. I turned on the radio and hummed to the tune of *Winter Wonderland*. By the time we left the city the sky had darkened and ragged clouds gathered. I hoped the snow would hold off until we arrived. But if the weather turned, I was prepared. I was so excited. The lodge brought home great memories. And some really bitter sweet ones of my mom.

My family first saw this historic lodge many summers ago when Jonny, Carrie and I were kids. We were exploring the famous Burgess Shale fossil beds, high on a mountain ridge. As my brother and sister competed over who had found the coolest fossil, my mom had discovered well below us and across a gleaming lake, a half-hidden lodge nestled among the lakeshore trees. The chalets looked silvery like the birches interspersed among the firs. And the dormered green roofs were the same shade as the lake. "What is that place?" she had asked my dad.

That place was the Emerald Lake Lodge. The following winter my dad took us there for Christmas, and wouldn't you know it my parents fell in love with it. In fact, when it came up for sale a few years later they bought the place, used it for a summer and Christmas refuge, and after an early retirement (age 52 for her, 53 for him) they moved there permanently to start up new careers as innkeepers. They spent their life savings renovating the place and now it was one of the most luxurious smaller lodges in the district. Unfortunately we lost my mom to cancer five years ago, so now my dad runs it with my twice-divorced sister.

Rocky was good on the two and a half hour drive. We passed Canmore and then Banff. We were inside Banff National Park headed in the direction of Lake Louise. It was only a hop, skip and a jump from there to my destination. Rocky slept most of the way until I stopped for gas when we arrived in the town of Field. It had snowed recently and there was a nice layer of fresh white over the sidewalks, old snow banks and lampposts. I let him out to make a yellow patch on an isolated snow bank. He stretched his legs and obediently followed me back to the car. We continued our journey through town just as the snow started to fall.

It was then that disaster struck. We were headed into the outskirts where the houses and businesses dwindled. I don't know what happened. I must have driven over a tack or glass or a really sharp rock. A thumping sound came from my rear left side. As I took a corner I felt a shudder like the wheel was going to fall off. Bugger. I had had the car serviced too. I pulled over to the side. There was very little traffic on this stretch of road leading to the wilderness. I had never changed a flat before. I was pretty certain I didn't know how. I wondered if the CAA would come to my rescue here. How big was the town of Field? Did they have a CAA office? I wasn't too far away from the lodge. I could call someone to come and fetch me.

I exited the car and circled around to have a look. Yup. Definitely a flat. The tire was compressed at the bottom.

I returned to the driver's seat and hauled my handbag off the rubber floor mat to dig out my cellphone. Just as I was about to call to ask if someone from the lodge could fetch me, Rocky started up a cacophony of barking at the window. I looked out, and saw a familiar figure strolling down the street. He was eating a pre-wrapped sandwich from a vending machine he'd purchased from the convenience store at the opposite side of the street. He was headed my way. My eyes popped out of my head. It was Jack.

Had my prayers been answered? Or was I dreaming?

Or was it fate?

He was wearing a buckskin shearling jacket and looked like a cowboy. But make no mistake. It was him.

I fluffed up my hair, adjusted the paisley wool scarf twisted around my neck. I got out of the car.

"Jack?"

"Hey Zamboni," he said. "Fancy meeting you up here." He grinned, but by the way he had made that last remark, I began to suspect that he wasn't surprised to see me at all.

"What are you doing here?" My first thought was that he was stalking me. But that flamboyant grin just did not come off as menacing. Besides if he was following me I was not one to mind.

"Actually, I'm spending the holidays up here. Thought I was going to be staying in town, but had an unexpected change of plans."

I was delighted, of course, and at the same time I wondered if I was part of those plans. Why would he come up here? Had I mentioned the name of my parent's lodge or the National Park in which it was situated? Was this a coincidence? Not likely. He *must* like me!

"Hey, big fella," he called to Rocky, who immediately plopped his paws onto the window ledge and barked. His eyes dropped to my car's rear left tire. "Looks like you've got a flat, Zamboni. Need some help with that?"

"I was just about to call my dad to pick me up."

"You don't want to leave your car here, do you?"

"No, I suppose not."

"Here, let me change that flat for you. You got a jack?"

I do now, I thought, and suppressed the giggle. *Sorry, Jack,* I said to myself. I went to look in the luggage compartment and then realized that I was clueless. Exactly what did a jack look like?

"Never mind," he said. "Be back in a flash." He was gone across the street to a Jeep Wrangler. So that's what he drove. I had never seen his car until now. He lifted the hatch and withdrew a wrench and what I guessed to be the jack. He returned to my SUV just as I was letting Rocky out. I was pretty certain he wouldn't appreciate being inside the car while it was being worked on. Jack gave Rocky the requisite pats and scratches around the ears, and then got to work raising the vehicle and removing the lug nuts. After a few moments of struggling with the flat tire, it came loose and he rolled it to the side of the road. He retrieved the spare from the back and replaced the flat with the good tire.

"Good to go," he said, wiping a smear of grease across his forehead.

How could that possibly be sexy? But it was. Ohhh, how it was. I drew out a tissue from my pocket and wiped the suntanned skin above his brow clean. He grinned. "You can dress me up, but you can't take me out," he joked.

I laughed. "Hey, you want to go get a cup of coffee?"

He glanced at the time on his smartphone. "Sure, guess I've got time. There's a place right across the street. Sorry, Rocky," he said. "No dogs allowed. Back inside. We won't be long."

Actually, it was a bookshop that also served coffee. It

was called the Bookworm Café and was a rustic store filled with used and out of print books, with a coffee bar and big cushy sofas and overstuffed armchairs for those who wished to sip and read.

I ordered a latte sans the whipped cream and caramel drizzle, while Jack ordered his coffee black. While we were waiting for our brews we moseyed down the shelves of books. There were a lot of classics and on one shelf, labeled **Reserved**, I saw my favorite Christmas story: *A Child's Christmas in Wales* by Dylan Thomas.

I glanced up and down the bookshelf, realizing that these books had been put aside for customers and were already spoken for. "I wonder if they have another copy of this," I said aloud. "My mom used to read this to us when we were kids."

"Your mom was very well-read."

My mother was Welsh, and the Welsh poet Dylan Thomas was one of her favorite authors.

I abandoned Jack to search for the book on the other shelves. It was clear that the titles were stocked alphabetically by the author's last name, so I had to amble down to the Ts before I found anything else by Dylan Thomas. Unfortunately there was only a copy of his *Portrait of the Artist as a Young Dog.* The title made me titter, as I knew this book had nothing to do with dogs and everything to do with a semi-comical, autobiographical view of the author's childhood, and teen and young adult years growing up in Wales.

I sighed.

"Problem, Zamboni?" Jack asked, sneaking up behind me.

"No, I just really wanted to find another copy of *A Child's Christmas in Wales.* The old copy my mom used to read to us has disappeared. I remember looking for it after she passed away, but couldn't find it. So I guess I forgot about it until now. It was a first edition, and had a cover exactly like that one." I shoved a thumb towards the

Reserved shelf.

"Well, I'm sure there are other used bookstores that might have a copy."

Perhaps, but I really had no time to look. "They're rare and hard to come by. Maybe I should search the basement of the lodge. It might be there."

By this time the barista had called out our names, our coffees were ready. I headed to the counter while Jack answered a text. He followed me after a few moments and offered me a ten to cover the coffees that I had already paid for.

"It's on me this time," I insisted.

"It's not like I paid for dinner the other night."

"It was a *work* dinner."

"Right, a work dinner."

Was he being sarcastic or just typically amusing? "Picking your brains for my article," I elaborated.

He smiled. "Right. I better pay for the coffees. You're making me look bad."

I laughed.

He tucked the ten-dollar bill into my side pocket.

If he put it that way, how could I object?

CHAPTER FIVE

I have never felt so happy. I glanced out the window to make sure Rocky was okay. He was sitting up looking out the window, but he didn't seem stressed. Neither was he barking. It was mild for the mountains, just hovering around freezing. Rocky had a nice thick winter coat so he should be okay for a half hour or so more inside the car.

I turned back to Jack and sipped on my latte. We were seated at one of the small tables for couples by the window. The door was behind me, which is why I neglected to see my pretty, bombshell of a cousin walk in. But Jack did. He waved a hand and I turned from absentmindedly twisting a lock of my dark auburn hair to identify the person he was waving at.

How did they know each other?

I was about to comment on the coincidence when the realization of who Jack was flooded my brain. How could I be so stupid?

She swept over to Jack and gave him a peck on the lips. I know I was staring. My mouth was open and I was frozen in that stance, half twisted in my seat. Jack—was Rocco. No matter how many times I repeated that in my head, it refused to sink in.

Ellie, in a stylish powder blue ski jacket, and tucking a blonde curl behind her ear, grinned at me. "Joy! I just called Carrie and she said you hadn't arrived yet. Now I know what's been delaying you. You've met Rocco."

She hugged his head to her ample bosom and flung herself over to plant one on me too. Ellie is one of those women who, for lack of a better description, could be said to be top heavy. She was not fat, just a little out of proportion, not slender like me, which by the way, makes me look tall even though I'm not, particularly. In fact, I think Ellie and I are the same height. However in the face department I think her blonde good looks are more attractive. Her presence had always made me feel insecure but her outgoing personality and sweet nature made up for any envy I might have possessed.

But right now all of that was irrelevant. I was sitting and she was standing. Yeah, that's right. I was so stunned I couldn't even stand up, so I got a mouthful of her chest in my face when she hugged me, same as Jack.

"You look surprised to see me, Joy. I told you I was coming, and that I was bringing my man."

"Yes, of course," I said, shaking my head. "I just didn't realize *this* was Rocco. He told me his name was Jack."

Ellie laughed. "Oh, it is. Didn't I tell you his real name? But nobody in the hockey world calls him that."

Nobody?

I stared at Jack—I mean Rocco. Okay. I have to confess I *can't* and will *never* be able to call him Rocco. From this day forward, if he becomes my cousin-in-law (I felt an inward, vicious, twinge of jealousy at the thought) I still won't be able to call him Rocco.

"Don't you follow professional hockey? What kind of a Canadian are you?" My cousin jabbed her hands on her hips.

Clearly not a very smart one—if I was incapable of putting two and two together. But…but he had opened a dog training school in Calgary. Ellie lived in Edmonton. It was a three and a half hour drive from city to city. There was something going on here. I could see it in Jack's eyes. I mean Rocco. Rocco's eyes. Okay, I give up. I cannot call him that. I just *can't.*

Ellie was still talking. "I was in the drugstore. Had to pick up some things I forgot to pack. Rocco was waiting for me after gassing up and getting something to eat at the vending machines. He sent me a text to tell me to meet him here."

I remained speechless. Did he know I was Ellie's cousin? Had he known from the beginning—from the moment we met? My surprise was changing to annoyance, and then to anger. Why? Why not tell me? Certainly, he couldn't have known that Ellie and I were related at first. But later? When I was babbling about going to Emerald Lake for Christmas? Had he guessed then?

One look at Jack's face and the rage faded. So what if he knew I was Ellie's cousin. I had flirted with him, not the other way around. He had invited me to take classes from his dog-training center. We'd gone out for coffee. All innocent. I was the one who had asked him on a date—and with Ellie's urging!

But the date was just part of my research. For my article. I felt an ache in my abdomen. My stomach was tied up in knots. I was having trouble convincing myself that that was all it was. If I *hadn't* been researching an article I would have done the exact same thing. I would have still asked him out. That's just the way I was. My sister Carrie was always telling me to think before I acted. She should know. She had the experience of two failed marriages. I sighed. I had had such a great time with Jack. If I were the type to curse I would be spitting all over myself right now. Who was to blame? Not him. Not even me. And certainly, not Ellie.

"I'm so glad you guys met up," she said. "What a great coincidence!"

Was it? Was 'coincidence' even the right word?

"Rocky's starting to get antsy," Jack said, his eyes aimed at the street.

I turned to look through the window and I could see that the dog was up on his hind legs checking out every passerby to see if it was me. "Yeah, I better go."

"Meet you up there," Ellie said.

I got up and waved a weak goodbye.

***

The setting of the lodge seemed more remote and even more beautiful than it had been in the summer when I first saw it. From the Trans-Canada Highway at Field I drove five miles north to a parking lot. Jack and Ellie were close behind me. In my rearview mirror I could see the jeep pulling up. I let Rocky out of the car and leashed him. For once he seemed determined to stick with me. Maybe it was the strange location and the wilderness all around, but he showed no interest except for a few brief sniffs of bare branches poking out through the snow.

No time to think about what had happened in the Bookworm Café. Jack Tinsle was off-limits to me. I was back to square one—just me and my dog. "Come Rocky!" I shouted.

There was no need to shout. He was right there at my heels. Jack's school had taught us both well. I didn't wait for Ellie and Jack to catch up with me. Plenty of time for mindless chitchat after I called the lodge from the check-in cabin to let the family know we had arrived. My brother, Jonny, came in the lodge's van to transfer us and our luggage down a snowy lane, across a small wooden bridge, and onto a spit of land where no cars were allowed, except those run by the lodge.

"How was the trip guys," Jonny asked after Ellie had made introductions.

"Not too much traffic," she answered from the backseat where she snuggled with Jack. My brother had directed his comments to the couple via his rearview mirror.

"Oh, I am so happy to be here!"

"Well that's nice, Ellie. We missed you not coming out last summer."

"Sorry. Rocco and I went to Europe."

"Wow. Living high on the hog." Jonny grinned. He turned to me. I was seated in the passenger seat beside him and was checking my appearance in the makeup mirror under the van's sun visor. I could see Ellie's head against Jack's shoulder. He was glancing casually out the side window.

Then suddenly he turned. His eyes met mine in the mirror. My brother's voice interrupted my daze. "You're quiet little sis. What's up?"

I slapped the visor up, ridding myself of the mirror and, simultaneously, the sight of Jack watching me. "Oh, nothing. Just got my mind on work." I told him that I had to spend part of my time here writing up my article.

"Well, you better make sure you find time for the family or you know what Carrie will say."

I smiled. I knew exactly what she would say. All work and no play... yadda yadda yadda. She should talk. When was the last time *she* went out for some fun?

Jonny parked and we got out to collect our luggage from the back. Rocky leaped out after Jack and Ellie. Jonny handed Jack his and Ellie's bags and took two of mine while I carried my handbag, my carryall and my laptop.

"Hope all this luggage means you're planning a long stay. Dad'll be happy."

I made no comment. I had no idea how long or short I planned to stay. The knowledge that Jack was Ellie's boyfriend had frozen my brain. Why go home if seeing him was now off-limits. The fact that he had opened a dog-training center meant that he had already moved to Calgary. And yet I had not heard that Ellie was planning to move. Certainly she would have told me. I was so confused I wanted to scream.

"Hey," Jonny jabbed me in the upper arm with his elbow.

"Ouch, what gives?"

"Wake up, Joy, before you step off the path and fall flat on your face."

I drew my attention back to my brother, severely annoyed. Couldn't he see I was suffering a crisis here? And then I thought better of my stupid thought. Intimate knowledge of my troubles was the last thing I wanted him to know. His advice would be to forget about Jack.

Rocky trotted over to my brother and looked up. He bent

down to pat him on the head. "So this is your new beau."

"What's Carrie been telling you?" I demanded, feigning offense.

"You don't want to know," he said, chuckling.

We plodded through the snow, my breath frosting in the air. Brick walkways, partially shoveled, winding between huge snow banks linked to the main lodge. "I see you've had a big dump of the white stuff already. The skiing must be fabulous."

"It's going to be a good season," Jonny said.

We stopped and Jonny lowered one of my suitcases onto the floor so that he could open the door for us. The central building was built in 1902 and had long since been refurbished with eighty-five guest rooms in twenty-four two-story chalets. As we walked in through the main doors, the eaves were fringed with icicles and the effect was that of a terraced mountain village forgotten by the world in the dead of winter.

Rocky shot past me into the lobby. The rest of the family heard the commotion and came out from wherever they had been to greet us. Everyone wanted to meet Jack.

Carrie's Lhasa Apso mixed breed designer dog trotted out to investigate all the noise. She took one look at Rocky and growled. "Hey, Wiggles," I said. "Don't you want to meet your new cousin?"

Wiggles gave a definitive No for answer, by growling even deeper.

Carrie scooped Wiggles up in her arms. "Just ignore her. She's a princess. She'll pipe down once she gets use to him." She squatted and stroked Rocky with her free hand.

I noticed Jack smiling at Carrie's treatment of her dog. A twitch started at *my* lips too. Carrie treated Wiggles like her baby.

Our rooms had views across the frozen lake. Mine was on the ground floor, next door to Jack and Ellie's. It had a small breakfast nook with a coffeemaker, a queen-size bed with a feather duvet, and a separate sitting room that led outside glass doors to a long veranda overlooking the spectacular scenery. Above me I could hear the sounds of footsteps on the stairs as my nieces and nephew raced between rooms where my brother's family was housed. He and his wife Kimberly had a four-room suite with their kids, Noel, Annie and Lucy. The kids had taken to Rocky, and were letting him chase them in fun.

My dad's chalet on the other side of mine was a two-story structure. After dumping my stuff in my room I went outside, trod through the ankle-deep, new-fallen snow and tested his door. He always left it unlocked. There were no thieves in the mountains he always said. I glanced up at the charming chalet. The bedroom, main bathroom, study and library were upstairs. Downstairs was the kitchen, dining room, living room and powder room. Dad's accommodations had been renovated when he and mom came here to live permanently. It was basically a house.

The interior was quiet when I stepped inside, stamping snow from my boots. The living room was large with taupe walls, beige carpet, and cotton Navajo area rugs, and this was where I found him, reading. It had a lake-view balcony and a fireplace where kindling and wood were piled high ready for use.

"Hi, Dad," I said.

"Hey, little girl. It's about time you got up here." He put down his book, and rose to give me a kiss. "Is Ellie here yet?"

"Yeah, we bumped into each other in town. I had a flat and her... her boyfriend fixed me up."

"Nice of him. But I always told you that you should learn to do that stuff yourself. What if there was no one around to help you?"

I gave him my best scowl. "Now, you sound like Carrie. And you know that's not true. There's always the CAA."

"In remote areas, you're not going to find a CAA tow truck anywhere nearby."

"Okay, Dad. I get it. Soon's I get home I'll take a course

in auto mechanics."

"Now, you're just being facetious."

"You worry too much."

"Then stop giving me reason to." He smiled. I know he really did trust me. It was just his way of letting me know he cared.

I stared out his window at the lovely snowy view. On the far side of the frozen lake the mountains rose like pinnacles of ice.

"Something troubling you, sweetheart?" he asked. "You're awfully pensive."

I tore my eyes away from the snow-dusted forest and the serenity of the mountain encircled lake. "Nothing a good meal and a glass of brandy beside the fire won't fix."

That was a lie, of course.

I assured my dad that I was fine, and after updating him on the most recent events of my life, sans any mention of Jack or his doggie school, I returned to my room to rest. I unpacked my things and then went to fetch Rocky from my brother's kids. I took him out for a short walk with my nieces and nephews who insisted on coming, and which on hindsight I realized had been a good idea. Their high spirits distracted me from my disappointment at learning that Jack was Ellie's boyfriend. I returned the kids to their parents, and Rocky and I went to our room for a quick shower. For me that is. Rocky was quite happy to settle down for a nap at the foot of my bed while I freshened up.

After drying my hair and dressing in clean clothes, I checked the time and left Rocky sleeping.

It was happy hour, and although I did not feel particularly happy, I headed to the Kicking Horse saloon, where I knew my family would have gathered. Dad and Jonny were already drinking pints of foamy Big Rock and Kootenay beer on tap. The kids were with their mom Kimberly and my sister Carrie, drinking Coke and ginger ale from cans and running around as young children do. I approached the oak bar—which was an antique, rescued from a Yukon roadhouse—while the huge fireplace toasted my cold toes.

I looked up as Ellie and Jack came in, her arm looped through his. I had a feeling this was going to be a horribly long night.

They ordered wine and insisted I join them. We did the small-talk thing and then went for dinner.

In the dinning room we were served what they termed Rocky Mountain cuisine—but what was actually classic French and innovative Californian done up with regional ingredients. We shared a game platter appetizer that included air-dried buffalo strips and wild boar pate, served with home-baked breads, crackers and relishes. For the main courses Carrie and Kimberly had oven-roasted wild salmon with caper berry butter, while Ellie and Jack tried the venison loin basted with soy sauce and olive oil and drizzled with fresh and sun-dried cranberry sauce (figures they would both eat the same thing). My brother and I had pork tenderloin medallions marinated in chili-flecked olive oil served with chayote, a pear-shaped squash. And dad had a steak. All through dinner it was more small talk. I tried to keep up with it but my eye kept drifting to Jack. He and my dad seemed to hit it off and they were discussing—can you believe it— dogs. I was waiting for Jack to mention his dog-training center. But the topic never arose. How was it that Ellie was ignorant of this?

Later the guys shot billiards on the antique table in the upstairs lounge. Carrie and Kim joined them, but I declined and went outside in the clear mountain night to sip a glass of brandy.

If Ellie was unaware that Jack had already opened a dog school in Calgary, did that mean he was planning to stay in Edmonton? Maybe it was one of those chain businesses where he had one in every major city in the province? He could certainly afford it. Professional hockey players made a ton of money. But it had seemed like he was personally running the dog school. The more I thought about it, the more I began to be suspicious of Jack. I was now more concerned for Ellie's welfare than I was for my own.

Or was I just fooling myself.

And yet, that was no way to keep a relationship going if he was lying to her. If he had two lives, she deserved to know.

But was I the one to tell her?

And was I just having these thoughts because I wanted Jack for myself?

"Boo!" someone said into my ear. I nearly jumped sky-high.

"What the—Jonny, you scared the bejeesus out of me."

"Sorry, Joy. But you were just so lost in your own little world. This article you're working on must be really important."

I had forgotten all about the article. I nodded. "It's how I make my living, big brother."

"What's it about?"

I was surprised he didn't already know. I told him the basic premise, how modern women were abandoning marriage and taking canine housemates instead. He scoffed.

That's exactly what I would have expected from a happily married man. Which made me miss Rocky. "Think I'll go get my dog," I said.

"Hey, sit down, Joy. What's really bugging you? I could tell from the minute I picked you up that something was wrong. You and Ellie are usually so close. What happened? Don't tell me you're jealous because she has a boyfriend and you don't."

I could have slugged him. I refrained of course. He had hit too close to the mark. But I had legitimate concerns. I wanted to run it by him to see if I was just making a mountain out of a molehill. But I was doubtful if any of this was my business. Or his.

"But it *does* have to do with Ellie?" he asked.

I nodded.

"Then talk to her."

How? Should I just tell her that Jack is living a double life?

It was too late for me to seek some quiet time with my favorite cousin. Here she came with her boyfriend in tow and the rest of my family not far behind. They all found seats on the patio and my brother proceeded to build a fire in the outdoor hearth to keep everyone warm.

Sister Carrie and sister-in-law Kimberly brought mulled wine and hot cider to pass around. This would have been one of my most memorable Christmas holidays had those been *my* shoulders Jack's arms clung to—instead of Ellie's. Nonetheless, for everyone else, it was a pleasant evening by the roaring fire under the star-spangled sky.

CHAPTER SIX

In the morning the lodge shuttle took those who wanted to ski to the slopes of Lake Louise just 25 miles west. The lake is famous for its turquoise color that is caused by glacial rock, ground into silt through erosion and suspended in melt-water. The mountain ranges surrounding the lake offer alpine and cross-country skiing, as well as heli-skiing and snowboarding. Other activities that visitors to the area engaged in were ice fishing, ice skating, snowmobiling, dogsledding, snowshoeing and ice climbing. Most of the latter activities were available around Emerald Lake where my dad had his lodge, but Alpine skiing was best at the Lake Louise Ski Resort. That was where my brother and sister, and Ellie and Jack went. Although Jack had told me he had never downhill skied, I was pretty certain that with his innate athletic skills, he'd be shushing like a pro in no time.

I had to remain behind to wait for my boss's photographer. Dad said he would text me when the man arrived, so I stayed close by and explored the local scenery in a short cross-country ski run along a shoreline trail that headed toward the Emerald Basin for a spectacular view of the mountains. I took Rocky with me.

When the photographer arrived, Dad texted me that he was on his way to pick the man up in the lodge van. I started back as soon as I heard because it would take me at least forty minutes to return to the lodge from where I was now.

I was almost there, but I was in a hurry, so when I saw the dark figure in a royal blue ski suit approach me from the opposite direction I thought little of it—until I almost skied passed him, and Rocky exploded into excited barking.

"Zamboni," I heard.

I stopped and turned as he rotated to greet us. By this time Rocky was all over him and he was squatting, petting the dog.

"Jack? What are you doing here? I thought you'd gone downhill skiing with Ellie and the gang?"

He looked particularly rugged and handsome with his face slightly flushed beneath his tan from the exertion of catching up with us. He stood up, and all six feet two of him hovered over me. "I wanted to talk to you."

I felt irrationally thrilled, but at the same time irritated by this admission.

He seemed unusually awkward. "I think I need to explain."

It was Ellie he owed the explanation to, not me.

"You don't need to explain anything. I'm not the one you're lying to."

It was true. There were no lies between us. They only felt like lies. His real crime towards me was in withholding information. But since I was practically a stranger, he owed me nothing. It was *his* life, and he was free to do with it as he would. But Ellie was a different matter.

"I can see that adorable scowl of disapproval on your face."

"Stop flirting with me, Jack." Talk about unfair, but I went silent. It could be that he had no idea how I felt about him. And if that were the case, he must never know.

"Since when was I flirting with you?" he asked.

I scowled. What was he implying? That I was imagining it?

"Okay, here's the truth."

Ha. That was a first. The thought was unfair, I know. But he deserved it.

His face darkened as he read the expression on my face. "Since when did I lie to you?"

"You never told me you knew I was Ellie's cousin."

"I *didn't* know. Why would I know?"

True, if Ellie had never mentioned me. And why should she mention me?

"But you *did* know. You weren't surprised to learn that I was your girlfriend's cousin when we were in the bookstore in Field."

That was hard to say. Girlfriend. Ellie was Jack's *girlfriend*. Bugger. Ellie had mentioned wanting to marry Jack—well, Rocco—but he was the same person.

"I only figured it out when I saw you in Field with the flat tire. I realized that the lake lodge you mentioned heading to for Christmas was the same place Ellie was taking me."

"So you decided to play it cool."

He frowned. "I'm confused... Decided... to play it cool—?"

You were leading me on! The accusation stuck firmly inside my head.

"What's going on, Joy?"

As if you didn't know. I refused to speak another word.

A light came on in his eyes as though he suddenly understood. I flushed. Bugger. He could read me like a book.

"I'm sorry if I made you think I was interested in you."

How dare you! How dare you feel sorry for me! Besides, I wasn't imagining it. I was not. *Just because you're too much of a jerk to admit that you were screwing with me. Yes, Jack Tinsle—or whatever your name is—you are a player.*

The look on his face made me squash the next thought. Maybe he was telling the truth. Maybe the flirting was imaginary. And I had made it all up in my head. Maybe all of this was just a stupid schoolgirl crush. I was thirty-two years old, for heaven's sake! Too old for puppy love.

I dropped to my knees and threw my arms around my dog. I had my own puppy to love. Jack Tinsle could go to the devil!

"Joy." That was the first time he had called me by my first name in a while. Rocky struggled out of my vice grip. He hated being squeezed.

I stood up. This wasn't about me. This was about Ellie.

"You lied to Ellie."

He nodded. "Well... not exactly."

"No. You just withheld the truth."

"She doesn't want me to quit playing hockey."

"*Have* you quit? And not told her?"

Jack was silent.

He *had* quit. Wow. Although a part of me was furious with him for deceiving Ellie, another part of me was impressed with his conviction.

His face had a hangdog expression. Not one of my favorites. "I don't want to play hockey anymore," he said.

Now here was where I was really perplexed, and I expressed my puzzlement out loud. "How is it that you could move to Calgary and open a business, and she not know?"

"Once in awhile the team trains in different parts of the country. She thinks I'm away, training."

All of a sudden Rocky started to fuss. I looked up to see my Dad and a strange man headed down the trail from the lodge. It was the photographer.

"I have to go," I said.

"Zamboni!" I paused at the urgency in his voice. "Thanks for keeping mum about my activities in Calgary."

What came out of my mouth next simply blurted out: "Tell her, Jack. Or I will."

***

I showed Graham Harlan around the lodge. Then we went into town for a lunch of bison burgers at the Yoho Brothers diner. I wanted a quiet place where we could talk, and had small chance of encountering my family until I had briefed the photographer on the article.

He was aware of the premise for my story. He made no bones that he thought the idea was stupid.

"Are you married, Graham?" I asked.

"Divorced," he said. "But I certainly don't want to replace women with dogs."

"Well, it's different for women."

"How so?"

It was complicated. And I knew if an explanation to Graham was difficult then a written treatise of my argument would be even less convincing.

"Do you have a dog?" I asked.

"A cat," he said.

"So, you like animals. Pets?"

"As much as the next guy."

"Well, since you're a guy, I can't really expect you to understand."

"Try me."

"Anything I say will only make you mad."

"Then wouldn't it be a good idea to run those things by me before you write it up and send it to Susan?"

This man, Graham Harlan, was a stranger. But he was smarter than he looked. "Okay," I said. I gave him the rundown on the deceptiveness of men. I told him the story of Ellie and Jack and me—without using any of our names. I changed our professions so that later when he met my cousin and her boyfriend he wouldn't know it was them. Or that the third woman in this triangle was me.

"So the tennis player is cheating on his supermodel fiancée with her best friend. She met him while walking her dog at the park. Is that right?"

"Yes," I said.

"Did they do the nasty?"

"What?"

"You know—did they actually sleep together?"

I was offended by his insinuation. "No," I snapped.

"Then what's the problem?"

"You don't see anything wrong with him quitting his career and establishing a new one in a different city and not telling his fiancée?"

"Frankly, Joy, the better question is: how is that even possible? How could he be running a business in a totally different city, and she not wonder where he was?"

Yes, that was the question.

"Beats me," I said.

"She would have to be pretty frickin' stupid."

"Hey—" I scowled, and stopped myself in time before I gave myself away. "Well, you wanted to know how my article could possibly be credible? Well, we women are full of stories like this. That's why we've given up on men and are choosing to spend our lives with pets instead. They are much more dependable, they never lie or cheat on you, and they give you unconditional love."

"Wow," Graham said. "Were you just dumped?"

"Shut up."

Graham lowered his eyes to his burger. He picked it up and took a bite. He continued to eat while I smoldered. This was not going the way I had planned. Now, all I wanted was for this jerk of a photographer to disappear. Why had Susan hired him?

"Listen," he said, putting down his half-eaten burger. "I get it. I was dumped too. But you don't see me going all misogynistic on you."

"Well, if we're going to be honest, you're not exactly Mr. Pleasant."

"Sorry," he said. He raised his camera and snapped a photograph of me.

"What the—what did you do that for?"

"You had an interesting expression just then. Here, look…" He turned the camera towards me and replayed the last shot.

Holy crow. He was good. That photograph captured my feelings with depth, but it wasn't an insulting or humiliating picture. It was beautiful in its honesty and its softness. No wonder Susan had hired him.

"How did you do that?"

"Experience. A practiced eye. I want to photograph these people who are going to be in your story while you interview them."

I nodded.

"And I want to meet this guy who has you all tied up in

knots."

"My ex is not here," I said.

"I *don't* mean your ex."

I glared at him. "What are you talking about?"

"Fine." He set his camera down. "I'm sure I'll know who he is when I see him."

I was quiet. He was sapping the life out of me.

CHAPTER SEVEN

"When someone does something hurtful to you, do something nice for someone else. It's the only way to fight back. Make the world the kind of place you want it to be."

I glared at him. Just who did this Graham Harlan think he was? Preaching to me like that? But as I gave him the evil eye I realized that Graham really was a nice guy. He was honest, maybe a little too honest, but his honesty did not come across as cynical.

"So who have *you* done something nice for lately?" I asked.

He shrugged.

I was going to give him my 'aha, so you don't practice what you preach' when my cellphone rang. I answered it after apologizing to Graham for the interruption.

"Yes, this is Joy Zamboni," I said. "What seems to be the problem?"

"Oh, no problem," the woman at the other end replied. "It's Sarah Krakowski at the Humane Society, the director of the pet foster program. I just wanted to let you know that we've found a permanent home for Rocky. Isn't that wonderful?"

My silence must have disturbed her. "Joy, are you there? Did you hear what I said? You no longer need to provide foster care for this particular dog." When I still said nothing, she got anxious. "Is something wrong? Is Rocky all right?"

"Oh, yes. I'm sorry," I said, shaking myself out of my unexpected discomfort. "I...I just wasn't expecting to hear from you so soon. I'm not home. Actually, I won't be back until after Christmas. I've brought Rocky with me to the mountains for the holidays."

"Oh, that won't do. The new owners, a family called Kinsley, want the dog for Christmas. He's a gift for their son."

"But I'm hours away..." My voice trailed off desperately and I could see that even Graham was concerned by my obvious agitation. It irked me to tell the woman at the Humane Society the truth. I did not—*could* not let Rocky go to someone else. I wanted him myself. After a few seconds of listening to her rambling away I broke into her monologue. I had made up my mind; the dog belonged to me. "Did you hear me, Sarah? I'd like to adopt Rocky myself."

It was her turn to be silent. Then she said, "I wish you had told me this yesterday. The prospective owners have signed all the papers and paid the deposit."

I hadn't known yesterday, or else *I* would have paid the deposit. "But..."

"Those were the terms of the foster care program. You must release the animal when we have found them a permanent home."

"But there are so many other dogs that need homes."

Sarah sighed on the other end of the line. "Look, I can see you've fallen in love with our Rocky, and perhaps he feels the same way. I'll talk to the family and see if they are interested in another pet, but if not, you understand that you will have to give him up?"

I nodded, grateful for the reprieve. "Thank you, Sarah."

"Glad to do it. But I'd hold off on the thanks for the time being. I can't make any promises. I'll get in touch with the Kinsley's and find out how they feel. Be in touch soon."

She disconnected the call.

"Bad news?" Graham asked.

I could see that he had finished his burger, and I had barely started mine. I picked it up, but put it down again almost immediately. It was cold, and I had no appetite. I just thought that eating would be a good excuse to forego conversation.

"A temporary setback," I said. "I'm sure it will all work out right."

He looked solemnly at me. "Well, sure. It's none of my business. Shall we get back to the article?"

I nodded, and picked up my glass of water to take a sip. My mouth was dry. It was difficult to speak. Finishing this article was now the last thing on my mind. I tried to discuss the details with him, and listened to his ideas for illustrating the text with certain types of photographs, but finally I had to confess to him that my mind was elsewhere. I excused myself and told Graham that I had to get back to the lodge. I desperately wanted to see Rocky. Fortunately, we had taken separate cars as he had planned to tool around in town after lunch, and I had things to attend to. I returned to the lodge. Rocky was waiting for me in our room.

"Hey, boy," I said. I hugged him, and for once he remained still while I lavished him with love. He licked my face and wagged his tail. "Let's go for a walk," I said.

Rocky was the perfect dog today. He walked obediently, just slightly ahead of me, and never tugged on the leash. We were on one of the trails that had been trampled down by winter hikers. I had chosen to go on foot, without cross-country skis or snowshoes because I wanted to be right there with my dog. My snow boots were ankle-deep in fresh snow. Rocky's long hair was knotted with snowballs. I was beginning to feel a little more at ease. I was worried for nothing. Surely the Kinsley family would choose another dog, a younger one perhaps. Don't most kids prefer puppies? Rocky was not a puppy. They didn't know him, the way I did. They had maybe met him once or twice in person. But if they had rejected him then, why choose him now? I know it was a serious undertaking, adopting the right dog. But if you waited too long, someone else might choose the one you wanted. And besides, the whole idea behind the Humane Society's foster program was to find permanent homes for the animals. I was offering Rocky a permanent home. Shouldn't I get first dibs? He was comfortable with me now.

We had grown accustomed to each other. He liked me. And I—well I was pretty sure I loved him.

They could *not* take him away from me. It made zero sense. It was like taking a child away from a home where it felt safe. And yet they did the same thing with children's foster care programs. But surely if the foster parents wanted to adopt the foster child, no one would thwart them?

Rocky turned and leapt up, flinging snow in the air. It was his way of telling me to throw him a snowball. I packed some snow in my hands and threw a ball at him, at which he jumped and snapped. I crouched down to grab more snow. Suddenly a snowball came flying past from behind me and Rocky flew towards it jaws wide open. The snowball crumbled between his teeth and I turned to see who had thrown it.

It was Jack.

"You still here?" I asked. "I thought you would have gone back to Lake Louise to ski with the others."

He no longer wore cross-country skis and like me was in snow boots. "Ellie and Carrie came back early. They went into town to do some Christmas shopping."

"Where's Jonny and Kim? And the Kids?"

"Gone ice skating on the lake."

At the mention of skating everything concerning Jack's deceptions came back to me. But it was no longer my problem. I had Rocky to worry about. "Did you tell Ellie about K-Nine?" I asked.

He hung his head sheepishly. "Not yet."

"You have to tell her, Jack."

"I will."

"Why are you so resistant to telling her that you want to live in Calgary and run a dog training center?"

"Because she hates the idea."

"How do you know?"

He sighed. "When we first started dating we told each other our dreams."

"So she knows what your fantasy job is. Training dogs.

Do you know what hers is?"

"She really just wants to stop working and have a nice house and kids."

So, he did understand her. "How did you two meet?" I knew Ellie was a huge hockey fan. She went to all the games and charity events that the teams attended.

"At a charity event for special needs children."

Yes, that was Ellie. But she had a special place in her heart for hockey and hockey players. Dare I say it? She was a bit of a Puck Bunny.

Jack could read the thought that was tumbling about in my mind. He smiled. "She really is sweet."

Yeah, she was. And unfortunately, so was he. They deserved each other and I would do well to stand back and give them some space to sort out their problems.

"I'm sorry, Jack. I should never have meddled in your issues. Whatever you do is between you and Ellie." I glanced down at Rocky. I had my own problems.

"What's wrong, Zamboni," he said softly.

I was on the verge of tears. It was stupid. He was only a dog. But the idea of losing him, after losing my prospects with Jack, was heartbreaking. I needed someone to love me. And Rocky loved me.

To prove it, he came up to me and shoved his snout into my hand. I dropped down to my haunches to kiss him on the head and he returned the sentiment with a few quick laps of a wet tongue. I smiled through my tears, and buried my face in his right ear to hide my distress from Jack.

"Joy," he said. "Stand up."

No. I would not stand up and let him see me cry.

He got down on his haunches until his eyes were level with mine. I refused to look at him and squeezed my eyes shut, still leaning my cheek into Rocky's neck. Jack cupped my face with his hands and drew it away from the dog. Rocky growled. I laughed. That was the first time Rocky had ever growled at Jack, whom he loved almost as much as he loved me. *Grrr,* he repeated.

Jack lowered his hands. "It's okay, boy," he murmured. Rocky quieted and Jack helped me to my feet. We stood face to face. What happened next was totally unexpected. I should have pulled away but I lost control. Jack's lips landed on mine, and his arms came around to my back, up to my nape and into my hair. The kiss was soft but firm, and quick. Because we both realized at the same time what we were doing.

"That did not happen," I said, wiping my lips with the back of my mitten.

He was silent.

He looked longingly at me and I felt like crying again. "No Jack," I said, when he moved to take me into his arms again. "Ellie loves you."

He nodded and a tiny whisper of a sigh escaped from his lips.

Did he not love her? Oh no. What was I going to do? Ellie was my cousin, my dear, sweet, beautiful cousin Ellie. I could not hurt her. I would *not* hurt her.

The one thing I remembered about that day was how the sun slanted through the snow-crusted branches of the trees, and how everything sparkled like silver.

"Oh, there you two are!" It was Ellie's voice, and both Jack and I took an instinctive step back from each other. "We've been looking all over for you. It's almost happy hour."

I did not feel terribly happy, not with the lingering sensation of Jack's lips on mine. I had to stop this before it progressed any further.

But the sight of them together, the confusion and unhappiness in Jack's eyes made my heart weep. I had my own problems and their problems were not mine, even though Jack had forced my hand.

And as I glanced back at the miss-matched couple I realized hopelessly that it was too late; I was already involved.

CHAPTER EIGHT

The next couple of days were excruciating as I waited for the Humane Society to call me back. I wrote and rewrote a draft of my article, always ending up tearing it up and throwing the sheets in the garbage bin. This should be easy, but the memory of Jack's kiss kept returning to haunt me. Rocky however never failed to remind me of the bitter truth—that dogs were much more trustworthy than men. I went into town to do some Christmas shopping of my own and when I got back to the lodge late in the afternoon, Graham Harlan, the photographer, had evidently hit it off with my sister. He had spent the last two days discreetly taking candid shots of my family when they weren't looking. I told him he would have to get their permission if he wanted to print any of them. I wasn't about to get on bad terms with my family for the sake of a magazine article. Screw how much it paid.

I was a little surprised to see Carrie and Graham having a drink together in the bar, since she had permanently sworn off men. Wiggles, her little dog, was sitting in her lap.

Ellie and Jack came in and I could tell by Ellie's high spirits that she was totally unaware of Jack's indiscretion. Although I had not seen too much of either of them since that incident in the woods, it was clear too that Ellie remained ignorant of Jack's business in Calgary.

It was one week before Christmas and Dad, Jonny and the kids had gone out to chop down a Christmas tree. Kimberly had obviously been busy making cookies and treats, as the whole place smelled of gingerbread, fruitcake and cinnamon. And overriding all of it was a lingering aroma of fresh popcorn.

I was determined to avoid Jack at all costs. We were in the Kicking Horse saloon where Jonny was now raising the tree. The kids were excited to decorate it. Rocky was excited too, he just wasn't sure why.

As I watched my dog going from child to child, curious as to whether the decorations in the kids' hands were edible, I knew that I needed him. I had to do everything in my power to keep him. He was part of my family now. Surely the Humane Society would understand.

It's ironic how fate works. Just as I was completing this thought, my cellphone chimed. I lifted it nervously to my ear.

"Joy," a familiar voice said. "It's Sarah Krakowski from the Humane Society."

"Yes, hi," I answered. "How are you?"

I guess I prolonged the inevitable with niceties because I could tell by the tone of her voice that it was bad news.

"I'm sorry, Joy, but the Kinsleys want Rocky. They wanted to adopt him a month ago when they first saw him, but were unable to because their house was undergoing a remodel, and you know how contractors are...it ended up taking longer than it was supposed to." She exhaled before continuing. "They'd like to have Rocky by Christmas Day. I know it's an inconvenience for you, but if you drive him back in the next couple of days you can still make it back to your family's lodge for Christmas."

I could barely speak. I know people who are not pet lovers don't understand what it means to have an animal you love taken away from you. They don't seem to understand that it is like having your child ripped out of your arms, against your will. But Sarah must understand. I inhaled unsteadily. "Sarah, I know this is asking a lot, but can I keep Rocky just a few days longer? I promise I will have him back to you by Christmas Eve."

"But how will you get back in time for your own Christmas?"

"It's only a few hours drive. Please, Sarah. It would

mean a lot to me."

She was silent for a moment. "Don't you think it would be easier on you if you brought him back right away? I realize how attached you've become, but really, Joy, you've had him for less than a month. Why prolong the agony?"

Because every moment with him means the world to me. I wanted to say that, but the words lodged in my throat. Because what I really meant was that when Rocky was gone I would be completely alone. My eyes flickered over to Jack who was sitting with Ellie on the sofa. Yes, I had a family, but they all had someone to love. Jonny had his wife and kids, Carrie had Wiggles, and Ellie had Jack. And Dad had a lifetime of memories with Mom. I had no one.

"All right," Sarah said. "But please get him here by Christmas Eve. And preferably in the morning."

"I will, and thanks," I said.

When I looked up, I caught Jack gazing at me. To my horror my cheeks were wet and my eyelashes glistened with tears. I turned away hoping no one else had noticed, and wiped my face with the backs of my hands. Ellie had joined Jonny and Kimberly who were trimming the tree with freshly strung cranberry garlands, pinecones collected from the woods and sprayed white like they were dusted with new snow, and popcorn strings. Carrie and Graham were stringing more popcorn.

In my present state of self-pity this was too much Christmas cheer. I got up from the armchair where I had been sitting and went to the bar where there was a box of tissues on the counter. Jack beat me to it, and plunked himself down on a barstool, and shoved the box towards me. The bar was far enough away from where everyone else was making merry by the Christmas tree, so no one could hear us.

"Go away... *Rocco*," I said.

He frowned. "You've never called me that."

"Well, it's high time I did."

He had no idea how hard it was for me to call him that. It was a nickname that friends and family used. And I was no friend or family to him.

"You have no idea how sorry I am."

I blew my nose and mopped my tears, and wondered irritated, whether my mascara was running.

He was silent, observing me.

"Stop staring at me. It's annoying."

He smiled. His voice came softly, "I am so sorry I hurt you."

I scowled. The one thing I found intolerable was to have someone feel sorry for me. It was bad enough that I had the ability to become filled with self-pity all by myself, but it was excruciating to have someone else express it as well.

You are so self-centered, I thought. Of course, you think this is about you. Just like a man!

I opened my mouth to contradict him but my throat was so tight with emotion that nothing came out except a froggy sounding croak.

I started to laugh as tears trickled down my cheeks.

He reached out to touch me, but I jerked back. "You're with Ellie," I said. "And if you start anything with me you'll draw attention this way, and *that* is the last thing I want."

He nodded, and sat back. His finger circled a knot in the wood of the bar. "If I had known I was going to make you so miserable I would have left you alone."

Yeah, you jerk, I wanted to say, but I hardly meant it.

He sighed. "I take that back. I couldn't have stopped myself if I tried."

Stop it.

I blew my nose, unconcerned if he thought I was crass. What difference did it make if I offended him. I could swear and belch and it wouldn't make him any more mine. It was better if I offended him and then he wouldn't want anything to do with me, and yet deep in my heart I wanted him to only know the best of me. But I must fight it.

I swallowed the lump in my throat and turned my teary eyes to him. "You are such a narcissist," I said. I suppose I did want to hurt him. But I tried to make the accusation sound like a joke. I shut my eyes for a second and let the last of the tears have their way; then I dried my face and looked around. Music was playing. At the time, the song was a total blur; I knew only that it was a Christmas tune. I turned back to Jack. He had that hangdog look on his face again. In my heart of hearts it pained me to hurt him even though he had really done a number on mine. I shook my head. And tried to smile. "This isn't about you, Jack. I'm not crying because you've broken my heart. I've had my heart broken before. It's… it's something else."

"Can I help?"

"I don't think so."

"What is it?"

"I don't see how it's any of your business."

He looked offended, but who cares? I wanted him to suffer. Oh, why was it when your desires were thwarted, it made your thoughts so contradictory?

"I suppose nothing about you *is* my business…." He sighed. "But I feel like it is."

"Don't say things you don't mean."

He looked at me long and hard. Finally, he said, "I have never said anything to you without meaning it."

I brought my hand to my forehead and closed my eyes. I had a headache to beat all headaches. "There is nothing you can do, Jack. Let's not talk about it anymore."

I rose to go to the bathroom to fix my face. The family must not see me like this. This would have to be my secret for a few more days. Like I said, I could not stand any more people feeling sorry for me.

CHAPTER NINE

The next morning I awoke early and took Rocky for a walk. On hindsight, allowing my emotions to get the better of me was a mistake. I should have stayed at the lodge and spent the few short days remaining with my dog. But I felt angry—and frustrated—and completely devoid of hope. The deadline for my article was looming, and I couldn't write a single word if my life depended on it. So I slapped shut my laptop and ordered a helicopter to pick me up and take me to a remote spot in the mountains to ski on my own.

I was an experienced skier but this was probably the stupidest thing I have ever done in my life. The helicopter pilot told me so himself. But he was an old friend. He was well acquainted with my wilderness and athletic skills, and we had known each other long enough for him to trust me.

He dropped me off on a beautiful quiet peak that sloped into a bowl of fresh powder. The day was clear, the sky a luminous blue. It was the kind of day where nothing bad could happen—except that everything bad had already happened to me. It should have been a dark, gloomy day to go with my mood. But no—the sun glittered blindingly in the sky illuminating perfect ski conditions.

I suppose my state of mind gave me a false sense of security, but when I launched myself from the peak I had no idea I was on a cornice of ice which unluckily for me just happened to break. Suddenly I fell, the momentum throwing my legs out from under me. I landed on my back, my skis twisting and detaching from my boots, my poles flying wide. The snow began to slide down from above and beneath me, burying everything in its wake. I did everything I could to keep from being buried alive, even swimming to stay on top of the snow, but to no avail. As I screamed for help, hoping the helicopter pilot would see me and respond snow fell into my mouth, choking me. I coughed and spit, keeping my head above the snow and pummeling at the stuff as it threatened to cover me entirely. If it did I would suffocate—so I punched through to create an air pocket.

The entire fall probably only took a few seconds but it felt like hours. I had stopped sliding and the snow had settled. I was alive.

Barely.

Movement was impossible. I felt no pain. Did that mean I had escaped uninjured? I tried to wiggle my toes and move my legs, but they were trapped by the weight of the snow. My neck was stiff, and I had managed to keep my face above the avalanche. I had just cheated death.

But I wasn't out of the woods yet. Getting out of this icy tomb on my own was unlikely. And if I failed to get loose in an hour I would freeze to death despite my cold weather gear.

Unfortunately, an overhang and the shadow of the mountain hid me. The avalanche had buried all of my loose equipment and nothing was left to indicate my location. Even from the air no one would see me unless they came down to look. My backpack with my avalanche beacon was still on my back. I tried to reach the cellphone buried in my pocket, but there was too much snow. I must keep trying and digging with my trapped hands.

By now the helicopter pilot must be frantic because I had disappeared. He would have called for a search and rescue team. All I had to do was wait.

The wait was relatively short, but at the time it seemed to last an eternity. I heard the chopping sound of the helicopter rotors and a few seconds later came a deep throaty barking. A search and rescue dog was among the team. Regardless, I was too weak to shout. I tried to call, but nothing emerged.

The avalanche had stopped for about twenty minutes. I

knew they would wait to ascertain the snowpack's stability before they came down. No point in anyone else being buried alive. After being dropped into the bowl by the helicopter, it took a few minutes for the rescuers to get oriented. They would have switched on their emergency beacons into receive mode. The helicopter pilot must have seen where I went under. He must know the approximate spot to hunt for me.

The sound of voices. Occasionally they stopped and all went quiet as the rescue team listened for my cries. I cleared my throat. I had choked on the snow and my voice was recovering slowly. Only a few pathetic croaks escaped.

At this point in my adventure I was almost passed out from the trauma and cold. It seemed like more than an eternity that I had been buried neck deep in snow. I kept passing in and out of consciousness. I almost felt warm again when the delightful dream of warm hands and strong arms came around me. But then I awoke and I realized it was only the pressure of the snow packed against my body. There were no soft lips on mine. No hard masculine chest for me to lean into.

And then I was off again into dreamland and the fear dampened and went soft. I was no longer afraid. He was there, touching me. Kissing me, the wet touch of his tongue on my lips. Was this a dream? It felt so real. I reached out to draw him closer. I felt strong muscles under my flattened palms. I was ready to sink deeper into the dream, when my consciousness broke though the foggy thoughts.

My rescuer wasn't who I thought it was.

I heard barking and a cold nose touch mine. Frantic licking all over my face, and then a dog's paws were working to dig me out. A few seconds later my human rescuers located me and, with shovels, they assisted the dog that had already removed the snow from around my throat and chest.

I blinked my foggy eyes. I knew that dog. My heart leaped with joy as Rocky clawed the snow frantically. Someone above him had a shovel and he was digging me out.

Actually there were three people. I recognized my brother Jonny, and the other man… was none other than—Jack. Then I saw Ellie. For as long as I live, I will never forget the look on her face. It was an expression of shock. Then horror as the truth dawned on her.

"Zamboni, can you hear me?"

I think I had passed out. My arms were free now and Jack had one of them in his hands. He had taken his ski mitts off and was rubbing the warmth back into my skin. When I came to he raised my hand to his cheek. I don't know how long I had lain there half buried in the snow. But finally I was freed and Rocky was jumping around trying to get to me as the others wrapped me in a thermal blanket, and airlifted me to safety.

***

"What were you thinking?" Carrie chided me, her arms loaded with hot chocolate, cookies and fruit. "You know better than to go heli-skiing by yourself. I can't believe that pilot even took you up there. He knows the rules. No one skis alone."

I was slowly recovering back at the lodge. "It wasn't his fault. I asked him to do it. Begged him. Please don't blame him, Carrie. It's not like he just left me there on the top of the mountain. He was waiting for me and saw me fall." I hesitated. "Does Dad know?"

"Not yet. He went into town with Kim and the kids." She set the food down onto the coffee table beside me. "Eat something. You need to get your strength back."

"I'm safe and unhurt. There's no reason he needs to know, is there? It will only upset him."

"You should have thought of that before you decided to do something so reckless."

I agreed. I was lying on the sofa in the Kicking Horse saloon. No one was there except my sister Carrie. Christmas was a slow period for guests, which was why the family spent the holidays at the lodge. Out of the corner of my eye I saw Ellie come in with Jack. They briefly glanced my way then went to sit opposite each other in armchairs next to the window. Now Graham followed. He sat down at the bar and began fiddling with his camera. Where was Jonny? I had to make Jonny promise to keep my mishap from Dad.

"Try to rest," Carrie said. She got up from where she perched on the edge of the sofa next to me, and her little dog Wiggles left with her. I was alone now, under a patchwork afghan blanket, with a cup of hot cocoa. I felt something nudge my hand, and I realized that Rocky was at my side. Oh no. *Rocky*. In all the excitement and my near death experience I had forgotten that I had to return Rocky to the Calgary Humane Society so that his new family could adopt him. My eyes welled with tears, and before I could mop them away, my brother Jonny came to check on my recovery.

"Are you injured?" he demanded. He did not raise his voice and chastise me as Carrie had done.

I shook my head, and placed the cocoa, untasted, onto the adjacent coffee table.

"But you're in pain."

"No," I mumbled. Not physically anyway. Rocky was up on his front paws licking my cheek, wiping away the salt of my tears.

"Then why the waterworks?"

I knew Jonny would understand. I knew *Carrie* would understand. But my energy failed me. The thing was: it wouldn't matter if I told them; nothing would change. The agony of losing Rocky would hurt just as much.

"You're worn out, Joy. It's not every day you get buried under five feet of snow."

"I was only partially buried," I said. "I could breathe."

"And thank goodness for that." He was about to say something else but changed his mind. He knew he might upset me by saying that I could have been killed. Besides, that was Carrie's job.

"Jonny—" I said, as he rose to leave from where he was perched on the side of the antique coffee table.

He smiled. "Relax. I *won't* tell Dad."

I sighed, and hugged Rocky's head to my chest. I had done a very stupid thing and it was going to take a long time for me to get over it. Dad would be upset if he knew—and for good reason—but I mustn't let him know how stupid his youngest offspring was. What good would that do for either of us? I felt guilty enough, and irresponsible. And I still had to tell him that I planned to return to Calgary for Christmas.

Yes, I had changed my mind. If I had to relinquish Rocky to the Humane Society then I wasn't going to return to the lodge afterwards. I was having a meltdown. My thoughtless behavior on the mountain was testimony to that. I could not, *would* not darken this most happy of holidays with my black mood and impending depression.

Besides, traumatized though I was after the avalanche had almost buried me, I was aware enough to notice Ellie's expression when she saw how furiously Jack had dug me out, and how desperately he had held my hand throughout the rescue. She knew something was going on between us, and that was why she was the only one that had neglected to express her concern. Granted, neither had Jack approached after seeing me safely home.

But Graham now wandered over and he pulled up an armchair to talk to me. "Susan called while you were… skiing," he said. "She was unable to get hold of you"—he glanced at my reposing form—"for obvious reasons, and wanted to know how the article is coming along. I said…it was coming…along."

I appreciated him not aiming his camera in my face and taking a candid shot of me just for kicks. I knew I must have looked awful. I also appreciated him not even mentioning my accident.

His head tilted slightly to the side to where Ellie and Jack were seated at the window. "The tennis player and the supermodel?" he asked, jerking his chin up. Actually it was a statement rather than a question. He commented with complete confidence. "And *you* I must conclude are the dog-toting third member of this trio."

"Did you get some pictures," I asked, ignoring the insinuation.

"I did. I need to get a picture of you, too. For the author headshot."

"Use a stock photo," I said. "I'm in no condition to pose for you."

He shrugged. "As you wish."

I was annoyed with his bluntness, his flippancy, and cast my eyes down. Why was it that this stranger was the only person who had a clue what was going on with me?

He scrolled through the shots on his camera, before coming to a stop. "How about this one?"

It was the pensive photo he'd taken of me the other day at the restaurant. It had captured something deep and responsive in me.

"Tell me the truth, Graham," I said, lowering my voice. "Am I wrong?"

He was thoughtful for a moment, plucked a chocolate chip cookie from the stacked plate Carrie had left with me and bit tentatively. "Depends what you mean by being wrong. Is it the 'forbidden love' thing you're referring to? Or is it that other thing—the mysterious secret that brings you to tears every time you think about it?"

"It's *not* a secret. And why are you always watching me? It is *so* aggravating."

"It's my job to observe people. That's what I do. How do you think I capture such moving photographs?"

"Not even the least bit conceited, are you?"

He shook his head, and finished the cookie in two bites. "Not even a little bit." He grinned, brushing crumbs from his shirt pocket. He sent a backwards glance at the quiet couple by the window. "Your cousin is really nice."

That was different. The first thing most people said about Ellie was that she was extraordinarily pretty. "That's why Jack loves her."

"Hmm. Are you sure about that?"

I glared at him. "They're sitting right there. If you speak any louder they will hear you."

"They won't hear a thing. They are so distracted and confused... the only thing they hear is the hum of their own brains and the beating of their hearts. Question is: for whom do their hearts beat?"

"You're insane, Graham."

He smiled, plucked another cookie from the plate. "Some people think so."

I moved the blanket aside and sat up. Strangely, I felt better—no thanks to Graham. Or maybe—*thanks* to Graham. He seemed to have an insight into life that made the little things not worth fussing over. Curiously, I decided to tell him Rocky's fate, and how it was tearing me apart.

He nodded in sympathy. "Maybe they'll have a change of heart."

I shook my head. "The Kinsley family wants him. I want to say I don't know why. But I *do* know why. It's the same reason that *I* want him. I have to return him and since keeping him longer isn't going to change anything, the sooner I do it, the better."

"You're leaving?" he asked. His voice had risen with the inquiry and I glanced furiously toward the window to see if Jack and Ellie and heard, but they were no longer there. They must have left as I was having my tête-à-tête with Graham.

CHAPTER TEN

It was the right thing to do. The Kinsley's son wanted Rocky. Who was I to deny a young boy the dog of his choice? I understood why he wanted this particular dog. Who wouldn't want a dog that was utterly devoted to you, who would risk his life to save yours?

I would miss him bitterly, but it was the right thing to do. It was the least reparation I could make to atone for the pain I had inflicted on my cousin Ellie. I will never forget the look on her face, even as I was coming out of unconsciousness in that avalanche of snow, when Jack held my hand. It was a lover's gesture.

They called it 'paying it forward.' *When someone does something hurtful to you, do something nice for someone else. It's the only way to fight back. Make the world the kind of place you want it to be.* That Graham Harlan, photographer, wasn't as much of an idiot as he pretended to be. And now I was taking advice from someone who was practically a stranger. Why had he suddenly come into my life?

I told Jonny and Carrie what had happened with Rocky, and that as the foster pet parent I was obligated to return him when a permanent home was found. Carrie was disappointed I had to leave and though I wanted to promise her I'd be back as soon as I could make it, I was hesitant that I would. There was still the article to write for Susan—if I didn't want to lose my job too. Jonny offered to come with me. I know he wanted to accompany me mostly to make sure that I would return. Carrie was nodding her head in agreement. She hated to always be the one who nagged me. "Are you sure you're up to the drive?" Jonny asked.

"By tomorrow I will be," I said. "Actually, I feel fine *now*."

Carrie was doubtful. But she went to the kitchen to make me a lunch for tomorrow.

I spent the rest of the day in my room with Rocky.

Just before dinner, I took Rocky outside.

My Dad was on the grounds shoveling old snow from the walkways.

"Hi Pumpkin," he said.

"Hi Daddy." There were times when we reverted to childish ways, where he talked to me like a six-year-old and I responded accordingly.

"I hear you have to give up Rocky."

I nodded, and fought grimly not to cry.

"Are you okay about it?"

I nodded again. "I never meant to keep him permanently."

"But now you've fallen in love, haven't you, sweetie?"

Little did he know just how true and inappropriate that assertion was. I exhaled against my will. And crouched down to bury my face in Rocky's fur. My father's line of questioning meant that neither of my siblings had mentioned my catastrophic skiing episode of this morning. I was grateful that they had respected my wishes.

Dad came over, jabbed the nose of the shovel into the snow and ruffled Rocky's ears. "Yeah, he's a great guy." He gazed down at me disconcerted. "So my daughters really *have* given up on men."

I glanced up and saw a mischievous gleam in his eye. He was half-joking, half-serious, and more than a little sad. "I'm sorry, Dad. We have our reasons."

"Things happen, Joy. Some things are not in our control. It doesn't mean you should give up."

I laughed miserably. "I seem to fall in love with the wrong men." I twined Rocky's leash around my mittened hand to emphasize my next words. "Dogs too."

"It's never wrong to love a dog. Even if you can't keep him."

That was true. Having Rocky by my side had taught me so many things about myself. One of which was that I could be strong.

"And as far as the men go, you're not talking about Lonny, are you?"

Sometimes my dad could be so insightful. My eyes shot up to his face in surprise. I lowered my lashes. How could he know?

Dad eased himself down to where I crouched at Rocky's level, leaning slightly on his upright shovel. When I stayed quiet, he said, "It explains why you and Ellie have barely said two words to each other since you arrived. Do you want to tell me what happened?"

This was a mother/daughter type of conversation, not a father/daughter conversation. I did not want to get into it. Besides—I had made up my mind.

"All right," he said, standing up to stretch his legs. He detached his shovel from the crusty snow. "I trust you, honey. You'll make the decision that feels right. But maybe, before you leave, you should talk to Ellie."

I nodded. "Thanks, Dad."

He kissed me on the cheek and resumed his shoveling. I took Rocky for a walk into the trails beneath the snow-laden branches of wild birches and evergreens.

The snow was packed on the woodland paths and my boots sank in very little. It had not snowed heavily now for a few days. I could hear the crunch of my own footsteps and the shuffle of Rocky's as he raced out ahead of me on a six-foot leash. I was tempted to let him run free. But what if he didn't return when I called him? Maybe that *was* what I wanted. For him to get lost in the woods so that I wouldn't have to give him to the Kinsley family. But that was selfish and stupid. Rocky could get injured and cold. What was I thinking?

There were footsteps sounding louder as I ran. I slowed

down, listened. They weren't mine. Rocky stopped at the tug of his leash and did a sudden about face. He started back toward me—tail wagging and eyes bright—like he was happy to see someone he knew. I rotated and saw behind me my cousin. Ellie.

Jack was nowhere in sight.

Her face was flushed. She had been following me and when Rocky had started running, she had had to race to catch up. I smiled at her, trying desperately to set back the clock to a time before I ever heard the name Jack Tinsle—or Rocco.

She stopped in front of me, unable to hide her unhappiness. She shook her head, her mouth working, trying to find the appropriate words to express her utter disappointment with me. She settled for: "How could you do this to me?"

Funny thing about this accusation. In all our lives as close cousins it was I who had framed this question in unspoken thought over and over. As kids she had the bubbly, vivacious personality, so it was she who got most of the attention. And when we were teenagers, she bloomed into a goddess. Problem was, she was so nice, so good-natured that she was more like an angel with a goddess' body. It was her sweet nature and genuine kindness that squashed any jealousy I harbored. But secretly I suppose I was always a little annoyed that she usually got her way, and that she always, *always* got the guy.

"I didn't mean for it to happen," I said.

I didn't even have to explain what I meant by that. From the look on her face it was clear she knew. "Don't worry, Ellie," I assured her. "I'm leaving. I have to take Rocco"—Oh crap, talk about a Freudian slip, I had not meant to say that—"I mean I have to take Rocky back to Calgary...to his new owners."

Ellie did not see how upset I was by this prospect. She was totally submersed in her own tragedy. "He lied to me, Joy," she said. "He set up a goddam business in Calgary!"

K-Nine. Yes, I knew. The dog school that changed my

and Rocky's relationship into something so enduring and wonderful that I could no longer bear to part with him.

"A dog school," she said. "He wants to train dogs!" She glared at me. "And you knew about it."

I know I was staring at her. She was upset about the dog school, not at me for falling for her beau. Was it possible that she was clueless?

"What did Ja...Rocco tell you?" I asked.

"He said he met you in Calgary—before I ever brought him up here."

"I see."

"No, you *don't* see. He wants to quit hockey."

I was patient, and silent. Ellie was very upset. But she seemed more upset with Jack than with me.

I tried to be calm as I answered her. How could they profess to know each other's dreams, and she be oblivious of this: "He doesn't want to play hockey anymore, Ellie."

My cousin was unfazed by my insinuation. "But why did he tell you, and not me?"

"He *did* tell you," I insisted.

She paused to gather her thoughts. They were clearly jumbled by her distress. "Yes, yes..." she murmured. "He did."

"Why do you care if he quits?"

"The point is, Joy. He has already quit. That is what he neglected to tell me." Her brows narrowed. Her eyes turned to me with suspicion. "But *you* knew."

I shut my eyes for a brief moment. It was my turn to collect my thoughts. That was untrue. He had lied to me as much as he had lied to Ellie. "I assumed his career revolved around dogs. He never told me he was a professional hockey player...." My thoughts returned to the wonderful days before I knew who he really was. There was nothing in our conversations that would have given me a hint that he was Ellie's boyfriend. "When did he quit?"

"Three weeks ago."

"In the middle of the season?"

"Yes. How could he humiliate me like that?"

I frowned. "Ellie. *He's* the hockey player. Not you."

"Everyone knew I was dating a professional hockey player."

I was confused by Ellie's reaction. Did she only love him because he was a hockey player? Was that why she never called him by his real name?

"And you," Ellie said. "You'd already met him. How could you keep this from me?"

"I didn't know that Jack was Rocco. I only met him because of my dog. As far as I knew he ran the K-Nine dog-training center. And before you accuse him of *any* thing, he did *not* know I was your cousin when we met. How could he?"

Ellie had that perplexed expression she wore when her expectations were unmet. Of course she would think he might have mentioned her to me, or I might have mentioned her to him. That was just the kind of self-focused thinking Ellie used. The world had always revolved around her. Why would she think otherwise?

Standing still for so long, I was getting cold. But it was obvious that we were far from coming to a satisfactory resolution. I could see my own breath frost as I elaborated on my previous statement. "You are not a dog lover. Why would it come up?" That was the gentlest way I could put it. It would never occur to Ellie that she wasn't a person that everyone would want to mention.

"He must have told you he was coming to Emerald Lake with me?"

I shook my head. "Why would he tell me that?"

"He had a girlfriend. Me."

It was interesting how she had responded in the past tense. I wanted to ask her what she meant by that. Part of me was hoping that it wasn't just a slip of the tongue and that she really had meant to speak in the past tense. I said, "I guess it was irrelevant."

"It's only irrelevant if you want someone to think you

are available."

My brain was frozen on this one.

"You should have mentioned me to him, Joy. You must have told him you were coming to the lodge for Christmas. He knew about your article."

So, he had mentioned the article to her, had he? I shook my head, as dumbfounded as she. Oh why had I involved him in my research for the article? Rocky started to whimper beside me. He was bored or impatient or cold—maybe all three. I glanced at my cousin who was rearranging a slipped scarf around her neck. I sighed. I knew exactly why I had involved him. The question was, did Ellie know?

Either way I understood, by the scowl on her pretty face, that things were going to end badly between us.

CHAPTER ELEVEN

They did. Far from ending well we almost got into a catfight like we did sometimes when we were kids. Those had always ended up as giggling pillow fights. This time we were nowhere near any pillows, nor were either of us in a giddy mood—and I could not picture us packing snowballs and chucking them at one another.

I left early the next morning without saying goodbye to Jack. I had already told my Dad and Jonny how early I was leaving, so they had said their goodbyes the night before. I was surprised when the photographer, Graham, decided to stay at the lodge, so it was only Carrie who was awake to see me off. "Call when you get home, and let us know when to expect you back." She glared at me when I hesitated from behind the steering wheel. "You *are* coming back for Christmas?"

To evade the question, I started the engine so I could pretend not to hear when she repeated the request. I waved goodbye from my SUV, Rocky belted into the backseat behind me, and watched my sister shake her head and then enter the lodge van. I gave her two minutes to leave ahead of me, before I flashed one more obligatory wave of the hand and put the car into gear.

I headed into Field to gas up. As I pulled into the second of the town's two gas stations I thought I recognized a Jeep Wrangler parked by the side of the road. It was near the Bookworm Café. If that was Jack's car I must avoid running into him. Since our altercation in the woods Ellie and I had dodged each other. She was angry with me because her boyfriend had chosen to confide in me rather than in her. As far as I knew they were still together. Since the rescue Jack had eluded me also. I realized now that I really should thank him. Furthermore my curiosity was getting the better of me. I was procrastinating, twiddling my thumbs trying to stretch out the time to circumvent leaving because the tank had already registered as full. I could see him in the window at the checkout counter of the bookshop. Maybe he was just getting a morning cup of Joe. If so, against my better judgment, I wanted to say goodbye.

I nervously crept up the stairs and opened the door after paying for the gas in my car. He was just exiting as I was entering the shop, and we once again tripped into each other's arms. Honestly, it was an accident. I had not expected anyone to be there on the threshold as I stepped through the doorway.

"Zamboni," he said, my face making a crash landing into his chest. I righted myself as quickly as I could, ignoring the hands that had come out to brace me. "Are you okay?" He smiled but made no joke about us always running into each other. Instead he said, "I was hoping to catch you before you left."

And I was hoping to leave before he could. And would have—if I hadn't spotted his car.

"I was just going to grab a coffee," I lied.

He had a red and green festive gift bag in his hand, trimmed with matching ribbons and a nametag—and nothing else. No cup holder with beverages for two. "Mind if I join you?" he suggested.

Actually I did mind. Somewhat. But on the other hand, there was nothing I wanted more than to see him again. "Where's Ellie?" I asked.

"Still sleeping."

"You left her in bed?"

He nodded.

"She's really upset, Jack."

"I know."

What else was there to say? We were still standing on

the threshold and I nudged wide the door, and he turned to follow me inside. We ordered two coffees: one black, one sweet and milky, and sat down at a table to wait. This time I relented without a fuss when he offered to pay. I added extra sugar from the packets on the table, and realized in consternation that it was the same table we had sat at the first time we were here.

"He glanced out the window and saw my Rav4 down the road." Rocky's head was just visible in the slightly opened side window.

"You're leaving," he said. It was a flat statement of regret.

Remorse?

Guilt?

Possibly all three.

I refused to relieve him of his guilt. I nodded.

He nodded too. "I heard about Rocky. I am so sorry, Joy."

He had not called me Zamboni. I sighed, grateful, and a little disappointed at the same time. When he called me Zamboni I felt there was something special between us. When he called me Joy, I knew he was serious. Whatever the tension between us, Rocky at least was safe territory. We could talk about *him*. My voice was low and strained but I knew I could say what was on my mind because Jack would understand. I sought his compassion, trying hard to control my voice. "It hurts so much, Jack. I don't want to let him go."

He frowned. "The adoptive family is set on this particular dog?"

I nodded because, try though I did, my vocal chords refused to work properly and my answer was muted. "I can't blame them."

"Yeah. Neither can I. Rocky is a special dog. He was amazing on the mountain. He leaped out of my arms, knew exactly where you were—and started digging."

The memory made a lump form in my throat. Knowing

about it was making things worse. And this—chatting with Jack, having coffee with him, pretending it was all casual and normal—was pointless. It would never be casual or normal for me. I loved him. And I shouldn't. I should just leave. Leaving Jack was going to be just as hard as leaving Rocky, and so I might as well cut the cord right now. Like Sarah from the Humane Society had said. Why prolong the agony?

I got up, coffee in hand. "I'm just going to pour this into a Take Out cup. I really have to get on the road. Traffic, you know." I tried to sound light and cavalier, but I was far from feeling it. "It was nice knowing you, Jack." The words came out hoarsely. "I don't think we should see each other again."

Silence from him as he rose to his feet. I attempted to leave but my muscles were paralyzed by my desire to stay. He looked down at me with that expression that turned my knees and my thoughts to melt water.

"I was afraid you were going to say that, Zamboni." He was also trying to keep things light. "But before you go—" He unhooked the festive gift bag he had looped onto the back of his chair. "Actually, I didn't come here for coffee. I came here for this...." He hesitantly extended the bag towards me. "I was hoping I would see you before you left. I'm glad we bumped into each other. I really *am* sorry if I hurt you. I never meant to."

I nervously fingered my coffee cup. Then I accepted the bag reluctantly. "It's not me you should be apologizing to, Jack."

"I know." He lowered his head, and then glanced up. "It's a gift. A Christmas present. Don't open it until Christmas Day."

So he knew I had no plans to return to the lodge for Christmas. How could I? *He* would be there.

I thanked him and made a quick exit. Rocky was waiting. I got into the car tossed the beautifully decorated bag into the backseat without looking to see what was in it, and rolled out of my parking spot. Jack remained standing on the porch of the bookshop watching me, and I quickly turned my eyes to the road. The sooner I made the break, the better.

***

The two and a half hour drive back to Calgary was not long enough. I almost took a detour and kept heading east, but I realized that I would only be delaying the inevitable. Why was it that when one thing went wrong in your life, everything went wrong? It was so unfair, so undeserved. Why couldn't things work out for me like they did with my brother? Or even my sister. At least with her, the choice to be single, to have a pet that belonged to her and no one else, and to run the lodge with my dad was her own choice. I hoped Ellie knew what she had in Jack. I hoped she recognized how special he was. As my thoughts rambled along these lines I began to see that maybe there was hope after all. It had happened for Jonny and my dad, and to Ellie. It could happen for me. I began to feel lighter as I drove to the Humane Society. There were other dogs. Rocky was special and dear to me. But he was spoken for. As was Jack. I had to move on. It was the toughest decision I had ever made. My heart just wanted to take Jack and Rocky and run away. But this was no TV movie. I had to let them both go.

Rocky did not understand when I led him into the building of the Humane Society. Sarah thanked me for being so understanding. The Kinsley's would be so happy. I was certain that they would be, but how would Rocky feel? It wasn't my call to make. I told Sarah that I would drop off his food bowls and toys in a couple of days. She told me not to trouble about it. The Kinsley's had money. They had already prepared for their new family member with brand new things.

She asked me if I wanted to look at the other dogs that needed adopting. "You could foster another one," she said.

I shook my head. "If I decide to have another dog, I think it will be a permanent adoption." I smiled at her sheepishly. "I don't think I'm cut out to be a foster pet parent. I had no idea I was going to love him so much." My voice cracked and I apologized, but I had to go. She understood. I gave Rocky one last kiss on the top of his head, before I made my escape. I had already cried too much this past week. It was time to get my act together.

I drove home and dumped my luggage in the middle of the floor. I went to my laptop and started typing. At last I knew exactly what this article was going to say.

No. Pets are not better life companions than men. They were just less complicated. But they made you worry and they made you love them just as much.

I tapped away furiously until the entire article was written. If Susan hated it she could lump it. It was my best effort. One of the best stories I had ever written. Thanks to Jack and Rocky. By the time I had finished it was almost midnight.

I emailed it to her. Then went to pour myself a glass of wine. Drinking wine by yourself was not nearly so much fun as sharing a bottle with someone you love.

I went to the bathroom to turn on the tub and make myself a bubble bath. I was going to indulge tonight.

As I sat in the fragrant lavender warmth of delicious bubbly water, sipping my wine, I knew I had done the right thing. I had also written the right story. There was no point in raging over life's sour grapes. It was like complaining about the rain. Or the size of your feet. Some things you could fix, and some things were acts of nature.

CHAPTER TWELVE

It was Christmas Eve. Susan was pleased with my article even though it wasn't exactly what she expected. It didn't turn out to be what *I* expected. But it was done and it would be published today.

My only dilemma now was whether or not to drive back to Emerald Lake to be with my family. I really wanted to be with them, but did I want to field questions about why it had taken me so long to return? I could always use work as an excuse, I supposed. That was something everyone would believe.

But the real truth was I wasn't ready to see Jack again. If he and Ellie remained together, if they got married, I would have to be able to see him without any of these feelings of loss and envy—and unrequited love.

Maybe it was just best that I concentrated on my next work assignment. Let this Christmas pass, and try for better next year. Susan had invited me to a Christmas Eve party at her home. Maybe I should take her up on it.

I took a shower and did my hair up into a stylish chignon. I applied a little more makeup than usual. Why was it that makeup felt like a barrier between you and the world? It wasn't really much of a mask. But it made me feel less naked.

What to wear. I had a sleeveless silver dress with a turtleneck. It made my neck look long and my arms look sexy. It was a strange combination when you thought about it, but for tonight it would do. I did not want to look like myself.

I greeted Susan's guests with forced enthusiasm.

Graham was there. I guess he had gotten enough of my family and had decided he should be with his own, until I learned he had none in town.

"Have you seen the article yet?" he asked. "I would have liked to run the photos by you before it went to print, but Susan was in a hurry. And of course, the editor has the final say."

I shrugged. Who cared? That assignment was passé. I had already moved on and had started research on an article on pets as fur babies. Yep. You got it. A puppy or a kitten as a substitute for a child. I already had my first interviewee lined up. She was a realtor, aged 29, unmarried, no kids, but—and this is the anchor of the story—she is taking parental leave to care for her newly acquired puppy. Her company is actually allowing her to take parental leave for a couple of months. How awesome was that!

"I heard about the new assignment," Graham said, sipping on a glass of bourbon. "I want in on it. Let me be your photographer."

"Seriously, Graham?"

"Seriously, Joy. In fact—you know what—I know someone whom you should interview for the article. Let me set you up."

"Okay. After New Years?"

"The new year—no, that won't work. This guy might not be around in the New Year if his business prospects flop."

"Well, why don't you tell me how he would benefit my story?"

"Sure. So, he's a guy in love with a girl but their family won't be complete unless they have a dog…"

"Don't they want children?"

"At this stage of their lives—no."

"So what's keeping them from getting a dog?"

He was about to continue with the story when my cellphone rang. "Excuse me for a second," I said. "I should probably get this." Graham nodded, and understood. I had been avoiding my family. And it was probably one of them, wondering where I was and why I hadn't been in touch. Guilt finally got the better of me, and I placed my wine glass down on an end table and dug my phone out of my black evening bag. "Hello?"

"Joy? It's me, Ellie." Her voice sounded cracked, broken.

"Ellie. What's the matter? You sound terrible." My first thought was that Jack had left her. Had broken her heart. How could he do that after what we had *all* been through?

"It *is* terrible. Awful. My life is falling apart. Oh Joy, I need you to come back. I broke up with Jack. I had to. Everything is just wrong now. He's gone. He left shortly after you did. Please come back to the lodge. I can't talk to Carrie. All she wants to do is feed me."

"Don't worry, Ellie. I'm on my way.

It was a good thing I'd only had one glass of wine. My driving would not be affected.

I told Graham I had to return to the lodge, made my excuses to Susan and thanked her for the party, which I was unable to remain at. She was too busy to be offended, and she also comprehended the high drama of being part of a Welsh-Italian family. "Take the entire week off, Joy," she said. "You did a bang-up job on that article. You deserve a break."

"Thanks," I said, but I was already halfway out the door, with Graham beside me.

"Just where do you think you're going?" I demanded.

"That was Ellie, wasn't it?" he asked.

I nodded.

"I like your family, Joy, and I don't have any of my own to spend the holidays with. Your dad invited me to come back for Christmas if I wanted to… I want to."

Just like Dad, I thought, inviting every Joe, Dick and Graham—*and* his dog.

"Fine. I have to go home to pack a few things. Are you taking your own car?"

He hesitated, and then said, "Thought maybe we could drive up together this time."

In hindsight I should have been a little suspicious that he wanted to return to the lodge with me. Especially when he wanted to ride in my car. But my mind was on Ellie and not Graham's personal agenda. So, I merely shrugged and said, "Pick you up in an hour."

The two-hour drive seemed like two days. It was already late, ten o'clock, and we wouldn't arrive until after midnight. Only advantage to night driving was that there was little traffic. It was strange driving back to Emerald Lake with Graham the photographer as my passenger rather than Rocky, my precious dog.

I could not think about that or I would cry again. Rocky was with a family that would take good care of him. Could they possibly love him as much as I did? But that was beside the point. Ellie needed me.

How long had I been away from the lodge? It must have been at least four days. My foot almost landed on the brake as a thought occurred to me. Hadn't Ellie said that Jack had left the same day I had? That meant they had split up on that very day. Why had Ellie waited this long to tell me? Granted, I had not been answering emails, texts or voice mail since I got home. I didn't want to have to explain myself. I had sent the family a message to tell them I was remaining in town for Christmas because of work obligations. And neglected to check my messages since. One of the reasons I had answered the phone tonight (other than guilt) was because I was at a party. All the noise of gaiety and jolliness would give my family members the impression that I was having a good time.

I had expected the call to be from Carrie or Jonny chiding me over choosing work over family, and had been prepared with my excuses. For the call to be from a tearful Ellie was a total surprise.

Graham and I had been silent for a few moments. The night scenery was speeding by and we were almost into the mountains. "So what's going on between you and my sister," I asked.

Graham grunted. He laughed. "Carrie? Are you kidding me? There's nothing that could get between her and her dog."

"But you *like* her. That's why you want to go back to the lodge."

"I like your whole family, Joy."

"But you like *her*."

"If you say so."

"Don't you?"

"Are you trying to play matchmaker with us? You're wasting your time."

He was probably right. Carrie's interest in men was superficial. As far as she was concerned, no man could measure up to the faithfulness, love and comfort of a dog.

I still found it hard to believe that Graham only wanted to spend Christmas with my family. Oh well, I had learned my lesson. Stay out of other people's business.

More times than I can remember I had told my sister: "if you spent a little more time minding your *own* business you would spend less of it minding *mine*." High time I listened to my own advice.

We pulled up to the parking lot where the check-in cabin stood. I glanced at my watch. It was half past midnight. Who would be awake? When I left the lodge there were no outside guests staying at the lodge on Christmas day. Bookings were made for the week leading up to New Years. I probably shouldn't call to have the van sent down to fetch us. Better if I just drove my SUV up there instead.

When we parked at the employee parking lot, a few lights were on in the lobby and golden lanterns glowed outside. Fortunately, the weather had cooperated on the drive up.

Graham and I each grabbed our luggage from the cargo area and I slammed the hatch shut. Inside, the only person waiting for me was Ellie. She was sitting in the lobby on the sofa near the fireplace that was dying. It was so quiet I could hear the crackling snaps of the burnt logs, which were crumbling to coals.

She got up and ran to me, and we hugged. "Oh, Ellie, I'm so glad you aren't mad at me anymore."

She sniffled, and dabbed at her cheek with a crumpled up tissue. The light was low in the lobby and made Ellie's skin look luminous and her hair shine like gold. Only Ellie could still look pretty when she was crying. "Are you okay?" I asked.

"Fine, now that *you're* here."

"I'm so sorry, Ellie."

"For what? What did *you* do?"

I glanced up and saw Graham watching us. He gave me a thumbs-up sign and left with his luggage to relocate his old room. I turned back to my cousin. "Is everyone asleep?"

She murmured something that I couldn't quite hear. She pressed my cheek into her shoulder. I swallowed my guilt before I confessed, "I *did* know, Jack—I mean Rocco— before we came up here. I should have told you."

She pushed me slightly away from her so that she could look me in the eye. She stayed quiet a long time before she spoke. "He was the guy you were talking about, wasn't he? When you told me you had met someone."

I nodded miserably. "I didn't know, Ellie. He didn't tell me he had a girlfriend."

She nodded. "I guess there was a reason for that."

"There was no excuse for that," I said, angrily.

"But you like him, don't you, Joy?"

"I don't like what he did to you."

Ellie sighed. She sat back down on the sofa and dragged me down with her. "If it's anyone's fault, it's my fault. I wasn't listening. I never listen. I always figure if I don't listen and just go ahead and pretend things are the way I want them to be, they *will* be that way." She looked at me, dry-eyed now. "Rocco and I. We had a lot of fun together."

Sure you did. I empathized. And I was pretty certain that he had not meant to play us against each other. But still….

She sighed. "I *wouldn't* have married him."

I looked up. "But you said you wanted to."

"I thought I did, but really, if you think about it, what do we have in common?" When I stayed silent, she smiled. "When you think about it, *you* and he have a lot more in common."

What was she saying? That she forgave me? That I had her blessing? But Jack was gone. And I wasn't sure I wanted him back. A man who did not tell the truth was not a man you could trust.

"Let's face it, Joy. He didn't really lie—to either of us. He just withheld information."

"Why? Why did he do that?"

"Maybe he was falling out of love with me and *in* love with you. Maybe he didn't want to hurt either of us."

I was silent. I studied Ellie's face. She had stopped crying and she didn't seem indignant at the idea that Jack could fall in love with me. There was no sign of anger or jealousy at all. Didn't I say that Ellie was perfect? She was beautiful and she was kind and generous. Even if the world did revolve around her.

"You're my best friend, Ellie," I said. "Let's not ever fight again."

She grinned.

"I think it's time you went to get your man."

"But I just got here!"

She frowned. "Right. Can't expect you to drive all the way back to Calgary. Again." She paused, and squeezed my hand. "Thanks for driving back to be with me."

"I wouldn't miss Christmas with the family. I just couldn't. I would have had to come anyway, whether you wanted me here or not."

"I was counting on that."

"Hey, what do you think of Graham?" I asked.

She smiled. "Don't you dare; I'm just coming out of a difficult relationship."

CHAPTER THIRTEEN

My sister Carrie Zamboni says, "Wiggles is special. She's there when I need her and never criticizes. People call her my fur baby, but really she is more like my partner. Humans need companionship and sometimes that is hard to find with a man. We want some big love. We want to be independent. Often the two don't go together. But with a dog that's exactly what you get."

That was an excerpt from my article just published in *Cats and Dogs Magazine*. Graham had a copy of it and had given it to me last night to read with my morning coffee. No one else was up. It was Christmas Day and I had never felt more excited—except when I was a kid.

I couldn't agree with Carrie's quote more. But here's something people don't think about when they get a pet for those reasons. You believe that your pet loves you, and you want that pet to love you and be there with you for the rest of your life. That won't happen. It can't. Their life spans are too short and you will be alone again. Sure you might be able to find another furry companion to fill that void, but you will have to do it over and over again. Carrie, my sister, is forty-one and has already had three dogs. When I had to take Rocky back to the shelter because another family had called dibs on him, my heart was broken. I couldn't have felt worse than if this were my husband or boyfriend being stolen from me. The feeling of loss is exactly the same. I miss talking to him.

But what I miss more is someone who can talk back. Sure, we only want a guy to talk back when he says what we want to hear. But sometimes the silence is too much, and a bark is only a bark. My dog can't understand when I have a problem or offer helpful suggestions. What he does for me is makes me know how much I'm needed. That is something men seem to fail at.

My conclusion? Dogs cannot replace the love of a man, anymore than a man can replace the love of a dog. It's different. And for some people—we need both.

Ellie was sleeping in, and Carrie was in the kitchen making breakfast. The kids were under the Christmas tree chomping on the bit, while Jonny and Kim tried to get them to eat something before it was time to open presents. I went to join them and saw the red and green, beribboned, Christmas gift bag from the Bookworm Café under the tree.

"Hope you don't mind, Graham," said as he crouched down beside me. "I saw that in the backseat of your car and brought it along. It looked like it was a Christmas gift."

"It is," I said.

"I couldn't help but notice that the tag says it's from Jack."

Well, I supposed Graham could hardly avoid seeing the words scribbled in broad black strokes. And since Jack was gone and I wouldn't be able to see his face when I opened this gift, I might as well open it now.

I fiddled with the ribbons drawing the bag together. I would prefer it if no one else saw this gift from Jack, especially not Ellie. I lifted it and went to a quiet corner of the room. The kids were busy trying to guess what was in their packages and paid no attention to me. The rest of my family was busy eating, drinking and chatting. I glanced up once to make sure I was unobserved and opened the gift bag.

Inside, wrapped in white tissue was the limited edition volume of Dylan Thomas' *A Child's Christmas in Wales*. I almost burst into tears. Inside the cover was a note that read:

Hope this makes your Christmas a little cheerier.
Love Jack

Ellie came through the door with two cups of coffee in her hands. She approached me and placed the coffees on the end table to my right.

"What have you got there, Joy?" She took the volume from me and smiled. "Your mom used to read this to us on Christmas Eve."

I was too choked up to answer her, and I didn't want her to know why. But I didn't have to tell her. Ellie could be perceptive when she chose to be. "It's from Jack?"

I nodded.

"Oh, Joy, we have to get him back. For you."

"I'm not leaving you or any of my family on Christmas Day, not even for him."

She grinned. She was about to say something witty when her eyes widened in surprise. "Maybe you don't have to."

She pointed out the window and I rose to have a look outside. A dark green Jeep Wrangler was parked beside my Rav4 in the lodge's employee lot. "Your dad's not going to like that," she giggled. "Two unauthorized vehicles."

I couldn't help but laugh. I wanted to run outside to meet Jack but I was too nervous, not knowing what I would possibly say to him. Graham saved me from that impulse by appearing at that moment to ask, "What are you two giggling about?"

Ellie pointed outside. Graham made a sound, not of surprise but expectation. He looked at me. "Remember that guy I thought you should interview for your next article on fur babies as substitute children? Well, where did I leave off.... Oh yeah. So, he's a guy in love with a girl but their family won't be complete unless they have a dog... and they don't want children at this stage of their lives when their love is so new—"

"Right I remember," I interrupted. "So what was keeping them from getting a dog?"

"Well..." He paused for suspense and when he saw me shaking my head in exasperation, he grinned. I kicked him playfully. It was Christmas Day after all; we didn't have all day to tell stories and play games. There was still the cooking to do. And Jack was about to come through the door. "The dog was promised to someone else..." He did it again, waiting like he expected a reaction from me. I tried not to tap my feet or to exhale loudly. Or even clear my throat. Then I lowered my eyes thoughtfully. Wait a minute, this was starting to sound familiar— "It was a family named Kinsley."

My eyes opened wide. I think my mouth dropped open, too.

"So the guy went to the family and asked them if they would consider another dog, a puppy, any one they wished. He would pay for it if they would do him this one favor. 'You see,' he said—"

I realized now that the entire room had gone quiet. "You're talking about Rocky," I broke in. He was also talking about Jack. I could see all the faces in the room suppressing smiles and I stood up, while Ellie grabbed my hand.

Graham smiled. "Well, maybe we should let the hero of the story tell you the rest of it."

By this time Jack had walked in. He looked so handsome in his shearling jacket and blue jeans. His skin had a high color like he had been rushing around doing things.

Clearly he had been listening. "'You see,' he said, taking up the tale. 'The girl he loved adored this dog. She'd been looking after the dog for a month. The dog rescued her from an avalanche—that's how much he loved her—and he missed her as much as she missed him. Would you please reconsider?' he asked the Kinsley family. Then the son looked at him and said 'you're Rocket T, the hockey player. He nodded and the boy asked, 'will you teach me to play hockey?'"

"What did you say?" Ellie asked. By now everyone in the room knew that Jack was the man in the story and that the girl he loved was me.

"What did I say?" Jack smiled gently at Ellie then turned his beseeching eyes on me. "I said only if you will give me your dog in exchange for another."

"And?" My entire family simultaneously demanded the boy's response to this request.

"And... he jumped for joy and said 'awesome!'"

There was silence as the clapping died down and everyone turned to focus on my reaction.

"Rocky is mine?" I was shaking I could hardly believe my good fortune. "Where *is* he?"

My dad walked in at that moment with Rocky on his leash. The beautiful Australian shepherd dog raced up to me and leaped up to my chest, almost knocking me over. "Oh my sweet boy," I said. "Oh, welcome home!"

Everyone made a great fuss over Rocky's homecoming.

The kids started to fuss over the delay in gift opening. "Can we open presents now, please? Auntie Joy has already opened one of hers."

It was then I looked down at the armchair where I had left the Dylan Thomas classic. My entire family was fixated on the tree and unwrapping gifts. No one's eyes were on Jack or me, and I lifted the volume to thank him.

Carrie took Rocky to join Wiggles for breakfast. Jack's eyes were firmly on mine. He still hadn't attempted to touch me or mention what had happened between him and my cousin. "Everything is all right between you and Ellie?" I asked.

"If by that you mean are we still friends. Yes." He smiled. "If you're asking whether we're still a couple, the answer is no. She asked me to leave."

I paused before I ventured my next question. "And then she asked you to come back?"

"Well, not exactly. It was Graham who thought it might be a good idea. He'd had a long talk with Ellie after we'd both left." He sought my eyes and waited before he continued. I knew this was hard for him. I knew he was conflicted and I knew that all along he was trying to fight his feelings and at the same time to do the right thing. "She didn't blame either of us," he said. "She blamed herself.

Which of course is absurd and I fully intend to tell her so. It was all me, Joy. I fell for you like a ton of bricks the day I laid eyes on you. That's why I never mentioned Ellie. Or that I was a professional hockey player. Or where I was planning to spend Christmas. I already knew I would be at your father's lodge unless I made a deliberate effort not to go. And that would have meant breaking it off with Ellie or lying to her."

There was an awkward silence before I said, "So you decided to lie to her."

"My intentions were good."

"The road to hell is paved with good intentions, Jack."

"Oh, I know. I found that out soon enough..." He stopped talking at this point and Rocky returned to us after feasting on kibble and leftover roast chicken. The dog nudged my hand with his snout and I obliged him with a gentle scratch under the chin. I could not believe Jack had managed to find a way to get Rocky for me. My heart was so full it felt like it would burst. I kissed Rocky's face, just before Jack drew me back to my feet to gaze into his beautiful eyes. "So what do you think, Joy? Do you have enough love in your heart to share between the two of us? I know Rocky's got it all over me. But I don't mind playing second fiddle." He lifted my chin up towards his lips. "Can you love such a flawed man as me?"

"I already do," I whispered.

Across the room by the Christmas tree I caught Ellie's eye. She gave me a thumbs-up, and then I saw Graham rise from helping my nephew unwrap a new snowboard. He came to Ellie and took her hand. They walked to the bar where a clump of mistletoe hung from the ceiling and then he kissed her.

Jack grinned. He'd caught the spontaneous act as well, and did likewise.

It was the best Christmas I had had since my mother passed away. We had the most glorious feast with roast goose, orange and chestnut stuffing, candied yams, cheesy broccoli and cranberry plum chutney. Dessert was even better. Carrie and Kim had made a Victorian Chocolate Orange cake for the adults and homemade candy cane ice cream for the kids.

After dinner we all sat around the fire, some on the floor, some on the big cushy sofa sectional to listen to Christmas carols and drink brandy. The kids were playing with their toys on the floor. My dad and Carrie were seated on the sectional with wiggles on Carrie's lap. Ellie and Graham had hit it off, and this time I don't think it was just wishful thinking. Kim and Jonny finally had a moment together and were standing by the window watching it snow. He opened the window briefly to catch a snowflake for his wife.

With the book under my left arm, hugging Rocky and my right hand laced with Jack's we snuggled in front of the fireplace, and I felt my mom's warm smile and glowing eyes looking down on us from somewhere above.

"Merry Christmas, Mom," I sighed. And I swear as Jonny closed the window, a breath of snowy air whispered "Merry Christmas to you, too."

Books by Daphne Lynn Stewart:

SOME ENCHANTED CHRISTMAS
This special Christmas collection of love stories for pet lovers contains *All She Wants for Christmas*, *Christmas in June*, *The Christmas Mix-Up* and *The Christmas Bunny*.

When Belle Rice rescues a runaway dog and returns it to its owner she falls hard for the dashing Christopher Winters. One thing impedes her happiness this Christmas—his girlfriend!

High school sweethearts Leigh and Matthew met at her grandmother's guinea pig shelter. Fifteen years later Leigh returns to film a Christmas documentary only to learn that Matt has moved on. But has she?

Danica Meriweather picks up the wrong pet carrier at the airport, and is thrust face to face with the man of her dreams. The problem? She never saw his face. Now she has his dog and he has hers!

For grad student Kendra Tyler, marrying Cabe Alexander, who monitors her rabbit studies, would solve all her problems. But she has a secret, and if he finds out it could end their romance.

Summer Destiny Series:
(Exclusively on Amazon Kindle)

Paradise on Deck: A Summer Destiny Romance
Do you believe in destiny? Ariel Stone does not until she meets handsome deck and landscape designer Ben Hammer on a cruise ship. While together they make a promise not to tell each other anything about their personal lives, but instead

to play a 'game' that Ben calls Destiny. "If it's meant to be we will meet again," he promises. When the cruise ends, Ben returns to his life and his girlfriend, and Ariel returns to her husband and her life as an interior decorator, only to learn that her husband has been having an affair. She meets Ben again, but this time it's different. She may be free, but Ben is engaged.

If Not For You: A Summer Destiny Romance
When a man loves a woman he will go to any extent to win her, but to what extent will he go to save her life? Leanne Constance meets Andy Briggs at a psychology conference in L.A. They both study relationships and the subject of "Love". Only one thing stands in the way of happily ever after. He lives in Berkeley California and she lives in Toronto, Canada. Both have important jobs in high profile universities and they are head over heels in love. What to do? To make matters worse, Leanne has a secret. When Andy discovers Leanne's secret he is horrified that he might lose her. Can he save her, and if he does, at what cost?

Acknowledgements

To my two little dogs Ming and Tang, thank you for inspiring this series of pet-focused love stories. Although both Ming and Tang have passed away, their memories are cherished in these tales of love. Thanks too, to Cathy Mansfield, Rebecca Little, and Janice Williams for agreeing to feature their cherished pets and pet friends in this collection. Many thanks also to my publishers at *Chicken Soup For The Soul* for providing the opportunity to write for them. Having a story published in this popular franchise set me on a new path of writing. And as always, thank you to my husband for his support and the lovely cover for this book.

About the Author

Daphne Lynn Stewart is a pen name used by fantasy/suspense author Deborah Cannon for her novelettes, a series of Christmas romances for pet lovers and her Summer Destiny series.

In 2013 she won an honourable mention for her short story *Twilight Glyph* in the Canadian Tales of the Fantastic contest and in 2014 her story "Tang's Christmas Miracle" appeared in *Chicken Soup for the Soul: Christmas in Canada*. Her career as a science fiction/fantasy writer began when she sold two short stories to Farsector SFFH magazine (2003). She has contributed to the *Canadian Writer's Guide* and is best known for *The Raven Chronicles*, a series of paranormal archaeological suspense novels and a time slip series for young adults, *The Pirate Vortex*. Recently she launched a fiction series of Kindle Short Reads called *Close Encounters of the Cryptid Kind*. Her most recent release under the name of Deborah Cannon is a critically acclaimed epic *The Pirate Empress*, a Chinese historical fantasy. She is also a book reviewer for the Washington Independent Review of Books.

She lives in Hamilton, Ontario with her archaeologist husband.

Made in the USA
Las Vegas, NV
12 September 2022